STRIKE FAST

DEA FAST SERIES

KAYLEA CROSS

STRIKE FAST

Copyright © 2017
by Kaylea Cross

* * * * *

Cover Art & Formatting by
Sweet 'N Spicy Designs

* * * * *

ISBN: 978-1974644681

Dedication

For all the single parents out there, doing one of the toughest—but most important—jobs of all on your own. This one's for you.

Author's Note

Dear readers,

Here we are at book 4 of the FAST series already! With any luck I tugged at your heartstrings with Reid's introduction in the previous story, so I hope you're as eager for him to find happiness as I was to give it to him.

Happy reading!

Kaylea Cross

FAST motto: "Contain, Disrupt, Dismantle"

Prologue

Forward Operating Base Bostick
Kunar Province, Afghanistan

DEA Special Agent Tess Dubrovski's heart thudded an erratic rhythm against her ribs, but her hand was steady on the stick as she guided the wounded Blackhawk through the dark sky to the ground inside the secure perimeter of the FOB. The moment the wheels touched down, her copilot initiated emergency shutdown procedures and she finally allowed herself to release a long, deep breath.

I'm still alive. Hard to believe after the ferocious ground fire they'd taken.

Ground crews converged on them from both sides with fire extinguishers at the ready, staying clear of the nose to avoid the low angle of the main rotor blades. Her crew chief had reported faint smoke in the cabin on the way back and she'd been forced to fly at a lower altitude due to a drop in power, but there hadn't been a fire, thank God.

With the sound of the engines powering down in the background, Tess leaned her head back against the seat and willed her heart to slow down. They were lucky to have made it to the FOB at all, let alone in one piece. Pushing her NVGs and visor up on her helmet, she ran a gloved hand over her face. It had been a damn close call tonight.

In the left hand seat, her copilot raised his own night vision goggles on his helmet mount and turned his head toward her, his expression tense. "That was some scary shit."

"Yeah, I'll never forget it." She pulled in a deep breath and just sat there while the noise from the engines wound down and the rotors slowed. "How many hits did we take, do you think?"

He snorted. "I lost count after the first dozen."

Her, too.

The crew chief popped his head into the cockpit from the back. "They're offloading the wounded now. I'll check the damage once they're out."

"Okay," Tess said. "How many were hit?" She'd done everything she could think of, used every trick she knew to evade the enemy fire, but no matter which direction she'd gone, they'd just kept taking ground fire.

"Two." He glanced between her and the copilot. "You both okay?"

"We're good," Tess said. Physically, anyway. But only thanks to their armor-plated seats and the helo's tough skin.

She still had no idea what the hell had happened out there. They'd landed without incident and picked up FAST Bravo and the others, including a high value target prisoner and two KIA. Right after takeoff from the LZ they'd taken a barrage of close range small arms fire from a rogue element embedded within the Afghan NIU force the DEA team had been working a joint op with. Seconds into their climb, rounds had penetrated the fuselage and struck two men on the other side of the bulkhead.

From what she could tell, the tail section had taken the worst of it. For a moment there, she'd thought the shooters had damaged the tail rotor. Then everyone onboard would have been screwed. Thankfully her door gunner had managed to clear off most of the enemy to avoid disaster, otherwise they'd all be burning in a mass of twisted metal back in those mountains behind them right now.

Her late husband's face flashed through her mind, along with an image of the wreckage they'd pulled his body from three years ago. Her stomach clamped so hard that for a moment she feared she might be sick right there in the cockpit.

With effort, she locked the bleak, painful memory away and focused on what was going on around her aircraft.

Icy January air rushed in through the open right side door in the back as the nine men of FAST Bravo carried the wounded and dead toward the cinderblock building. At the sight of those black body bags, her hands started to shake. Tucking them under her thighs, she took slow, deep breaths in an attempt to calm down.

She'd been in tight spots before, on a couple of missions back during her army days when she'd deployed over here. But never this tight. And that had been before Brian had been killed.

Tonight, while the bullets had been flying, she hadn't had time to be scared, her entire focus on flying the aircraft and getting them out of range of enemy fire. Now that it was all over, her nervous system was making up for lost time.

Only after all the passengers had disembarked did she unbuckle her harness and exit the aircraft through her cockpit door. She was steadier now, her heart rate back to normal as she stepped out onto the bare, frozen ground.

In the dim illumination of the base perimeter lights, she got her first look at the damage they'd sustained. It wasn't pretty.

"Jesus Murphy," she said under her breath.

A moment later her crew chief walked around the end of the tail and came toward her. "How bad?" she asked.

"Bad. Check this out."

She followed him around to the other side of the tail section, and her breath caught. Light streamed through the dozens of bullet holes in the tail boom. A chunk was missing from one blade of the tail rotor. More holes raked the entire right side of the aircraft, right up to her seat in the cockpit, and the engine housing was peppered with holes as well.

Tess swallowed. Shit, it was a freaking miracle the bird had continued to fly.

Movement flashed in her peripheral vision. A man was climbing out of the Blackhawk's cabin with some gear draped over his shoulder. When he straightened, recognition hit her. SA Prentiss, one of the FAST Bravo members. Tall, dark and handsome, the first man who had captured her curiosity and interest in a long time...and the absence of guilt that normally accompanied a thought like that about another man startled her. What did it mean?

Didn't matter, because she was pretty sure Prentiss didn't even know she existed.

He nodded at them and started to turn for the building. Tess pulled her helmet off as she talked with her chief, and Prentiss stopped. Seemed to stare at her for a moment, his broad-shouldered silhouette backlit by the light coming from the building behind him.

Her pulse quickened as they studied each other across the open space. Did he recognize her? She'd spotted him around Bagram with some of his teammates a couple times over the past few weeks, and of course he'd been at the pre-mission briefings she'd attended. It was impossible not to notice him, but not once had he even made eye contact with her at a briefing or meeting. Maybe he was married, or otherwise engaged. Or maybe she was just too plain to draw his attention.

She summoned a smile, tired as hell now that her adrenaline level had crashed. "How's your team?" she called out, feeling the need to say something. *Yep, I'm the pilot commander.* None of the wounded were from the FAST team, or her chief would have told her.

"We're all fine, thanks to you," Prentiss said in his deep, southern drawl. Even his voice was sexy. She'd spent a lot of time in the Gulf region during her training days, and from his accent she'd place him either from coastal Alabama or Mississippi.

He eyed the shot-up helo before meeting her gaze once more. At this distance she couldn't see his features that well, but her brain had no problem filling in all the gaps, easily conjuring up the square jaw and dark blue eyes she found so captivating. "Your bird sure took one hell of a beating out there."

She gazed at the Blackhawk fondly, grateful for the amount of protection it had given them. Wasn't the first time she'd required it, and wouldn't be the last. Risk came with the territory in her line of work, and she wouldn't give up her position within the Aviation Division or flying Blackhawks for the world. "She did. But she still got us home."

"No, *you* got us home. That was some damn fine flying."

She shrugged off his praise. She and her copilot had merely followed procedure to the best of her ability. The door gunner deserved the most credit. "Just doing my job. And I've got a great crew." Mostly, though, they'd just been damn lucky. And after everything that had happened tonight, she didn't feel like talking to anyone. Even the mysterious, sexy man in front of her right now. "Have a good night."

"You, too." Without another word, he turned and

strode for the cinderblock building.

Tess gazed after him for a long moment, cataloguing the outline of his tall, strong body and the way he moved. Confident. Sensual.

Get back to work, Dubrovski.

She gave herself a mental slap as her crew chief continued their conversation, and expelled a breath as the weight of exhaustion hit her. She had a ream of reports to fill out and questions to answer before they could return to Bagram. Only then could she be alone to crawl into her bunk and process everything that had happened. And reimagine the terror her husband had felt in those moments before the helo he was in crashed into the mountains three years ago.

But they wouldn't be returning to Bagram on this bird.

Tess eyed the shot-up Blackhawk once more. She was too badly damaged to fly back to base, so they'd have to hitch a ride with another crew. And at the moment, she was more than okay with being a passenger instead of at the controls for the return flight.

She headed for the main building with her crew chief, deep in thought. She'd learned something surprising about herself tonight. Based on her reaction to seeing Special Agent Prentiss a few minutes ago, maybe she was finally ready to move on from Brian's death.

Even if she had no one to move on with.

Chapter One

Four months later

Reid pulled up to the curb in front of the two-story, Colonial-style brick house in the middle of Georgetown, the most expensive neighborhood in the D.C. area. There wasn't a snowball's chance in hell he could ever have afforded this kind of place on his salary as a DEA agent. Lucky for his ex, her businessman boyfriend had a lot more money than he did.

He didn't get out of his car and go to the front door, just pulled out his phone and texted Autumn. He'd discovered years ago that it was way easier for everyone involved if he and his ex didn't have to see each other during pick-ups and drop-offs.

He had joint custody of Autumn, but with Sarah still bitter about the divorce and forced to assume all of the parenting duties while Reid was away—and he was away a lot, either for training or deployments—he'd learned to keep a low profile with her. All their limited communication was via text or email, or through their lawyers. Which sucked, not only because it was a pain in the ass, but because it was a damn waste of money for them both.

The front door popped open a minute later and Autumn bounded onto the porch with her little pink overnight backpack strapped to her shoulders. She waved as she hurried down the steps, an excited smile on her face that made his chest tighten even as he grinned. He'd known nothing about kids or being a father before she'd arrived nine-and-a-half years ago, and now he couldn't imagine life without her. She was the light of his life, hands down. There wasn't anything he wouldn't do for her.

He leaned over and popped the passenger door open for her. "Hey, baby girl."

"Hi, Dad!" She tossed her backpack onto the backseat, then ducked into the front to wind her arms around his neck. "Missed you."

Reid gave her a squeeze, inhaling the scent of her shampoo. "Missed you too."

Autumn hopped out and slid into the rear seat while he set the front one back into position. She was still too short to sit up front with him. "I brought my new craft kit with me. We can do it after we get home from the movie and dinner."

Inside, he grimaced, but he merely smiled, glad she'd have something to occupy herself with for the next several hours. "Yeah, about that…"

She stopped in the midst of doing up her seatbelt to look at him. "What?"

"I have to stop by HQ for a little while right now."

She groaned. "Now?"

"I know, it sucks, and I'm sorry. But I have to go in, there's an important meeting. I didn't want to cancel our night together though, so I thought I'd just come get you, take you with me, and we can catch the movie when I'm done."

She buckled her seatbelt and flopped back against the seat with her arms crossed, looking so much like her mother but with his coloring, it startled him. "Fine," she muttered, gazing out the window.

Reid fired up the engine. "Shouldn't take too long," he said trying to put a positive spin on things. He swiveled to look back at her. "It's a nice day out. Wanna drive with the top down?"

She shrugged and didn't look at him. "I guess."

The amount of attitude she managed to inject in those two syllables damn near made him chuckle. He was in so much trouble when she hit her teens. "Okay."

Without another word he hit the button to open the convertible top and it folded away into the back, smooth as butter. Pulling away from the curb, he reached down and turned on the stereo, where he had a special playlist waiting, and cranked it.

As soon as the bass line for one of the bubblegum pop songs she loved blasted through the speakers, he glanced in the rearview mirror and caught the reluctant smile tugging at her mouth. Reid smothered a grin. Worst music in the history of music, but if it put a smile on his kid's face, that was all that mattered.

By the time he reached FAST headquarters in Arlington just across from the Pentagon, Autumn was singing along to the music and bobbing her head in time with the beat.

Mission accomplished.

He parked in a spot out front of the building just as Maka pulled in beside them in his big-ass black, raised pickup. Reid nodded at his teammate. "Hey, who's that?" he said to Autumn.

"Uncle Kai!" she squealed, and frantically unbuckled her seatbelt.

Reid had just enough time to switch off the ignition

and pop the passenger door for her, then she was out like a rocket, practically hopping up and down as she waited impatiently for Maka to climb down from his truck.

"Hey, if it isn't my best girl," Maka said, his bronze, rugged face breaking into a huge smile as he reached down to scoop Autumn up in a giant hug.

The contrast in their size was almost comical, but Reid had to admit there was something endearing about a guy Maka's size hugging his daughter with such genuine affection, those huge arms wrapped around her protectively. It always made him proud that all his teammates loved her and would watch out for her.

"Nice tunes, by the way." Maka shot Reid a knowing grin. "Didn't know you were into that sorta stuff, man."

"Guy's gotta have some secrets from his teammates," Reid said, climbing out and grabbing Autumn's backpack, then his gear in the trunk.

The instant Maka set her down, Autumn reached up for both his hand and Reid's. "After Dad finishes with his meeting, we're going to see the new Pixar movie," she said to Maka. "You wanna come with?"

"Oh, man, I wish I could, sweetie, but I've already got plans later."

Autumn peered up at him, a frown tugging at her eyebrows. "You have a girlfriend?"

Reid burst out laughing at her astonishment.

Not the least bit offended, Maka grinned. "Yeah, I do. We've been seeing each other on and off for a while now."

From what Reid had gathered, the "relationship"—if one could call it that—with Shelley was a total shit show, but there must be a reason why Maka kept getting back together with her. And Reid wasn't exactly a relationship guru, so what the hell did he know. She must be damn good in bed for his buddy to put up with all the drama, though. Since he didn't exactly have the equivalent of a

PhD when it came to making things work with the opposite sex, Reid had never asked his buddy about Shelley.

"Oh, there's Uncle Zaid!" Autumn said as they entered the building. She tugged free of their hands and raced over to Khan, who stopped and held his arms out to her with a big grin.

"Hey, princess. How are you?" Khan said, wrapping her up in a bear hug.

"Good. Dad and I are going to a movie after he's done here. You wanna come? Uncle Kai can't, because he's got a date or something."

"Is that right?" Khan shot Maka a wry look. "I'd love to go, but I've got a date too."

"With Jaliya?"

She and Khan had eloped over in England back in March. Everyone on the team had been stunned by the suddenness of it, except for Reid. Of all of them, Khan was the most level. He knew what he wanted, and when he'd found Jaliya he hadn't wasted any time in making her his. Reid had never seen his buddy happier.

"Yes. You like her, right?" Khan asked Autumn.

"Of course! She's awesome. And I like that she knows how to use a gun."

Reid's heart almost burst with pride. "She's her daddy's girl," he murmured, watching her chatter on to Khan.

Maka scratched his chin, watching her. "How long you figure until she starts dating?"

That wiped the smile off Reid's face. "Dude, she's only nine."

Maka shrugged his massive left shoulder, shifting the thick black, tribal tattoos roping down the length of his arm. "Okay, so that gives us, what? Another five years or so until the boys start sniffing around?"

The thought was absolutely terrifying. "Jesus. Five

years?" The last nine had already flown by way too fast. And soon he was going to have to worry about horny teenage boys?

Maka nodded. "I was about fourteen, yeah. You?"

Reid scowled. "Yeah." And unfortunately he knew too well *exactly* how teenage boys thought.

His buddy clapped him once on the back. Hard. "Don't worry about it yet, brother. Let's go get this briefing done so we can spend some quality time with our ladies."

Reid rescued Khan from getting his ear talked off, and held Autumn's hand as he escorted her to the kitchen. "I think there are some of those cookies you like. Unless Uncle Kai ate them all. And you can have some milk with them—" He stopped in the doorway to the kitchen when he saw the blond-haired woman sitting alone at the table, her profile to them as she read a newspaper.

What was *she* doing here?

Agent Dubrovski looked up from the paper, gave him a quick smile before focusing on Autumn. "Hello. Who's this?"

It had been months since their paths had crossed overseas, and he'd never imagined bumping into her again stateside.

He shook himself and found his voice. "My daughter, Autumn." Was she here for the briefing or something? That didn't make sense, since she was a pilot, and the last time he'd seen her had been at the FOB in Afghanistan back in January. What a hell of a night that had been.

"Hi, Autumn. I'm Tess."

Tess. Reid let his gaze wander over her as she got up and came over to shake Autumn's hand. He hadn't been able to get an up-close look at her before, and at the FOB it had been too dark to see her face clearly, but he sure was curious about her. She and her crew had saved his entire team that night.

She was tall for a woman, around five-nine or ten, and

maybe in her early thirties. The dark jeans she wore hugged the womanly curves of her hips and thighs, and the deep blue T-shirt emphasized the generous swell of her breasts.

Seeing her in civvies was a hell of a lot different than seeing her in a flight suit and combat boots. Though on her, both were equally hot. She had a lush, ripe body, curvy in all the right places, made to fill a man's hands. How the hell he'd never noticed her back at Bagram was a mystery.

"Do you work with my dad?" Autumn asked, shaking Tess's hand politely. Reid noticed Tess wasn't wearing a ring. Was she single?

"Sort of. We worked together overseas a few months back." She glanced up at him, a hint of humor in her light green eyes. Faint laugh lines fanned out from the corners and a light scattering of freckles dusted the bridge of her nose and cheekbones. He'd noticed she was quick to smile, her lips full and kissable.

"Are you on the FAST team too?" Autumn asked.

Tess chuckled softly. "No. I'm a pilot."

Autumn's eyes widened. "You fly planes?"

"Helicopters. Big ones."

His daughter grinned. "That's so cool."

No, it was downright hot.

"It really is, yeah," Tess said with another smile, and straightened, a slight dimple appearing in her left cheek. Realizing he was staring, Reid forced his gaze back to his daughter.

"I had to come here with Dad because he's got a meeting. But after that we have a special date planned."

Yeah, so special she'd invited Maka and Khan along, Reid thought with a mental snort. "Right, so you can sit over there and have some cookies while you wait," he told her, and headed for the cupboard, his entire body attuned to the woman standing behind him.

As soon as he opened the cupboard, he bit back a curse. Of the dozen packages of cookies that had been there the last time he'd checked a couple weeks ago, just one remained. And when he pulled it open, there were only two cookies left.

"Maka, you giant pig," he muttered under his breath, turning back toward the table. "Sorry, there are only a couple left. You want milk with them?" he asked Autumn.

"Can I have some tea?"

He blinked at her. "You drink tea now?"

She shrugged, already in the process of opening her backpack and unloading her things onto the table next to Tess's seat. "Mom took me out for a tea party a month ago. It was super fun."

Right. Tea. "Okay, I guess so." He'd never made tea in his life. He searched the cupboard until he found a teabag, then took down a mug and filled it with water. Plopping the teabag in it, he put it in the microwave to nuke it.

"Eww, Dad, that's not how you do it."

Reid cranked his head around. "Why not?"

Autumn rolled her eyes as though he was an uncultured hick. "You're supposed to boil the water in a kettle first, then pour it over the teabag and let it steep."

Steep?

Agent Dubrovski walked over and gestured to the microwave door, amusement gleaming in her pretty eyes. "May I?"

He held up a hand and backed away. "Be my guest."

She gave him a sideways glance as she took the mug out. Damn, she was pretty, in a low-maintenance, fresh-faced way. "Isn't your meeting starting soon?"

"Yeah, in a minute."

"I can stay with her if you want. One of the analysts is my ride, so I have to wait here until after the briefing anyway."

He hesitated. He didn't even know her. Didn't seem fair to expect her to hang with Autumn, and he wasn't sure if his daughter would be comfortable with it. He never even introduced Autumn to the women he dated. Though to be honest, he didn't date them so much as he hooked up with them over the past two years. Easier that way, and less bullshit to put up with. "You sure?"

"Absolutely. I've got three nieces back home." She shot Autumn a grin that was so genuine, warmth spread through Reid's chest. "Been a while since I had some genuine girl time."

Autumn's eyes lit up. "You like to do crafts?"

"*Love* doing crafts."

Reid rubbed the back of his neck, feeling a little out of his depth. Truth be told, even though he was looking forward to spending time with his daughter, he hadn't been super pumped about the crafting portion of the evening she'd planned for later on. And Autumn sure seemed to like her, so... "Okay with you, Autumn?"

"Yes, for sure. You go on," she said without looking up from emptying bundles of what looked like yarn and other supplies onto the table. "As you can see, I came prepared."

Reid didn't miss the jab. He'd picked her up without bringing anything to amuse her with because he'd planned to let her watch TV here while he was in the meeting. "All right."

He shifted his attention back to Agent Dubrovski, struck again by her understated beauty. And combined with that body... Yeah, he must have been fucking blind not to notice her before. "Thanks a lot. Shouldn't be too long, hopefully."

She shrugged, the ends of her golden hair brushing her shoulders. A lock clung to the top of her breast, dragging his gaze there like a magnet before he forced his eyes back to her face. "No problem. See you soon."

Reid made it to the briefing room just as the meeting got underway. All eight of his teammates were already in their chairs facing the front of the room. He took a seat between Khan and Hamilton, the team leader, and listened while their commander gave them a rundown of the latest intel.

"First off, thanks for coming in on your day off," Taggart began. His dark blond hair was spiked at the top and front and he wore dress slacks and a button-down, all spiffy-looking. Must be taking the wifey out on a hot date after this. "I'm gonna keep this brief, and update you on the latest on the *Veneno* cartel."

The current bane of their existence. FAST Bravo's recent deployment to Afghanistan had been…eventful, but positive. They'd managed to bag a famous smuggling lord known as The Jackal, who worked with the *Venenos* and turned out to be the head of the Afghan forces that FAST Bravo worked with on ops.

"Our recent deployment to A-stan helped curb the majority of the flow of opium out of there to Mexico, but now the drug runners are just smuggling their shit north over the border into Tajikistan, and from there to China before shipping it into the U.S."

This came as no surprise to anyone in the room. Seal off one avenue, and the smugglers simply used another. The war on drugs was never ending, and frustrating as hell. Sometimes Reid wondered whether they had any affect at all on diminishing the flow of illicit drugs around the globe.

"As you know, the entire purpose of General Nasar acting as The Jackal was to earn enough cash to pay for a heart transplant for his young son. Even though he didn't raise the funds and got locked up, someone in the *Veneno* organization stepped up and made the operation happen. Found a donor on the black market and paid for the procedure personally. All our sources to date have indicated it was *El Escorpion*."

The fabled and mysterious head of the *Veneno* cartel. As far as the DEA knew, no one within the cartel even knew exactly who he was, except for perhaps the top two or three people. Even the top lieutenants had never met the man in person.

"I asked you all in today because we're gearing up for Emerald Warrior in just over a week."

A joint training exercise held in the southeast U.S. where FAST trained with other SOF elements like SEAL Team Six, Delta, the FBI's Hostage Rescue Team and others, to increase cross-unit proficiency and streamline things when they worked missions together.

"It's a happy coincidence that we'll be working along the Gulf Coast, since the agency is currently searching for Carlos Ruiz, one of *El Escorpion's* lieutenants. Some of our agents tangled with him last year. He was wounded, but recovered. So he's got a grudge against all of us, and he'd love the chance to get even if he can." Taggart paused, his thick arms folded over his chest as he glanced up at the screen behind him.

One of the analysts brought up a picture and a list of bullet points. Ruiz was a rugged-looking Hispanic man in his mid-thirties maybe, with wavy, coffee-brown hair and hazel-green eyes.

"This asshole is a real piece of work, even by cartel standards," Taggart continued. "Likes to live the high life, rumored to own a big spread of land in the Sinaloa region, and he's got a sadistic streak that is right up there with the worst we've seen from the Mexican cartels. Word is, he's responsible for the recent kidnapping of American reporter Victoria Gomez and the killing of her family. The FBI isn't sure if she's still alive or not, or if she's still being held captive by Ruiz and his men."

Staring up at that picture, burning the image into his mind, Reid hated the human piece of shit on sight. He remembered the reporter's story, because it had been all over the news when it first happened. She'd disappeared almost two weeks ago after her family had been slaughtered by those sadistic animals in southern Florida, and nobody had heard anything since.

He sat there committing every detail of the bastard's face to memory while Taggart carried on with his report, giving them all the background info the agency had on him.

"He's suspected to be operating in southwestern Florida right now, or maybe into Alabama, and he's our priority target. If we get a lock on him, we're going after him." Taggart turned back to face them, his turquoise gaze intense. "Memorize his face and the pertinent details. He's going to be heavily armed and will likely have a protective detail made up of at least a half dozen *Veneno* enforcers with him, all hand-picked by him. And if it helps as a point of reference, Dillon Wainright was his head enforcer."

Everyone glanced at Logan Granger, seated at the end of the row to Reid's right. Wainright was the asshole who had terrorized Granger's girl, Taylor, last year. Reid was glad she'd shot the bastard dead that day.

"Ruiz is impatient," Taggart continued. "He's abrupt and ruthless, and that goes for dealings with his own men as well as anyone who gets in his way. Or anyone he *suspects* might get in his way. He's reputed to have either personally killed or ordered the killings of over a dozen high-ranking rival cartel bosses." Taggart paused to scan the room, giving his next words added weight. "This guy is marked for death by other cartels, so the fact that he's stayed alive this long has to tell you how tough a target he is. He's got money, resources and plenty of contacts to protect him." He raised his dark blond eyebrows. "When we get the call about him, we need to be ready to go in hard and take him out."

Hell yeah. Arms folded across his chest, Reid's hands bunched into fists against his ribs. As far as he and his teammates were concerned, Ruiz and the rest of the *Veneno* cartel were living on borrowed time.

Chapter Two

⬦◇◈◇⬦

"When did you start flying helicopters?" Autumn asked, frowning in concentration as she glued a plastic googly eye on the ball of fluff in her hand.

Half a dozen pom-pom puppies sat perched in a row in the middle of the table amidst a mess of crafting supplies. Tess had no idea how the company had managed to fit it all into the box in the first place.

"I was twenty-two. Just after I finished college."

Autumn looked up at her from across the table. "You learned to fly there?" She didn't have an accent like her dad. Her mom must be from up north.

"No, I got my bachelor's degree in science there. I learned to fly after that, once I was in the army. But my science degree made it a lot easier because of the math, and because I already understood the physics of flight."

The little girl looked impressed. "Wow, that's neat." She went back to placing the puppy's eye. "I've thought about joining the military when I graduate from high school."

Tess paused in the act of winding yarn into a ball, surprised. "Yeah?"

She nodded. "That way I could get my college paid for, like my dad did. And it would be pretty neat to learn how to fly a Blackhawk. My parents and grandparents told me they'd pay for my school if they can, but that's a lot of money. I'd feel bad."

Tess frowned at her, momentarily at a loss for words. "How old are you?"

"Nine. I'll be ten this December."

Holy shit. When Tess had been nine, she'd only been interested in My Little Pony and what kinds of candy she could afford to buy with her weekly allowance. Never had it crossed her mind to think about going to college someday, let alone how she was going to pay for it. "Wow, that's… You're looking ahead. That's great."

Autumn shrugged. "I want to have a nice house and be able to travel when I grow up. So I need to have a good job and earn lots of money."

Jeez, this kid was starting to give her an inferiority complex. "Where would you like to travel to?"

"Europe, for sure. Maybe Antarctica, because I like penguins. Dad and I just went to the Wizarding World of Harry Potter a few weeks ago. It was my Christmas present."

"Just the two of you?"

"Yeah. My parents are divorced." Her tone was matter-of-fact.

"Oh." She squelched the leap of excitement inside her. Divorced didn't necessarily mean he was single. Or available. "And did you have a good time there?"

Autumn's face lit up and she stopped working on her pom-pom puppy. "The best. I'm a huge Harry Potter fan. Have you read the books?"

"No."

Autumn looked scandalized. "None of them?"

Tess bit back a laugh. "Not a single one."

"But you've seen the movies," she said with a frown. "Or at least some of them."

"Nope, afraid not."

Autumn sat back, an expression of disbelief on her little face. "What? I thought you said you have three nieces."

"I do, but they're a lot older than you, mostly all grown up now, and into different stuff." And they sure as hell hadn't been this mature at age nine. Autumn was scaring her a little.

She gave Tess a dubious look and returned to her crafting. "Well, if you don't like to read you should at least watch the movies, they're awesome. Anyway, Dad took me to The Wizarding World of Harry Potter." She sighed, shook her head, her eyes wistful. "It was just like being in the movies."

"That good, huh?"

"Amazing. Even Dad liked it."

Tess didn't know the man, but she thought it was incredibly sweet that Reid had planned the trip and taken his daughter to a place that clearly meant so much to her. "Sounds like fun."

"Yeah. I don't get to see him all that much, so it was cool to have a trip with him. He's a good dad. Even if my mom doesn't think so," she added.

Tess's ears perked up. "She doesn't?"

"Nah. They don't get along. My mom's always mad at him, no matter how hard he tries."

Interesting, that Autumn would defend him. And it sounded to Tess like she got caught in the middle a lot. "I'm sorry. That must be hard."

She shrugged. "I'm used to it. I just don't like it when my mom says bad stuff about him. He loves me and he's doing the best he can."

He had a sweet little protector, that was for sure. "That's good. I know he has to be away a lot, for work."

Autumn nodded. "Do you go away a lot too?"

"Yes." The Aviation Division was based out of Fort Worth, but she moved around wherever she was needed, including overseas. And she was glad for the ever-changing scenery, because keeping busy had saved her sanity in the years since Brian died. "I go home to Nevada when I can to visit my parents and my sister and her family, but I don't get to see them as much as I'd like."

Autumn gave a solemn nod. "It's a sacrifice families like ours have to make so that the world can be a better place."

The little girl's maturity was astounding, although that last bit sounded exactly like something a parent would say to their child to explain their situation. Tess didn't quite know what to make of it. Maybe Autumn just had a crazy high IQ or something.

"Hey, how'd you guys make out?" a familiar male voice drawled from the doorway.

Tess looked over her shoulder just as Special Agent Prentiss entered the kitchen, a half-smile on his ruggedly handsome face. Her heart beat faster at the sight of him. He was a little over six feet, and broad through the chest and shoulders, his arms well-muscled below the short sleeves of his T-shirt. "Good. We've been busy making a pack of pom-pom puppies."

"I see that." He went straight to Autumn, set his big hands on her little shoulders and bent to kiss the top of her head as he took in their efforts. "They're pretty cute."

"Yes, and I made you this one," she told him, picking up a floppy brown-and-black one with ears that stuck straight out of its head, a little pink felt tongue lolling out of its mouth. "It's a German Shepherd."

"My favorite," he said, cradling it in his palm.

"I know," Autumn said, her voice full of pride. "So are

you done now?"

His eyes crinkled at the corners when he smiled, and the obvious warmth between the two of them made him even hotter to Tess. "All done."

Autumn turned to her. "We're going to dinner and a movie now. Or maybe a movie and then dinner. You wanna come with us?"

Taken aback by the offer, it took Tess a moment to respond. "Oh, I couldn't—"

"Please? You told me you like Pixar movies."

"And you told me it's a special father-daughter date," she pointed out.

Autumn waved the protest away with one hand. "That was before." She turned those dark blue eyes on Tess, eyes exactly like her father's. Oh yeah, this kid knew how to work it. "Pul*eeeze*? It'll be so much fun."

Unsure what to say, Tess glanced at Prentiss for help. She expected him to maybe clear his throat awkwardly or look away, but instead he raised his eyebrows at her in question and waited.

Wait. Did he *want* her to come? Or was he just being polite and hoping she'd say no? God knew she had no plans, other than a hot bath and curling up to watch a movie in her hotel room. "I...guess I could."

"Yay!" Now that she'd gotten the answer she wanted, Autumn hopped down from her chair and began cramming all the crafting supplies back into the box. "Dad, can you find an open box for the puppies? I don't wanna squish them."

"I'll take a look around."

"I'll help," Tess said, and jumped up to follow him across the kitchen. His scent trailed back to her, citrus and spice. Damn delicious. Autumn hadn't mentioned a girlfriend in the picture. Was he seeing anyone? It would be weird to go to the movie with them if he was, and a guy like him wouldn't have a shortage of women to date.

He reached into a cupboard, found a cereal box and began tearing one side off to make a tray for the yarn puppies. He had such strong, capable hands. Hands that could render someone helpless or even kill them, but could also cradle a yarn puppy and touch his daughter with complete gentleness. He was part protector, part nurturer, and part warrior.

Put that together with that rugged face and powerful body, and he was enough to make her ovaries explode.

Yikes! Down, girl. You don't even know him.

"Are you sure about this?" she asked him quietly. "I don't want to crash your date." *Plus we don't even know each other.* It was kind of weird to just up and go to dinner and a movie with him and Autumn. Right?

"Nah, it's fine. I appreciate you hanging with Autumn, and she obviously really likes you." He paused to look at her, and her pulse increased at seeing that rugged face up close. "But don't feel like you have to."

The perfect amount of dark brown stubble covered his jaw and cheeks, giving him an ultra-masculine look. His eyes were a deep, dark blue toward the outside of the iris, then changed to an almost powder blue near the pupils, and surrounded by thick, dark lashes. Gorgeous, arresting eyes she could easily fall into.

Get hold of yourself. "Okay then," she murmured. "I can have my ride drop me off on her way home. Where's the theater?"

"Just come with us. I'll drop you back at your hotel after dinner. Sound okay?"

Ah… "Sure." Tiny butterfly wings began to flutter in her stomach, something she hadn't felt in ages. It had been three years since she lost Brian, and she'd be lying if she said she wasn't lonely. But she'd never reacted to a man quite this strongly before. This was visceral. Primal. She'd briefly dated a guy for a couple months up until her recent deployment to Afghanistan this past winter, but things had fizzled out pretty fast while they were apart, and within weeks of her being overseas he'd told her he wanted to start seeing someone else.

It had hurt at the time, but it wasn't like she'd been in love with him, so she'd let him go and focused on work. Lately, though, work, travel, and time with her family back home weren't enough to fill the void.

Her family worried about her being on her own all the time, so she lied to them and told them she wasn't lonely. She wasn't going to settle for just any man who came along just to have someone to hold her in the night. And she'd been alone long enough now that she'd gone through her grieving and was finally ready to find someone to share her life with.

Reid handed Autumn the modified cereal box. Once the yarn menagerie was safely stored in their new home, they all walked out to the parking lot together, Tess texting her friend to say she had a ride. "How long are you in town for?" he asked Tess. He was a full head taller than her, his size and muscular build making her feel small by comparison. As well as intensely, amazingly feminine in a way she hadn't for so damn long.

"Just another few days, for some meetings prior to our upcoming training op."

At that he shot her a surprised look. "You doing Emerald Warrior with us?"

"Yes. Well, a week of it, at least." And she hoped that meant she would see more of him while they were down there. Based on what she'd seen so far, she'd love to get to know him better.

"You like convertibles, Tess?" Autumn asked, holding her dad's hand. It was adorable, seeing such a big, muscular alpha male holding that little hand.

Tess swore her uterus cramped, but reprimanded herself. He was divorced. So clearly, he wasn't perfect. She had to remember that and stop being so dazzled by him. "I love them."

"Good. Wait 'til you see my dad's car."

Tess glanced at him but he just smiled and kept walking. Then she spotted the shiny, vintage black Mustang convertible sitting next to a massive, lifted pickup, and grinned. "That yours?"

"Yup." The hint of a smile played around the edges of his mouth.

The black paint gleamed under a fresh coat of wax, and because the top was down she could see it was a standard. It was clear he took good care of it. "*Nice*." There was something so sexy about a man who could handle a stick shift.

He raised a dark eyebrow at her in surprise. "You like cars?"

There was that little flutter in the pit of her belly again. "I like *nice* cars."

At the grin he flashed her, any remaining awkwardness melted away, and she was glad she'd accepted the impromptu invitation to go with them. They were essentially strangers, but this was already promising to be the most enjoyable night she'd had in a long time.

Chapter Three

⬤————◇◇◇◇————⬤

Music blared from the secluded house, so loud that the thump of the bass reverberated in Carlos's chest and covered the thud of his cane on the concrete as he walked to the front door. The aging bungalow was set back a long way from the road. Spanish moss gleamed a pale, ghostly gray in the moonlight as it hung from the gnarled branches of the cypress trees that surrounded the property and arched over the low roofline, giving it added privacy. The location was perfect for their needs.

Out here there were no neighbors, no passersby to nose around and spoil the fun.

Going by the amount of noise coming from inside, his guys were having one hell of a party, and he wasn't going to miss out on a night's entertainment. They'd carried out his most recent orders perfectly, executing three traffickers who had tried to screw him, so he didn't mind them letting loose for the next couple days. He felt perfectly safe here. This backwater area out in the Louisiana swamp was so isolated there was little chance anyone would find him even if they were out hunting him.

Still, one couldn't be too careful. His list of enemies was longer than his erect dick, and he wasn't taking any chances. Not when he'd finally started living the kind of high-roller lifestyle that had been denied him until a few months ago.

The smell of booze and pot hit him the moment he opened the front door, mixing with the underlying stench of B.O. and piss. He wrinkled his nose in distaste and shut the door behind him while his two bodyguards stood outside on the covered porch. He didn't mind the boys having fun, but getting wasted to the point of no longer caring about personal hygiene was gross.

In a room off the run-down foyer that looked like it hadn't been touched since the early eighties, four of his enforcers were sprawled out on the peach-and-green sofas and scarred hardwood floor. Each had a naked woman on their lap, one wearing a slave collar to signify that she wasn't there willingly. When Carlos met her frightened gaze, she cowered away from Javier and tried to cover her naked breasts as she lowered her head, shame etched into her face.

Carlos ignored her and stood facing his men. He'd lost several of his best guys over a year ago when they'd been killed by DEA agents up in D.C. Those who remained weren't nearly at the same level as the dead men, but they were good enough, loyal, and enjoyed what they did.

The four of them called out to him with the joyful tones of the sloppy drunk—or the wasted high. "What are you lazy fuckers up to?" he said in Spanish over the music, unable to keep from grinning. From the looks of things, they'd been partying for quite a while already. The room was full of ashtrays overflowing with discarded weed buds, along with empty beer cans and liquor bottles.

"Reaping the rewards of working for you, boss man," Javier said, his gold front tooth flashing as he grinned.

One arm locked around the cringing woman's shoulders, he squeezed her naked breast and laughed when she tried to slap him away. "She's new. You know I like 'em feisty."

She was pretty enough, tits still firm, decent body. They could get a good price for her with their next shipment. Along with one very special addition.

Carlos flapped a dismissive hand at them as he turned away, his mind on other things. "Carry on."

He was here to check that special addition in person. Had driven all the way here from Tallahassee just to see her.

In the kitchen, he found his head enforcer next to the fridge, helping himself to a massive burger in one hand, and a bottle of beer in the other. Stone cold sober, as usual. It's why Carlos had made him head enforcer. Carlos had enough to do without having to babysit his guys.

Carlos nodded at him and shouted over the music. "Antonio. How's it going?"

"Good, *patrón*," he answered, stuffing his mouth full.

Carlos surveyed the rest of the open concept great room that looked as shabby as the rest of the place. Six more of his guys were in the living room and kitchen. Three of them were busy entertaining the whores they'd picked up, one was mostly out of view as he fucked a woman in the corner, and the last two were snorting coke at the kitchen table.

He wrinkled his nose again. He enjoyed his booze, fine cigars and liked to party with the best of them, but he never touched dope. Ever. He'd seen too many stupid assholes ruin themselves by partaking of their product and getting hooked. It always ended the same way. Either in self-destruction, or a fellow enforcer sent to end them.

The guys doing lines at the table were taking a huge risk in getting addicted on that shit, especially given how potent their labs were making the stuff, cutting it with poison like fentanyl, which could easily kill someone in small concentrations. They liked to live life on the edge, riding the razor-sharp between getting high, and turning into yet another junkie created by their product. A tightrope very few could walk without falling off.

Not Carlos's concern. It was Antonio's job to monitor them. If any of their men got hooked and could no longer be trusted to carry out their duty, he alerted Carlos, and they were dealt with immediately.

But people throughout North America were looking for a more potent high, and the old stuff wasn't cutting it anymore. For the cartel, the trick was finding the tolerance threshold that the average human could handle. Culling the herd with overdose deaths was okay to a point, but it made no business sense whatsoever to kill off every potential customer who tried *Veneno* coke or heroine. Making it strong enough to hook them on the very first try, but not kill them, was the key.

Again, not his department. His job was to expand the cartel's territory and eliminate the competition wherever he found it. By whatever means necessary.

As for his men…

Carlos swept his gaze over the great room once more. The couple in the corner must be near finishing, because there was a lot of thrashing going on now. A shrill female scream pierced the racket blaring from the speakers of the ancient stereo and a lamp fell, smashing to pieces on the floor.

He sighed inwardly, feeling like an old man in the midst of a wild frat party. Even though he was only thirty-four, he felt ancient compared to these guys, most of whom were in their early twenties. As long as they did their jobs when he gave them orders, Carlos didn't care what they did in their spare time, or with whom. They were a means to an end, rabid dogs he'd brought to heel and kept leashed with the lure of money, product and free women.

In exchange, when he needed something done he unleashed them, and they reverted back to their natural state. Soulless killers, every single one of them. So sadistic it made people's blood run cold. And he was the only one who could control them. If that changed, he had them put down. Simple. Every one of them knew the rules, and the arrangement suited Carlos perfectly.

He turned back to face Antonio, growing impatient. "Where is she?"

Antonio shoved the last bite of burger into his mouth, chewed it fast. "Out back."

"Alone?"

"Yeah. She tried to escape the other night and damn near made it, so we've been training her to be more obedient ever since." He flashed a satisfied grin. "She's a slow learner."

Carlos grunted, his fingers flexing around the head of his cane, that familiar, deep ache shooting through his leg. "I want to see her." This bitch had nearly ruined him and he wanted to see her suffering. "Show me."

He followed Antonio through the living room, past the naked couple collapsed in a heap in the corner, and out onto the back porch. The brain-numbing noise of the music muted once the back door was shut.

As they walked across the grass of the private backyard, Carlos glimpsed the outline of a wooden shed tucked amongst the trees near the rear fence. Even though it was eleven at night the humidity was high enough to have him sweating by the time they reached the outbuilding.

At the base of the wooden steps, Antonio switched on a flashlight, illuminating the heavy chain and padlock on the weatherworn door. He unlocked it and shoved it open.

The smell of hot, stale piss nearly made Carlos gag. He pulled a handkerchief out of his pocket to cover his nose and mouth as he peered inside. His eager gaze followed the beam of light to where it revealed a naked, dark-haired woman lying on a filthy bare mattress in the middle of the floor.

She was chained to the floorboards by a metal collar around her neck. They'd hogtied her, hands and feet bound together behind her with rope.

Couldn't be too unbearable, since she appeared to be asleep. Then again, they'd probably drugged her with something. "Wake her up," he ordered, his heartbeat drumming in his ears.

"Hey," Antonio said gruffly, stalking over to nudge her bare leg with his boot.

The brunette stirred and raised her head slightly. Her features were distorted from the bruising and swelling, but it was definitely her.

Victoria Gomez, the Mexican-born reporter from Houston who had not only exposed him, but almost cost him his life when a rival cartel had targeted him because of a story she'd broadcast. Three of Carlos's best men had died in the shootout trying to protect him, and every day the pain of the healed bullet wounds in his right leg reminded him of the suffering she'd caused him.

"Wake up, bitch," Antonio snapped in Spanish.

The woman cracked one dark eye open, the other swollen shut. It took a moment for her bleary gaze to focus on them, but when she did she glared up at them with such hatred and malevolence it sent an involuntary shiver up Carlos's spine. Excitement blended with the buzz of warning at the back of his head.

Seeing her bound, naked and helpless sent a rush of power through him. *She* was the victim now, and deserved everything they did to her.

He took a step forward, intending to bend down and grip her jaw between his fingers so he could stare into her eyes, but his foot slipped on something. Looking down, he saw the wet sheen on the old wooden boards near the edge of the mattress and nearly gagged before he jerked away from the puddle of piss.

"For Christ's sake, clean her up," he snarled to Antonio, retreating to the doorway.

Disgusted, he limped down the steps and wiped the bottom of his shoe on the grass. Fucking nine-hundred-dollar Italian leather, and now he'd have to throw them out. No way he'd wear them again, now that they'd been tainted by that bitch's piss.

When he turned around, Antonio had dragged a hose out from behind the shed.

Standing in the doorway, his chief enforcer opened up a jet of cold water on the bitch. She shrieked and ducked her head to try and shield her face, but that was all she could do to protect herself.

Antonio held the flashlight in one hand as he continued to hose her down from head to foot, leaving her dark hair plastered to her head and naked body gleaming on the soaked mattress. Carlos's dick hardened and a bolt of excitement flashed through him. Even half-starved she had a body on her that would net them thousands.

He would use her before they sold her, once his men had enjoyed her for a while, but not now. He would never touch her when she was so filthy and repulsive. When he was ready for her he'd have her scrubbed clean first, waxed, her makeup and hair done up, and wearing some sexy lingerie he could cut off her with the blade he always carried with him.

More blood surged to his swelling cock as he imagined the expression on her face when he pulled the knife out and advanced toward her while she was bound and helpless. It had been a long time since anything had excited him half as much.

When she was prepared the right way, and tied to a bed in some luxury hotel in New Orleans, then he could savor every tiny cringe as he unwrapped her, enjoy her terror and loathing as he did whatever he pleased to her. Whatever pleased *him*.

Only after he'd taken his fill would he sell her, so that he could have his revenge and show her the price for exposing him, plus make a profit on her.

And if she died before that happened, it wasn't the end of the world. One less loose end for him to worry about.

Smirking as Antonio finished hosing her down and shut off the water, Carlos stalked back up the steps, his cane loud on the wood in the enveloping silence. The bitch wasn't so gutsy now, soaking wet and shivering in her miserable prison, pinkish rivulets of blood trickling down her wrists and ankles from where the rope had cut into her flesh during her struggles to free herself.

"That's better," he said, standing at the edge of the waterlogged mattress to tower over her. He liked seeing her helpless and shivering. Not so brave now—

She whipped her head around and spat at him, the wad of saliva landing with a revolting splat on the toe of his left shoe.

He clenched his jaw as primal rage roared through him. No one disrespected him that way. *No one*. He took a menacing step toward her, cane raised, ready to bash her sneering face in, then stopped at the last moment because of the look on her face.

Acceptance. Relief.

He saw it in her eyes. She knew he was going to kill her. *Wanted* him to use the cane and put an end to her torment.

His hand shook on the cane as he sucked in a shuddering breath. He refused to end her torment so easily after what she'd cost him. He wanted her to suffer a lot more yet before she eventually died in some hovel of an Asian bordello when her pimp decided she no longer was worth the cost of keeping her alive.

A slow smile curved his mouth, and he reveled in the first hint of fear that crept into that dark, bruised eye.

"Get Javier," he said softly to Antonio. "Might as well not let her go to waste, now that she's all clean again."

Pivoting on his heel, he limped back down the sagging wooden steps and across the overgrown lawn, the music from the house getting louder and the rage-filled screams from the shed growing fainter behind him.

Chapter Four

Reid pulled up in front of Tess's hotel twenty minutes after dropping Autumn off at her mom's place, trying to think of a way to stall. Or even pondering asking Tess out, which didn't make any sense because they lived in different cities.

Although that could be a good thing, too. The thing was, he hadn't expected to enjoy Tess's company so much, and now he didn't want the evening to end.

He wanted more time with her, to get to know her. And if part of it was because a tiny bit of him was desperate to stave off the inevitable moment when he was left alone with his demons as the anniversary of his best friend's death loomed like a black hole before him... Well, he was far from perfect.

"Thanks for letting me tag along on your father-daughter night. I had a good time," Tess said to him, reaching down to unbuckle her seatbelt.

"Yeah, me too." Watching her undo that belt and prepare to get out of his car made dread congeal like a cold, hard lump in the pit of his stomach.

The idea of going home alone to his apartment right now rattled him enough that his heart rate kicked up. This time of year was always the hardest on him, as well as the Christmas holidays.

This past Christmas he'd been at Bagram with his teammates, and had plenty of things going on to keep his mind occupied. Until Khan had eloped a few months ago, Reid had spent a lot of time with him, in part because his teammate didn't drink. Now, Reid was on his own with downtime on his hands, and the urge to hit up the nearest liquor store just to numb the memory of Jason's death a little was like a living thing inside him.

"And thanks for dinner. Next time, my treat," Tess added.

It encouraged him that she was open to a next time. "Sure." Things had gone way better tonight than he'd anticipated. The movie had been pretty good, then he'd taken them to Autumn's favorite Italian place for dinner. He'd expected to suffer through a couple hours of awkward pauses during the meal since they didn't know each other, but that hadn't happened.

Throughout dinner Autumn had chattered to Tess like they were old buddies, and Tess had kept up with every shift in the conversation, talking to and treating Autumn as a little adult rather than a child. That earned her major points right there. Too many adults talked down to kids, and kids could always sense that forced fakeness a mile away.

Not Tess. She was kind, with a good sense of humor, and clearly had a soft spot for kids. More points for her.

It was actually kinda funny—he'd avoided introducing Autumn to the few women he'd gotten involved with since the divorce, and here Tess had forged a connection with his daughter right off the bat. Not that he and Tess were involved, of course.

But he was starting to think he'd like to be. And he

wanted the chance to see how much more than just physical attraction was going on here. Because shit, yeah, their chemistry was powerful.

Tess popped the passenger door open and shot him a questioning look. "See you at HQ tomorrow, maybe?"

"Maybe." He'd only be called in if something big came up because the team was scheduled to have the day off.

She gave him a little smile and started to slide out, and a spurt of alarm shot through his chest at the prospect of being alone with his memories the rest of the night. He'd been dry for almost nine years now, but it was a constant battle. Not a day went by when he didn't crave a drink, even though he'd gone through programs and had a fellow vet for a sponsor. Days like *this* were even worse. And he was the kind of recovering alcoholic that if he had a single drink, he'd likely fall headfirst off the wagon and not even realize what happened.

"You wanna go for a walk or something?" he blurted. He told himself he wasn't being selfish, wasn't using her as a distraction or a crutch. He genuinely liked and was drawn to her. Although as far as distractions went, Tess was a goddamn powerful one. "There's a nice promenade in front of the hotel that goes along the waterfront."

She stopped and faced him, her hazel-green eyes searching his.

He liked the way she looked at him. Direct. Nothing coy or practiced or calculated about her. Tess was classy. Mature.

Real.

Maybe that's what it was that drew him so hard. She wasn't trying to be anything other than her authentic self. As someone who was still learning to be comfortable in his own skin without alcohol, he admired that a lot.

He was pretty sure she felt the pull too, or at least he hoped there had been a gleam of interest in her eyes a time or two across the table tonight. But no flirting from her, not even after they'd dropped Autumn off. He'd always enjoyed being the pursuer, and it had been a damn long time since he'd needed to be, let alone felt the urge to.

The idea of enticing Tess was arousing as hell and excited him in a way he didn't even understand. His instincts were urging him to pursue her, and for once, he didn't question them.

A grin spread across her face. "Sure. A walk sounds great."

Inwardly, he sighed in relief. *Perfect.*

He got out with her, locked up the car and fell in step beside her as they headed around the north side of the hotel and onto the brick-paved path that ran along the bay. Antique lampposts lined the walkway, spilling warm yellow light onto the path and surface of the water, making it ripple with a million sparkles.

To stem the urge to touch her, he stuck his hands in his front jeans pockets. "I'm glad you came with us tonight. Autumn was thrilled."

Tess tucked a lock of golden hair behind her ear as the breeze blew it around her face. "I'm glad I did too. And she's a great kid." She shot him a sidelong grin. "Like a fifty-year-old woman in a little body."

He laughed at the spot-on description. "Exactly. It's just…"

She tilted her head to the side. "What?"

It had been bothering him for a long time now, and he didn't feel stupid telling Tess about it. She was easy to talk to. "Sometimes I think she's way too mature for her age. And she worries too much. Way more than a little girl should."

"About what?"

"Everything." He wished Sarah had honored his request and kept her from watching the news, but that was yet another battle he'd lost in the raising of their daughter and there wasn't much he could do about it since Autumn lived with Sarah eighty-percent of the time. "And a lot of the time she worries about me."

Tess didn't say anything, just kept glancing at him as they walked.

He let out a breath. "Not sure if she told you, but her mom and I split a long time ago."

Tess nodded. "She mentioned it."

"Well, to be honest, things didn't end well." And how did he put this without sounding like an asshole? "My ex is still pretty angry about it."

"So the divorce wasn't by mutual agreement?"

"Sort of. She was the one who finally filed, but I guess some part of her thought I'd never actually go through with it."

"Ah."

He glanced at her, curious. "You married?" She didn't wear a ring, but that didn't mean anything.

"No, widowed, actually. I lost my husband a few years ago."

Oh, shit. "I'm sorry."

"Thanks, me too. He was a good man, and I was lucky to have him as long as I did. We met in college."

Silence followed her response, and for the first time that evening, it was an awkward one. He wasn't sure whether he should ask more about it, change the subject, or shut the hell up.

"What happened?" he finally asked, going with his gut. He wanted to know her better, and losing a husband must have had a big impact on shaping the person she was.

"He was killed in combat in Afghanistan. His squad's helo was shot down."

He winced. "God." She must think about that every time she climbed into the cockpit. And when he thought of their near escape during that firefight in the mountains back in January, he felt even worse for her. That had to have stirred up a hell of a lot of shit for her, but he'd never have guessed that when he'd spoken to her right afterward. She'd seemed perfectly calm, standing there next to her shot-up aircraft.

"Yes. Anyway," she said with a wave of her hand. "You were talking about Autumn worrying too much."

"Right." It was a relief that she changed the subject again, since he felt uncomfortable and tongue-tied and had no idea what else to say about her loss. He wasn't good with that kind of stuff, emotional stuff. One of the many faults Sarah had found in him. "She's only nine, but she's smart, and she can tell things aren't good between her mom and me."

"In what way?"

Every way. He couldn't say that aloud, though. Not without sounding like a bitter douche. "My ex bears the brunt of the parenting because I'm away so much. I get why she's mad about that, but she tends to, ah, interfere with my efforts to maintain a good relationship with Autumn."

"Really?" She sounded surprised.

He nodded but didn't elaborate. He didn't want to bitch to her about his problems. "Autumn sees it and tries to run interference whenever she can. I don't want that for her. And when I'm away, even for training, she constantly worries that something will happen to me. If I don't text or email her every day, she thinks the worst."

"It's because she's bright. She understands the risks of what you do."

"Yeah, and I don't know how to keep her from worrying."

"I don't think it's something you can protect her from, Reid. It's one of the ways she expresses her love for you." Tess aimed a soft smile at him, and damned if it didn't set off a burst of warmth in his chest. "She told me all about the trip you guys just took. She'll remember it for as long as she lives."

He hoped so. "It was awesome to spend so much one-on-one time with her. I never get more than a couple days at a time with her at most."

"And your ex agreed to let her go, so that sounds promising."

He grunted. *Not really. I had to fight like hell to make it happen.* But enough of him bitching about his problems like a little pussy. That was the opposite of sexy, and he was trying to get Tess interested, not turn her off him for good. Though he'd sworn off relationships since the divorce, he could see himself trying something like that with Tess. They clicked on so many levels.

"What about your family?" he asked.

"My parents, older sister and her three girls live back in Nevada. We're pretty close and I fly home to visit whenever I can. You?"

"Just my aunt, who raised me." She was watching him again, and he sensed her silent question so he continued. "My mom's sister. She and her husband raised me, down in Pascagoula."

"Oh. Did you spend much time with your parents?"

He shook his head. "Never really knew them. They were both killed in a car wreck when I was ten months old, and my aunt wound up taking me in. She was sixteen years older than my mom, so she'll be eighty-five this year. She's really slowing down lately." It was going to hurt like hell when she went. She was his last living link to the family he'd lost.

"Why did you join the DEA?"

"I wanted to stay in the action, and I wanted to make FAST. I'm not exactly a desk job kinda guy."

She chuckled. "No, I can't imagine you behind a desk. You were SF before, right?"

He nodded, surprised. "You been asking about me?"

The hint of a smile tugged at the corner of her mouth. "Maybe. You worried?"

"No." Pumped that she was interested enough to ask about him, more like it.

"I'm former army too."

He smiled at her. "Hooah."

"Hooah," she said with a laugh that made something swell in the center of his chest.

He couldn't remember ever connecting with a woman like this before, or so easily. Not even Sarah, who he'd married and had a child with. Before everything had gone to hell.

He told her a couple funny stories about his SF days, enjoying making her laugh.

Tess shook her head as they kept walking. "You sure haven't had it easy, have you?"

He half-smiled at the teasing note in her voice. "Guess not." Although a lot of the shit he'd gone through was self-inflicted. "But not as tough as a lot of people have it."

Up ahead, a jazz group was playing in a lookout built into the promenade, the slow, sultry strains reminding him of home as they drifted on the warm night air. "You want to sit and listen for a bit?" he asked, gesturing to a bench nearby.

"Sure."

She sank down on it next to him, the outside of her thigh pressing against his and her delicate pear scent swirling around him in a delicious cloud. They listened to the music for a while. A few minutes in, Reid glanced over and caught the vestiges of a bittersweet smile on her face. "You okay?"

"Yes, it's just this song. It was one of Brian's favorites."

Oh, great. He hadn't meant to upset her. "You want to head back?"

"In a little while. It's good to remember him. Hurts

more if I don't."

Her words were like tiny daggers in his heart. Because she was dead on about that.

She frowned slightly, turning more fully toward him. "What's wrong?"

"Nothing." He cleared his throat, glanced toward the band before turning his attention back to her. "How long ago did he die?"

"Three years ago."

He nodded slowly, his heart beating faster. Another connection they shared. He was starting to lose count of how many they had. "It never really goes away, does it?"

Her gaze sharpened on his. "No."

"And it's tough to move forward, because if you do, it feels like you're forgetting the person you lost, and the guilt is just as hard."

Tess stared at him in astonishment for a moment. "Who did you lose?"

It shouldn't have surprised him that she was so perceptive. He hadn't wanted to talk about this, but she'd just opened up to him, so he had to give her something in return. "My best friend. Jason. We served together in the same A-Team. He was like a brother to me."

"Oh, I'm sorry. When?"

"Ten year anniversary is coming up in a couple weeks." And he was fucking dreading it. May nineteenth was an entire day of torture he was forced to endure each year, when his demons were strongest and the temptation to slide back into a bottle had him on the verge of giving in.

Tess reached for his hand, startling him, and laced their fingers together. It was scary how natural it felt. How comforting. "Tell me about him."

Because he was more comfortable with her than he had been with anyone in ages—other than his teammates, who still didn't know all the details or how bad his alcoholism had been—Reid did. He told her about how he and Jason had met during Robin Sage and how Jason had pushed his ass through to the finish. How Jason had loved Adam Sandler movies and smoking cigars and bass fishing.

But he couldn't tell her about how Jason had died after that last deployment to the hellhole in Helmand Province almost a decade ago. The pain of it was still too fresh. Too raw. He wasn't ready, maybe wasn't capable of baring his soul that way.

Tess's expression was soft as he finished. "He sounds like a great guy."

"He was." Jason had been the best friend Reid had ever had. And when Reid had lost him, nothing else in his life had mattered anymore. He'd let the darkness take him, because he'd thought he didn't deserve to be happy if Jason was gone. The guilt had damn near killed him.

"You still miss him a lot," Tess said, sliding her thumb gently back and forth over the back of his hand.

Reid squeezed in silent thanks, and something about the way she watched him, that she truly understood where he was coming from because she had experienced loss, made him continue. "I...wasn't in a good place after he died. Didn't handle it too well, and I had a child on the way."

He'd wound up a high-functioning alcoholic who got next level drunk when he went on a bender, which back then was all too often. Because the booze at least temporarily numbed the pain. "I got out of the army, eventually got my life together—" But only after a monumental struggle and the destruction of his marriage—"and applied to the DEA. I made a lot of mistakes before that, though."

He didn't tell her about the drinking, or how bad it had gotten, because it was still embarrassing as hell. And he didn't want to scare her off. What woman in their right mind would want to get involved with a recovering alcoholic? Let alone one who had gone through what Tess had?

She squeezed his hand. "Everybody handles grief differently. We all make mistakes."

How had she handled it? He bet she hadn't tried to drown her sorrows in alcohol the way he had.

"And if it helps, whatever your faults, Autumn doesn't hold them against you. She adores you. Anyone with eyes can see that."

That made him smile. "She's the reason I kept going." Like corrosive acid, the survivor's guilt had all but eaten what was left of his soul. Until Autumn was born and he'd found a reason to get his shit together. A reason to start living again. "I'd see that little face looking up at me, and that was all the kick in the ass I needed to get back up again."

"Because you're a warrior, and you love your little girl."

"I love her to death." There wasn't anything he wouldn't do for her. He loved his job, but not even in the same realm as what he felt for his daughter. Push came to shove, he would give it up for her if he had to. And some days, it seemed like that was the right thing to do. He'd missed out on so much already, being away so often. He didn't want to miss the rest, too.

"I noticed. And it's adorable." Tess cocked her head, that endearing little smile in place.

God, she was pretty, the night breeze gently blowing her hair around her shoulders, her cheeks the same soft pink as her lips. She didn't wear much makeup. Didn't need it, and it only would have covered up her natural beauty. Her low-maintenance style was just another thing that set her apart from every other woman he'd been with.

"She's a lucky little girl to be that loved," Tess said.

"Nah. I'm the lucky one." She'd saved him, no question.

The band finished their last song and began to pack up their instruments.

As the quiet closed around them, Reid cleared his throat. "Should we head back?"

"Sure." Tess released his hand and stood, hugging her upper arms as the wind tugged at the hem of the thin sweater she wore.

Without a word, Reid took off his leather jacket and draped it over her shoulders. She glanced up at him with a grateful smile that punched him straight in the chest, and tugged the halves together. He wished he was still holding her hand.

They didn't talk much on the way back to the hotel, and he started to regret having revealed some of his baggage to her. Talk about a downer of a conversation, and he hated to think she was sad now, about to be alone with thoughts of her dead husband for the long hours that stretched ahead. The nights were always the longest.

All too soon they reached the hotel lobby doors.

"Well." Tess slid his jacket off and handed it to him, the lantern-style lights throwing bright gold highlights on her hair and illuminating her green eyes like gems. "Thanks for a great evening."

He closed his fist around the jacket. "I'm glad you came." The instant he said that word, an image of her coming in an entirely different way highjacked his brain. Spread out on her back, naked, her hands in his hair while he pressed his face between her thighs and took his time getting her off.

As though she'd somehow picked up on what he was thinking, she stared at him, pupils expanding in a telltale reaction of arousal she couldn't hide.

A low, primal growl built in his chest as heat roared through him, shunting a rush of blood straight to his groin. Them working for the same agency and having contact on ops should technically put her off-limits, but he didn't care. All he cared about was what was happening between them and the crazy intense pull he couldn't resist.

He stepped closer, reading every subtle sign her body gave him as he closed in. She didn't move except to tilt her head back, those pretty green eyes locked on his, her lips parted ever so slightly as though she couldn't quite catch her breath.

Lifting a hand, Reid cradled the side of her face in his palm, letting the pad of his thumb sweep over the petal softness of her cheek. Tracing the line of freckles that extended from the bridge of her nose and reining in the impulse to kiss each one. "Have dinner with me tomorrow night at my place. I want to cook for you." Maybe it was too soon to ask, but she knew he wasn't an axe murderer and had to trust him on some level.

She blinked, as though waking from a trance. "You cook?"

He half-smiled. "I'm not a chef or anything, but I won't poison us."

Her lips twitched and her eyes gleamed with silent laughter. "Okay then."

Yes. "I'll pick you up at seven."

A tiny nod, and her eyes still fixed on his for a moment before they dropped to his mouth. Reid couldn't stop himself from dipping down to capture those soft lips.

She let out a soft, nearly inaudible gasp as he settled his mouth over hers, and reached for his shoulders. Lust slammed into him so hard it dazed him.

He dropped his jacket on the ground and slid that hand into the back of her hair, holding her in place as he molded his lips to hers. Slow. Firm, giving her the barest stroke of his tongue across her lower lip before he gently nibbled on it a moment and lifted his head.

Tess made a sound of protest and gazed up at him through heavy-lidded eyes, her fingers still gripping his shoulders, her lips shiny from his tongue. Reid couldn't help bending to take another taste, then released her, stunned at the almost electrical charge crackling over his skin.

Jesus.

They stared at each other from less than a foot apart, the constrained sexual tension heating the air between them, pulsing with the promise of what would happen if they took things farther.

Before he could give into temptation and risk pushing too hard too soon, he bent to scoop up his jacket and straightened, never taking his eyes off her. "Seven tomorrow."

She nodded, still seeming a little dazed. "Okay. See you then."

He gave her a slow smile, the sweet ache of desire spreading through his body. He wanted her. Badly. Loved knowing he'd just affected her so much with a kiss. "Sleep well."

She gave a slight nod, the hint of a smile, and then walked through the revolving doors. Inside she paused, looked back at him, the heat in her eyes making the hunger burn hotter. He stood where he was, raised a hand in farewell and watched the fluid movement of her curves as she walked away, already impatient for tomorrow night.

As for tonight...

Instead of tormenting himself with thoughts of Jason and battling the demon in the bottle, he was going to fantasize about the woman who'd just rocked his world with a single, innocent kiss.

Chapter Five

—⬥⬥⬥⬥—

"You wanna grab a bite?" Kai asked Prentiss the next afternoon, grabbing a towel and mopping at his face. They'd burned a shit-ton of calories with that workout, and he was freaking starving. Normally Khan worked out with them on their days off, but he and Jaliya had something going on today, so it was just Kai and Prentiss. And once they got down to Emerald Warrior, they'd be slammed and wouldn't get much if any time in the gym.

"Sorry, man, can't. Got plans."

"Plans?" Well now. "What kind of plans?" He'd just had Autumn last night, so it couldn't be that.

"Why are you so fucking nosy?" Prentiss shot back with a half-hearted scowl.

"Because I like to be kept in the loop." He draped the towel over his shoulders and followed his buddy toward the gym door. "So?"

"Dinner plans," Prentiss said without looking back.

Kai raised an eyebrow. "You've got a date."

No answer.

It was killing him. "Dude, come on. You haven't been on a date in like, six months. Who is it?"

"How the hell do you know the last time I went on a date? Maybe I went on one last night."

"Did you?"

"None of your damn business, Maka."

Oh, it was serious when he used Kai's last name. "It's that hot helo pilot. Am I right?"

Prentiss sighed and twisted the combination lock on his locker. "Not telling you shit."

"You don't have to, because that just answered my question." Kai saw a hell of a lot more than the guys gave him credit for. He wasn't only interested in food all the time. He'd seen Agent Dubrovski at headquarters yesterday, and noticed Prentiss chatting her up prior to the team meeting. "Saw you putting her into your Mustang last night, brother."

"She hung out with Autumn while we were in the meeting, and Autumn asked her to come to the movie with us after. I couldn't say no."

So defensive. "It's all good, man. So, what's the plan? Where are you taking her out to eat?"

"I'm making dinner."

Kai stopped dead at that and swung his head around to stare at him, utterly betrayed. "Wait, you *cook*? Since when?"

Prentiss snorted. "Since always."

No way. "We've been teammates for four damn years, and you've never once made me a meal. What's up with that?"

"It's because you're a grown-ass man who can cook for himself. And besides, with the amount of food you put away I couldn't afford to feed you anyway. Beast."

Kai chuckled and rubbed a hand over his stomach. "I'm a big guy. Takes a lot of fuel to keep this machine in prime condition."

"Yeah, and the rest of us know it. So you can fuel that machine on your own dime."

Kai shook his head, unable to smother a grin at the sarcasm. "Why you gotta be so cheap all the time?"

"Because I have a daughter to support and eventually put through college," he said dryly.

Yeah, okay. Good one. Kai unlocked his own locker. "What's she like? Dubrovski. I mean, aside from hot and crazy talented in the cockpit."

"She's nice. Genuine."

Those five syllables might not sound like much, but from Prentiss, they were high praise, especially since they pertained to the opposite sex. He hadn't had an easy time with his ex since the split. It was good to see his buddy willing to put himself back out there on the dating market again. "Awesome." Kai hoped it went somewhere.

Prentiss grabbed his gym bag and shut the locker. "What about you, don't you have plans with Shelley?"

Kai barely stopped himself from making a face at the mention of her name and broke eye contact. "Nah. We're taking a break." Maybe a permanent one this time, hell if he knew.

Prentiss looked at him, and even though he didn't say anything, his reaction was clear. *Again?*

Avoiding his gaze, Kai grabbed the stuff he needed for the shower and shut his locker. Ironic, him being embarrassed about how things were with Shelley considering Kai had made it no secret how he felt about Prentiss's bitch of an ex. But Shelley had a vindictive streak when she was pissed off.

"It's fine," he muttered, for some reason feeling the need to elaborate. But it wasn't fine, actually. It was exhausting. Always drama. The constant ups and downs made him feel like he was on a freaking rollercoaster. But then she'd do something so damn sweet and kind, and the make-up sex was so damn good, he'd forget about all the bad stuff and believe that things would be better going forward.

Except it never was for long.

Unsurprisingly, Prentiss let it drop and thumped a hand on Kai's back. "See ya tomorrow."

"Yeah, brother." Kai was looking forward to a night chillaxing on the couch by himself. Just him and some quality time with his flat screen.

Freshly showered and changed into clean clothes, he climbed into his monster of a truck and drove back to his place, already planning what he wanted for dinner. He didn't have much in the fridge and didn't feel like doing a big grocery shop on the way home, so he'd just order in from his favorite barbecue joint and watch some rugby.

The moment he stepped off the elevator onto his floor of the apartment building, the smell hit him. The delicious, mouthwatering aroma of homemade gorgeousness that was coming from apartment 7F. He inhaled deeply. Damn, that woman cooked like a goddess.

Stepping inside his condo, he tossed his keys onto the kitchen counter and turned to head to his bedroom, but stopped dead when he saw he wasn't alone.

Shelley sat on his living room couch, watching him with her arms crossed and a pissed-off expression on her face.

He tensed and stifled a groan. What was she doing here? He thought she'd slammed the key he'd given her onto the kitchen counter yesterday before she'd stormed out, but maybe not. Or she'd had another spare made.

"Hey," he said in a neutral tone. He'd learned to test the waters with her after a fight, gauge her mood. Right now, she looked like she wanted to smack his face.

Her jaw flexed once, her blue eyes cold as glaciers as she stared him down. "Where've you been?"

Instantly his back went up. He hated it when she questioned him like that. As though she didn't trust him.

"The gym," he answered, keeping his voice level. If he didn't, things would escalate fast.

When he didn't offer anything else, just stared at her from across the room, hurt crept into her expression. "I thought maybe you'd call me so we could talk this out."

Oh, man, the thought of freaking talking about "this" any more made him want to stab himself in the eye just so he'd have an excuse to leave. "You wanted space." She'd screamed the words at him yesterday on her way out the door. "So I was giving it to you."

She let out a humorless laugh. "What I *want*, clearly I can't have." She pushed to her feet, stood there facing him in the short black dress that hugged every curve of her killer body, her long, dark hair cascading over her shoulders in shiny waves, her makeup done to perfection.

Stunningly beautiful. And yet for some reason so damn insecure inside it baffled him.

"I'm tired of being the only one willing to fight for us, Kai."

And I'm fucking tired of fighting, period.

Sick of always trying to reassure her, to continually prove he cared and wasn't cheating on her. He wasn't stupid enough to say any of that aloud, though.

"What do you want from me?" he said, tired all of a sudden. This part drained him. It didn't matter what the hell he did, he could never do or say enough to make her feel secure about their relationship. And the truth was, he was tired of trying. He just wanted a peaceful relationship. Was that too much to ask?

Her eyes flared. "I want you to love me! That's all I've ever wanted, and even though you say the words, you don't act like it. You don't show it the way I need you to. I still come in last, even after being with you for almost a year. I've waited for you through missions and weeks-long training exercises, and a four-month-long deployment, yet I still—"

"I can't help it that I'm away a lot. It's my job," he said, voice tight. He loved his job, had worked his freaking ass off to make FAST, wouldn't give it up for anything. "You knew going in that that was the deal. I told you straight up how it would be." He was actually looking forward to the training exercise next week, just to have a break from this.

"Yeah," she said bitterly. "I guess I'm just too fucking stupid to realize that you'll never be able to give me what I need."

He had no idea what she wanted him to say to that, and the truth was that right now all he wanted was for her to leave. "Look, I've had a long day. Maybe you should just go."

Shock flickered across her face for an instant before anger burned in her eyes. "You want me to go? *Fine.*" She snagged her purse from the coffee table and marched past him, the scent of her expensive perfume trailing in her wake.

The familiar scent of it had once spiked his heart rate and libido. Now it almost made him cringe.

She opened the door and stopped, her back rigid. Nailing him with a hard look over her shoulder, she paused there. "You'd better think long and hard about what you want, Kai. Because you're this close to losing me for good," she said, holding her index finger and thumb an inch apart.

With that parting shot she flounced out and slammed the door shut behind her.

Kai sighed into the sudden quiet, struck by the stark sense of relief washing over him. Things had been great between them for the first few months, but the constant bickering over stupid shit had taken its toll. Nothing he did seemed to make her happy for very long. Seemed to him that she was pissed-off and hurt more often than not these days.

Damn, maybe *he* was the one who needed the space and not her.

A knock at the door had him biting back a frustrated growl. He didn't have the patience to deal with this bullshit any more tonight, but if he didn't she'd just use her key and barge in again.

He yanked it open, ready to tell her to leave him alone, but stopped when he saw his food goddess neighbor standing there instead. "Abby. Hey."

"Hey," she said, twisting her head to look down the hallway, her pale blond pixie cut gleaming in the lights. She had on black yoga pants and a snug athletic jacket that hugged her fit, but curvy body. "I thought I heard Shelley's dulcet tones a minute ago." She faced him, the top of her head coming to the center of his chest, her vivid blue eyes lit with a trace of wry amusement. "But the door slam confirmed it."

His face heated and he barely resisted the urge to rub the back of his neck. This was so damn embarrassing. Half the people living on this floor were probably aware of the drama. "Sorry about that," he muttered.

"Hey, not my deal." She shrugged and held up the container in her hand. "I'm just off to the gym but I thought I'd drop this off. It's beef stroganoff over egg noodles."

He didn't have to ask whether it was homemade, and his mouth was already watering. "Thanks, you're an angel," he said, taking it from her. It was still warm, too. Homemade comfort food like this would so hit the spot right now, and Abby's cooking was always awesome. It reminded him of his grandma, who had raised him. "Smells amazing."

Abby leaned a shoulder against the doorjamb, her head tipped back so she could meet his eyes. "Your text said you wanted to talk to me about your schedule?"

"Oh, right." He'd sent it last night. He gestured over

his shoulder. "You wanna come in for a sec?"

"Sure." She stepped inside and followed him to the kitchen, smelling of the light, clean scent of shampoo and soap instead of perfume. "You going out of town again?"

"Next week for about ten days." He reached into a drawer for a fork, glanced at her. "You want some?"

"No thanks, already had some and I'll be eating it for the next week anyway. So, you want me to look after Goliath and grab your mail while you're gone?"

"That'd be great, if you could." They helped each other out like that whenever one of them was away.

Although he was gone a whole lot more than she was, so the arrangement was pretty lopsided. Kai tried to help her out whenever he could to make up for it, fixing things around her apartment, dropping off a bag of her favorite coffee or whatever. Actually, she did way more for him than Shelley ever had, and that was a hell of a sad statement about his so-called girlfriend.

"Sure, no problem."

Abby was always like that, always willing to help without making it a big deal. No guilt trips, never made him feel like he owed her or anything. No drama. God, she was such a breath of fresh air compared to Shelley now that he thought about it. "Thanks. I appreciate it."

Another shrug. "Just text me when you're on your way home so I don't accidentally barge in on you."

He wouldn't mind if she did. He liked talking with her, because she was so easy to be around. "I will."

She gestured to the fork in his hand. "I'm waiting for you to take a bite," she said with a grin.

He was happy to oblige. Sliding a mouthful of tangy sauce-smothered beef, mushrooms and noodles into his mouth, he let out a deep groan of appreciation and gave her an adoring look.

One side of her mouth tipped upward. "Good, right?"

"It's awesome. I can taste the love."

"That's my secret ingredient for every dish."

"I know it." He forked up another bite.

Abby glanced around the kitchen/living room to where Goliath swam in the special tank Kai had outfitted over in the corner, then focused on him once more. "So you and Shelley are back together again?"

His hand froze around the fork. "Ah…no, we're…taking a break." Actually, he wasn't sure what the hell they were doing anymore, aside from being miserable most of the time.

She frowned and shook her head a little, concern etched into her face. "Are you okay?"

"Yeah, I'm good. And Shelley's great," he said, not even sure why he felt the need to defend her. When things were good, they were awesome. They just weren't good all that often anymore. "She's just…tired of me being gone so much."

Among other things. He didn't exactly blame her for being upset. Very few women were okay with the frequent and sometimes long-term absences his job demanded. And since they were only dating, there was a lot he didn't—couldn't—tell her.

Abby's shrewd expression told him she wasn't buying it, then her face softened. "You know, I don't talk about this much, but I got out of a toxic relationship a while back. We were together three years and I was sucked in so deep I didn't see how bad it really was. And, if I'm honest I guess deep down I just really didn't want to be alone, so being in a bad relationship was somehow better than being by myself.

"But then one day I realized how dysfunctional and codependent it was. I finally understood that I deserved better. That I'd been enabling it." She took a deep breath. "Once I figured that out, there was no going back. I left him. It wasn't easy, but my life is a thousand percent better now. Looking back, I can't believe I wasted three years of my life on someone who was never going to treat me the way I deserved."

Kai stared at her in stunned silence. Was that what he was doing? Enabling a toxic relationship? He floundered for something to say, squirming inside. So much of what she said rang true for him, too. It was like she saw right through him.

Abby took pity on him by shrugging and giving him a quick smile. "Anyway, don't worry about your place, I've got it covered. I'll see you when you get back."

"Thanks. I'll give your container back after I wash it."

"Okay. See you." She let herself out and left him standing there in the kitchen with a container of delicious food in his hand and a strange, hollow sensation filling his chest as a light bulb went off in his brain.

Jesus Christ, she was right about everything. He'd been enabling a toxic relationship for months now, and it wasn't the first time. All four of his serious relationships had followed a similar pattern, and every single one of them had dragged on way too long in the same hellish cycle. Why did he pick women that were no good for him?

Kai frowned, suddenly angry with himself. Shit, he *did* deserve better. He knew damn well that Shelley was never going to change, never become secure in her own skin and in his loyalty to her.

It was time to get real, stop hoping things would get better, man up and do something about it.

Chapter Six

Tess smoothed a hand down the front of her coral-colored, knee-length dress and took a breath before pushing the doorbell. She couldn't remember the last time she'd had butterflies before a date—maybe a few in the beginning of her one and only relationship since her husband died—but they were fluttering like crazy in the pit of her stomach right now. Reid had promised to pick her up, but things had gone late with her last meeting so she'd texted and told him she would take a cab over.

Reid pulled the door open a moment later, wearing jeans and a deep blue shirt that matched his eyes, and gave her a slow smile that made her heart do a slow somersault. "Hi."

"Hi." She thrust the bottle of wine at him, mentally muting the whisper of uncertainty in her brain that wouldn't shut up. *What are you doing? Do you even know what you're doing? You think getting involved with another man whose job puts his life in danger all the time is a good idea?*

Okay, no to that last part. But what was she doing? She

was *living* for a change, rather than just existing. That kiss had left her body aching and restless. Reid had woken something inside her, made her feel alive and attractive in a way she hadn't in a damn long time, and she refused to spoil this by overthinking it.

While staring at the ceiling last night, yearning for the weight and heat of that strong body atop hers, she'd made up her mind to simply go with this and see what happened. It wasn't like they were going to get serious—she was only here for another day, and she was based over a thousand miles from him.

"I brought you this instead of flowers. But I confess it was for partially selfish reasons, since it's my favorite kind." A glass or two would shut that damn whisper up completely.

"Come on in and I'll pour you a glass," he said, stepping out of the way.

She slipped off her heels inside the door and followed him into the kitchen, breathing in the scent of something spicy and rich. "Do I smell Mexican?"

"You do," he said, looking up from uncorking the wine. "Is that okay?"

"It's great. What did you make?"

"Chicken enchiladas with roasted tomatillo sauce, and a black bean and vegetable salad."

She lifted her eyebrows. "Wow. I was expecting steaks. Or maybe Hungry Man dinners."

His boyish grin made her heart trip. "I looked up a recipe online. Hope it doesn't suck."

So cute, that he'd picked it out for her. "Anything that smells that good can't suck."

He handed her the glass of wine. "For the lady."

"Thank you," she murmured, warmth spreading into her cheeks from the way he looked at her. Like he was already thinking about what would happen after dinner, and she'd bet it involved more than just kissing. It was a lot different being alone with him, without Autumn to act as a buffer.

With a kitchen towel draped over one broad shoulder, he turned back to the ingredients he'd laid out on the counter.

"You're not having any wine?" she asked. She knew she should have bought beer instead.

"No, I'm good with water," he said, and she watched in amazement as he picked up a husked corn of cob with a pair of barbecue tongs and began roasting them on a grill pan on the stove.

"This feels so fancy," she said, smiling as she sipped at her wine. And decadent. Other than her husband, who hadn't liked being in the kitchen all that much, no man had ever cooked for her before.

"Like I said, it won't be gourmet." He looked back at her over his shoulder, those stunning, deep blue eyes locking on hers. "But I hope it'll make an impression."

Mission already accomplished. Her bare toes curled around the rung of the stool she sat on. Mouth dry, she took another sip of wine. "Can I help with anything?" she asked when he went back to roasting the corn.

"Nope. Almost done here. Tell me about your day."

"Just some meetings with my bosses, and I met my new flight crew. They seem great. One of them's former air force, and the rest are former army. What about you?"

"We had the day off, but I hit the gym with my buddy Kai this afternoon."

Since his back was mostly to her she allowed herself to enjoy the view, drinking in his broad shoulders and the muscles stretching the fabric of the shirt, the way his jeans hugged his trim hips and hard butt. Yes, she could appreciate all the time and effort Reid must put into keeping his body in that kind of condition. "He's the big one, right?"

One side of Reid's mouth turned up. "Yeah. He tried

to invite himself over for dinner tonight, but he would have eaten everything I had and still been looking for more so I told him forget it."

"Then I'm glad he's not here, because I'm *starving*."

She hadn't meant to make it into an innuendo, but when he looked over at her again, there was such heat smoldering in his eyes that it damn near made her stop breathing for a second. "Yeah? Good. I'm hungry too," he said, his voice dropping an octave.

Oh my God. Could she even handle it if they wound up in bed together tonight? She wasn't sure she'd survive it.

She sat there on her perch, greedily drinking in the sight of him moving so comfortably around his kitchen while he sliced the grilled corn kernels off the cob and mixed them with halved red grape tomatoes, diced avocado, black beans and whatever else he had in the salad bowl. Once he'd tossed it all together with the dressing he had mixed together in a glass measuring cup, he pulled a casserole dish out of the oven and sat it on the counter.

Tess leaned closer, inhaling deeply. "It smells delicious." She couldn't wait to eat it.

Wielding a spatula, he eyed her from next to the counter. "Just how hungry are you?"

Fifty-fifty chance he was talking about food. "I haven't eaten since eleven this morning, so, pretty damn hungry."

With a nod, he scooped out two steaming, golden brown enchiladas onto a plate and added a mound of the salad. "Let's eat at the table," he said, carrying her plate into the eating nook where he'd set the table and lit candles.

It felt romantic and intimate, and she couldn't help but smile as she sat down. "This looks beautiful."

"You're the only woman besides Autumn to have ever eaten here, so I wanted it to be special."

What did it signify, that she was the only woman he'd allowed into his inner sanctum, other than his daughter? She wasn't likely to forget this anytime soon.

Once he was seated with his own plate, she raised her glass. "To surviving our recent deployment to Afghanistan."

He smiled at her dark humor and tapped his water glass to her wineglass. "Cheers."

"Mmmm, this is so good," she said in between bites. How sexy was it, that a man as professionally accomplished as him could cook, too?

After dinner, she started to help him clear the table but he refused and refilled her wineglass before banishing her from the kitchen while he cleaned up. She sat on the leather couch opposite the TV and talked to him while looking around at the clean, uncluttered space as the anticipation about what might happen in a few minutes built inside her.

A few framed photos graced the mantel and side table. Mostly of him and Autumn at various stages of her life, including a recent one of them on their trip to Universal Studios. Autumn was atop Reid's shoulders wearing a black robe and holding a wand proudly overhead, while Reid grinned up at her, hands securely locked around the front of her shins, his eyes hidden by a pair of dark sunglasses. It made Tess smile.

A few others of Reid and his teammates were scattered around as well. Then she spotted another photo on the mantel, and her heart squeezed. It had to be from his army days because Reid was wearing desert-pattern BDUs and clean-shaven, his arm around the shoulders of another soldier around his age.

Reid joined her a few minutes later with another glass of water. He sank down beside her, close but not touching her, and draped a casual arm along the back of the couch. "You could have turned on the TV," he said.

"No, I've been looking at your photos. This one's my favorite," she said, pointing to the one of him and Autumn at Universal.

He grinned. "That was a great day. Worth every penny to see her face when we got to Hogwart's Castle."

"I'll bet." She paused to sip her wine, debating her next words, but finally decided just to say it. "Is that Jason?" she asked, nodding to the picture of him and the other soldier.

His smile slipped and he tensed a little. "Yeah. On our last tour in Afghanistan together."

"Were you there when he died?" she asked gently.

His jaw clenched and he lowered his gaze to the water glass he held in his lap. "No. He didn't die in combat."

"In training?"

He shook his head. "Hanged himself a few months after we got home."

"Oh, Reid…" She put a hand on his shoulder, feeling awful, the muscles rock hard beneath her palm. "I'm sorry, I shouldn't have asked."

"No, it's okay." He fidgeted with the water glass. "I knew he was in a bad place and tried to do what I could to pull him out of it. He promised me he'd get help." He pulled in a deep breath. "I knew something was wrong that night. He wouldn't answer his phone so I went over there. And I found him hanging in the shower."

Oh, Jesus. "That's terrible."

He nodded. "I think the worst part was telling his wife. They'd been having problems and she was out of town staying with her mom when it happened. I drove all night to get there, and when she saw me at the door she started screaming."

Tess couldn't stand not being able to comfort him. She set her wine down and wrapped both arms around him, pressing her cheek to his shoulder. Relief and warmth spread through her when he curled an arm around her and tucked her into his side. "I'm so sorry that happened."

"It was hard, not gonna lie." He ran his fingers through the ends of her hair, the motion tender yet arousing, too. "I told you last night that I didn't handle it well."

She tipped her head back to look at him, sensing he was about to say something important.

He nodded at the glass in his hand. "You probably noticed I've been drinking water this whole time. And that's because I had a drinking problem."

The bluntness of the admission took her aback, but she also found it incredibly brave. "You did?"

He nodded once. "A bad one. Started drinking heavily after Jason died and everything kind of went into a downward spiral after that. I've been dry a long time now, thanks to Autumn coming along, but I can't pretend it's not still inside me." He turned his head and met her gaze, and the bravery of that struck her deep inside. "So if you were wondering what happened with my marriage, that was a big part of it. That and me being gone a lot, starting from when I began trying out for FAST."

There were always two sides to the story. "You seem to have done a good job at getting your life back together again."

"So far so good, yeah."

She rested her chin on his shoulder, admiring him for his honesty. "Thank you for telling me. Why did you, by the way?" He certainly hadn't needed to. He could have kept it from her, but given enough time she would have wondered why he always abstained.

He avoided her gaze as he answered. "I wanted you to know what kind of man I am before things went any farther."

So she could make up her mind whether he was worth the risk or not. He didn't say the words, but they were clear anyway.

Tess slid her fingers into the back of his hair, caressed

his scalp gently as she leaned in to nuzzle his cheek with the tip of her nose. "I think I've already seen enough about your character firsthand to have a pretty good idea of what kind of man you are," she murmured against his stubble.

She'd seen him protecting his teammates during that harrowing extraction. Knew the stringent standards that FAST members had to maintain in order to make the teams. And she'd seen the love he had for his daughter. Those things, combined with him having just volunteered his deepest, darkest secret to her up front on his own without excuse or apology, told her he was worth the risk.

He turned his head to face her, surprise clear in the depths of his deep blue eyes. "And you still want to be here?"

The hint of vulnerability coming from such a strong man turned her heart to mush. His drinking may have been a huge contributing factor to the dissolution of his marriage, but the divorce had obviously hurt him deeply.

She smiled and leaned in to brush her lips across the corner of his mouth. "I absolutely do." Whether it was smart or not, she couldn't deny it.

His water glass thudded on the coffee table an instant before his hands slid into her hair and his mouth covered hers. She sighed and sank a hand into his hair, her other going to his shoulder to anchor herself. God, the way he kissed—a heated seduction of lips and tongue she had no prayer of resisting. Her head swam as he deepened the kiss, his tongue caressing hers.

The distinctive notes of the Harry Potter theme song broke through the fog in her mind.

Reid eased back, stared at her. A ringtone coming from his phone.

"Autumn?" she guessed, trying to clear her head. The man was lethal with his mouth.

He nodded, his eyes all smoky, his voice rough with desire. "I'll call her back."

Tess shook her head and put a hand in the center of his chest, pushing back. What if it was important? "No, answer it."

With a low groan, Reid straightened and dug his phone out of his pocket. "Hey, baby girl. What's up?"

Tess watched him as he talked, loving the alertness about him, how he gave Autumn his full attention even though he had to be fighting the effects of that smoldering kiss.

"Oh. Yeah. One second." He held up a finger to Tess to say he'd be back in a minute and disappeared around the corner. She assumed it was to have privacy, but he didn't lower his voice so she could still hear what he was saying. "Found it. You left it in your dresser drawer." A pause. "What, tonight? Ah, honey, I... Hang on."

He reappeared a second later, standing so tall and sexy on the other side of the room, one hand covering the bottom of the phone. "Autumn left her wand here and she needs it for a birthday party first thing in the morning."

"Oh." So their date was over, then.

With a soft chuckle, he uncovered the bottom of the phone. "Yeah, it's Tess." He raised his eyebrows at her. "I asked her over for dinner and we were about to have dessert."

Oh yeah, she was craving more of that dessert right now.

His lips quirked at whatever Autumn said. "Yeah, I'll ask her. Hang on." He spoke to Tess. "She wants us to drop it off."

He wanted her to come with him? "Sure, fine with me."

He raised an eyebrow. "You sure? From here it's a twenty-five-minute drive each way."

"That's okay." Spending an hour alone in the car with him sounded good to her.

He lifted the phone back to his ear. "All right. We'll

be over in a while. But don't make it a habit to leave things behind when you come over. I won't always be able to drop everything and run it over to you."

Whatever Autumn said in reply made Reid grin, and Tess was struck once again by how gorgeous he was when he smiled, the harsh edge to his features completely melting away. "Okay. We'll leave now. Keep your eyes peeled for us." He put his phone into his pocket and faced Tess. "You sure about this? It wasn't how I'd planned the night to go."

"It's fine," she said, already heading back to the kitchen to grab her purse. And probably for the best that they got out of his place for a while at least. Being alone with him here tempted her mercilessly, and this would give her a little more time to decide whether she was ready to sleep with him.

In the elevator on the way to the underground parking garage a minute later, an idea struck her. "How about we take Autumn out for dessert somewhere? A sundae or something."

Reid glanced at her in surprise, then his expression shuttered and he seemed to hesitate.

"It was just an idea," she said quickly, wishing she hadn't opened her mouth. "Never mind."

"It's not…" He sighed as they stepped out of the elevator and started toward his Mustang. "I love the idea, but Sarah will never go for it."

Tess frowned. "Why not? We would drop Autumn off right after."

"But it wasn't on the schedule," he explained, frustration creeping into his tone. "If it's not scheduled, she won't allow it."

Wouldn't allow the father of her child to take Autumn out for an ice cream at eight o'clock on a Friday night, even when she was just sitting at home doing nothing? "Oh."

He put her in the front passenger seat of the Mustang, then settled behind the wheel. As he was reaching to turn the key in the ignition, he paused. "Screw it. I'll try." He pulled out his phone and shot off a quick text before firing up the engine.

The radio came on low to a classic rock station. "This okay by you?" he asked.

"Yep."

He slanted her a grin. "That didn't sound convincing. Seriously, what do you like?"

"Country, but I don't mind this."

Without a word, he reached for the dash and switched it to a country station for her. The buzz of nerves inside her eased when the familiar strains of one of her favorite songs came on. "Better?" he asked in a wry tone.

She couldn't help but smile. "Yes."

"Top up, or down?"

"Down."

He hit the button and waited for the convertible top to fold back before pulling out of his spot and steering toward the automatic gate on the garage. As soon as they were rolling down the street with the wind in her hair, she closed her eyes and tipped her head back, inhaling the fresh night air tinted with the scent of backyard barbecues and fresh cut grass. She felt lighter inside, freer than she had in forever.

Happy.

The thought startled her. Until that moment she hadn't realized she'd been *un*happy. But maybe she'd been simply going through the motions of living, instead of actually enjoying life.

She tapped her fingers on her thighs to the rhythm, started humming under her breath. If she'd been on her own she would have busted out singing.

Reid's phone chimed. She watched as he picked it up and read the message. His mouth thinned, his jaw tensing beneath the thick, dark stubble.

"No good?" she asked, heart sinking at his expression. He shook his head. "Nope."

She opened her mouth to say how ridiculous it was that his ex wouldn't let him take Autumn out for a spontaneous dessert date, but held it back. "Is it because I'm with you?"

"Nope. This is just how she is."

"Wow. That sucks."

"Sucks *big* time," he muttered, shoulder checking to change lanes. "Even more for Autumn than for me. But short of burning up a bunch of my savings on more legal fees, there's nothing I can do."

That wasn't fair. Reid seemed like a great dad who wanted to be a bigger part of his daughter's life, and Autumn adored him. "Why does she do it?"

"To punish me."

She mentally flinched at the bitterness in his tone. Would his ex really be so small-minded and vindictive as to withhold Autumn from him, just to get back at him? *You don't know him very well. Not fair to just take his side when you don't know the rest of the story.*

"She blames me for our marriage failing. She resents me for making her a divorcee."

Tess was silent for a minute, then attempted to lighten the mood with small talk, but she sensed Reid's lingering frustration and decided to stay quiet as they neared the upscale neighborhood where Autumn lived with her mom. The colonial house looked like something out of a magazine spread.

"Did you live here?" she asked him, unable to stem her curiosity.

"No. This is Max's place. Sarah's business tycoon boyfriend."

Ah. So she'd moved on physically, but not necessarily emotionally. At least not enough to forgive Reid and try to make the best of the co-parenting situation. Tess might not know Sarah's side of the story, but it was hard not to dislike the way she was handling things by depriving her daughter of Reid's company when they so clearly wanted more time with each other.

The moment they pulled up at the curb the front door flew open and Autumn bounded down the steps, her long, brown ponytail trailing behind her as she ran down the brick walkway to the street. "Hi!" she said, her face flushed with excitement when she neared the Mustang.

Tess opened her door and stepped out, surprised and heart-warmed when Autumn grabbed her in a welcoming hug. "Well hello again to you too," she said with a laugh, returning the embrace.

Autumn shot her a grin and let go to scramble into the front seat and wrap her arms around her father's shoulders. "Thanks, Dad," she said as he handed her the wand.

"Welcome."

Autumn eased back and looked between him and Tess. "Can I go for a drive with you guys? It's not my bedtime yet."

Tess's heart ached when Reid's expression froze for a second before he put on a forced but believable smile. "Sorry, baby girl. Maybe another night."

Autumn went into instant pout mode. "Aww, come on, please? Just a short one? You've got the top down and everything, and I found out yesterday that Tess and I like the same music. We can sing for you."

Tess bit her lip and didn't say anything, feeling sad for them both. And the moment was even more bittersweet because Reid didn't blame his ex in front of Autumn.

Instead he gave her a gentle smile and stroked a strand of hair back from her face. "Can't tonight, sweetheart."

"But Tess leaves tomorrow. I might not ever see her again," Autumn said, looking up at Tess.

Tess met Reid's surprised gaze, and nodded. "I fly back to Fort Worth at noon."

Reid turned his attention back to his daughter. "I'm sure you'll see her again. We can set something up for when she comes into town next."

While her heart leapt at him talking about a next time, she was still preoccupied by the unfairness of the situation. She had half a mind to march up to the front door and speak to Sarah herself, see if she could sweet talk the woman into changing her mind, but it wasn't Tess's place and she had no right to interfere.

Autumn's face fell and she slumped in the passenger seat. "Yeah, okay."

"Hey," Reid said, gently chucking her on the chin with his fist. Autumn tried not to smile, but failed. "We'll ride with the top down when I come to pick you up for your sleepover when I get back from my training thing. Okay?"

"Okay," she muttered, and slid out of the car to face Tess. "When you come back into town next, will you come with us?"

Tess didn't want to lie to her, and didn't want to be condescending. She glanced at Reid for help, and the way he watched her so intently made her insides tingle. It was as though he wanted her to promise to come back.

She smiled at Autumn, a little overwhelmed. There was a lot to take in here, with Reid's job, child, ex, and past alcoholism. Her gut instinct was to let whatever happened happen, but it would be smart to be cautious when this much baggage was involved, especially on the first date. "I don't know exactly when that will be, but yes. I promise." As long as your dad still wants me around, she added silently.

Autumn grinned and threw her thin arms around Tess's waist. "Thank you. And maybe sometime you could take me flying?"

Aww, hell, that was Tess's weakness. She could

become attached to this kid all too easily. "That would be so awesome."

"I get to come too," Reid said.

Tess met his gaze, and smiled at the admiration she saw written there. Guys thought it was cool that she flew Blackhawks, but few understood the risks her job entailed. Reid was one of them. "That's up to Autumn."

"He can come too, as long as it's not a girl's only thing," Autumn said.

"What she said," Tess told him, and the grin he gave her was like a punch to the solar plexus. He was charming enough in his own right. These two together were a deadly combo she had no prayer of resisting, and she didn't want to.

"Oh! Almost forgot," Autumn said, digging into her pocket. She pulled out a white pom-pom dog and handed it to Tess. "This is the one we made together. I thought you could put it on the helicopter dashboard. Her name's Winter."

Oh, dammit... Tess took it, heart aching as though someone had wrung it out like a wet dishrag. "Winter will look awesome in the cockpit. Thank you."

"Welcome. See you guys. Love you, Dad," Autumn called as she started back up the pathway.

"Love you back," Reid answered.

Tess waited until Autumn waved from the front porch and disappeared into the house before sliding back into the car, Winter the fluffy white pom-pom creature cradled in her palm, its little plastic googly eyes staring up at her. "Oh, my heart," she said to Reid.

"Yeah, I know. She's an expert at tugging the heartstrings," he said, firing up the engine.

Smiling, Tess set Winter on the center of the dashboard next to the German Shepherd Autumn had made Reid, both of them right up against the windshield so they wouldn't fly out. They both laughed as the little black pupils bounced around with the car's motion. "She's such a great kid, Reid."

"She is," he agreed, his voice full of fatherly pride. "I keep hoping things will get better the more Sarah sees me trying, but... So far that's not happening."

Tess reached across the console for his hand. He shot her a grateful smile and laced his fingers through hers, squeezed in silent thanks. "Where to now?" he asked. "Want to go back to my place?"

Her body hummed with a low-grade arousal that would burst back into flame with a single kiss or caress. She wanted Reid, even if she could only have him this once. "Hmmm. My hotel's closer."

He met her gaze, and the sudden flare of heat in his eyes started a delicious throb between her legs. The slow grin he gave her made her insides shiver in anticipation. "You're right. It is."

Chapter Seven

If she'd thought she'd been nervous before, her anxiety level was way higher when they arrived at the hotel fifteen minutes later. Tess's heart thudded against her ribs as Reid parked out front and turned slightly in his seat to look at her.

"Want me to walk you up?"

He'd just given her an out if she wanted to use it. And that melted her heart. "Yes."

He nodded and pushed his door open, and her belly flipped as she watched six-foot-plus of gorgeous male climb out and walk around to her side. His dark blue gaze held hers as he reached for her hand and gently pulled her to her feet to stand in front of him.

She expected him to kiss her but instead he took her face in his hands, staring into her eyes for a long moment. Searching for something, she didn't know what, while her pulse beat out of control and her entire body tingled.

That voice in the back of her mind whispered again. *If you sleep with him, you won't be able to walk away after.* She'd never been a no-strings girl in the first place, and something about Reid made her want to take the risk of getting attached.

Finally, she raised a hand to curl her fingers around his solid wrist, and he bent his head to brush a soft kiss across her lips that left her entire body tingling. His hands stayed on her face, his thumbs gliding along her cheekbones as he kissed her lower lip, her upper one, then the tip of her nose. So tender and full of reassurance, as though he understood her silent battle, it shook her inside. Then he straightened.

Speechless, she stared at him, returning the smile he gave her when he dropped one hand down to grasp hers and lace their fingers together. "Come on. I'll take you up."

Her thoughts were scattered as they rode the elevator up to her floor, and even when they reached her room, she still wasn't sure what she wanted. Her attraction to him was off the charts crazy, she liked him as a person, and she admired the man he was.

Could she sleep with him and keep her heart out of it? And if not, could she deal with all the complications getting involved with him would bring?

Doubt and nerves began to take the upper hand as she pulled out the plastic key card to unlock her door. Her fingers were clumsy, unsteady as she slid it in the slot and fumbled to pull it out in time. A red light appeared on the door lock mechanism, indicating she'd messed up. Blood rushed to her cheeks and she mentally cursed as she tried it again.

A warm, strong hand appeared over her shoulder and closed over hers. She stopped, every cell in her body aware of that big, powerful body standing a mere foot behind her.

"You don't have to ask me in," he said in a low voice.

Tess closed her eyes as embarrassment washed over her. "I'm just...I guess I'm a little nervous, that's all," she said breathlessly. Had she ever felt an attraction this intense before? If she had, it certainly hadn't happened this fast, not even with Brian.

Before she could find the guts to turn and face him, Reid plucked the card from her fingers, slid it into the slot and unlocked the door for her. Pulse pounding, she walked through into the cool, air-conditioned room, the faint scent of her perfume hanging in the air. Housekeeping had been in earlier. Her bed was turned down and the bedside lamp was on, casting a warm, inviting glow over the sheets.

Tess stared at it, her mind and body at war.

Reid was right behind her as the door clicked shut, closing them in alone together and locking the rest of the world out. "Tess. Look at me."

His deep voice was like a gentle, intimate caress to her senses. Gathering her nerve, she slowly turned around, a shockwave of desire blasting through her as she faced him.

He shook his head once, those blue, blue eyes on her face. "Why are you nervous?"

A nervous laugh bubbled up. "I don't know." *Because I don't do this. I barely know you.*

And because I'm afraid that I could fall for you.

Even with all his baggage, even though his job was every bit as dangerous as Brian's had been. More so, in many ways. And that scared her because she was a sensible, practical person. She liked to think things through. But Reid made her want to leap without looking.

One of his hands came up to cradle the side of her neck, his thumb rubbing over her frantically beating pulse point. "Are you nervous? Or afraid?"

"Not afraid," she said softly. Not of him. Only of this frighteningly intense physical pull she'd never experienced before, and of the consequences she would have to face in the aftermath. All the complications that came with him would still be there, and she'd be emotionally attached and unwilling to walk away.

"Good," he murmured, and dipped his head. She closed her eyes and tilted her face up to his, expecting to feel his mouth on hers a moment later.

Instead she gasped as the warmth of his lips touched the sensitive spot beneath her left ear. He kissed it, parted his lips and scraped his teeth across it gently before the warmth of his tongue touched her skin.

Tess made an involuntary sound of surprise and pleasure and tipped her head to the side, her hands coming up to curl around his upper arms, a thrill racing through her at the sheer power of the muscles shifting beneath her hands.

Reid took advantage and opened his mouth against the side of her neck, the delightful prickle of his stubble a stark contrast to the smooth glide of his lips and tongue. "You smell so damn good, I could just eat you up," he whispered.

She shivered in his hold, her nipples beading tight and a hot throb pulsing between her legs. It had been so long since she'd felt a man's body against hers. An eternity since she'd felt a man's hands moving over her, caressing, arousing. After having only her own hands to bring herself pleasure for so long, the thought of a man like Reid touching her so intimately made her tremble.

Reid made a low murmuring sound and slid his free hand up into her hair, his fingers squeezing a fistful of it as he stepped into her body. Tess closed her eyes and let out a moan at the feel of him pressed flush to her, hard and warm, his hold both possessive and protective.

Her heart thundered out of control while his mouth blazed a path down one side of her neck, across her collarbones and up the other side. Her fingers bit into his upper arms when his tongue found the erogenous zone where her neck and shoulder met. Reid paused there, sucked at the tender spot, damn near making her eyes roll back in her head.

By the time he kissed his way up to her jaw she was dizzy and breathless, her lips eagerly searching out his. But he held her head in place, refusing to let her move as he nibbled his way across to her chin, then the corner of her mouth.

Tess made a soft, desperate sound in the back of her throat and grasped his face in her hands to bring his mouth to hers. The moment their lips connected a bolt of pure, sweet desire shot through her. Her breasts were swollen and heavy, the folds between her thighs growing slick. Aching for his touch.

Reid let out a low growl and backed her up against the nearest wall, pinning her there with his weight. She wrapped her arms around his neck, keeping one hand in his hair to fuse their mouths together. His tongue slid across her lower lip. Teasing. Making her crave more.

She met it with her own, sliding, caressing, and when he eased it into her mouth in an imitation of what was to come, her entire body clenched with need. Over and over he stroked the inside of her mouth, sucked at her tongue gently, keeping control of the kiss the entire time, never letting her take over. Some part of her had known that he would take the dominant role in bed, and she reveled in knowing she was about to experience it fully.

Needing more friction, she pulled him closer and rubbed her breasts against the rock hard planes of his chest. Reid hummed against her lips and shifted his stance to bring his hips square between her legs, the sudden pressure of his erection against her covered mound making her whimper. He cut off the sound with another deep, searing kiss, and rocked his hips, slowly dragging his thick length along her swollen center.

Tess jerked her head to the side as pleasure radiated outward from where he stroked her, sucking a ragged breath between her parted lips. This was so freaking intense, and a little frightening. She couldn't remember teetering on the brink of losing control like this, and not with a man she barely knew.

Reid stopped rubbing against her and simply pressed forward with his hips, the thick length of his erection snuggled up to her throbbing core as he kissed his way back across her jaw to her ear. Unhurried, sensual enough to make the breath clog in her throat. The hand holding her hair slid down her shoulder, down to her ribs and up again to gently cradle the curve of her breast. Tess bit her lip and quivered in his grasp, her aching nipple grazing his hot palm through two layers of fabric with every uneven breath.

"So sweet, Tess," he groaned, gently nipping her earlobe. "I wanna unwrap you so bad. Peel that dress away so I can kiss you all over, and slide my tongue into you."

God! She shuddered at his graphic words, her body totally on board with that plan and her mind supplying the movie in a string of rapid high-resolution images.

He made a low, gruff sound and placed a hot, open-mouth kiss to the sensitive spot on the side of her neck before raising his head and studying her. Tess stared up at him through heavy-lidded eyes, her lips swollen, her aching nipple grazing his palm. The heat in his eyes, the tightness of his face and the hard ridge of his erection were all at odds with the tender way he cradled her breast and the care he'd taken in arousing her.

With his other hand still grasping the back of her neck, he stroked his thumb across the straining nipple, watching her eyes the whole time. Tess bit her lip but couldn't stifle a whimper of pleasure as need knifed through her. She strained up onto her toes, needing more friction. Just...more.

"I know, baby," he whispered, pressing a tender kiss

to her parted lips, the soft stroke of his tongue making her crazy.

Except he lifted his head and let his hand drop before easing his body away.

No! She made an unintelligible sound and swayed forward, tried to pull him back, but he merely smoothed his hand over her hair and dropped another brief kiss to her upturned lips.

She blinked up at him, confused, on fire. "What—"

"I'm not taking you to bed tonight."

Shock cleared some of the haze of arousal away. "Why not?"

The corner of his mouth kicked up, and then he sobered again. "Because I like you, a lot, and when we first got up here you were nervous. That tells me you're not ready, even if your body is. And since we sometimes work together, I don't want you to regret sleeping with me or feel awkward around me later." He ran his thumb across her lower lip, light as a sigh, and she kissed it. "I need to know you're sure, and not just giving into this because of the chemistry happening between us." He leaned forward to rest his forehead against hers, a smile in his voice. "But hell, our chemistry is off the charts."

It was. She didn't know what the hell to say to his reasoning, so she let out a shaky laugh to cut the tension.

He murmured in agreement and paused to kiss the tip of her nose before easing back. She felt cold all of a sudden without the intense heat of his body against hers, and was grateful for the support of the wall at her back because her knees were so damn weak.

"You sure you don't want to stay the night?" she asked, still a little breathless. Having him hold her in the night would be so damn good.

He shook his head, his dark eyes intense. "If I climb into that bed with you, there's no way I wouldn't wind up inside you at some point."

Her insides clenched. It sounded like a damn good idea to her, but he was right about one thing; she needed to be sure before they took that step, and she admired him for giving her the space to make it. Even if her body hated her freaking guts right now.

His palm caressed the side of her face, then he lowered his hand. "I'll call you before I see you down at Emerald Warrior."

She nodded, not knowing what else to say. It was a huge exercise, and while they might catch glimpses of one another here and there, she doubted they'd be able to spend any time together in their off hours. Still, a chance was better than nothing. "We'll figure something out."

"Damn right, we will. This isn't over, Tess. Not by a long shot." He aimed a sexy smile at her as he took a step toward the door. "Dream about me."

Like she had a choice? "Okay." Although dreaming required her to be asleep, and with how tightly wound her body was right now, that wasn't likely to happen for a long time.

But she'd sure as hell be fantasizing about him, and the moment when they finally did something about the hunger raging between them.

****

Morning sunlight filtered through the palm fronds that arched across the cabana next to the pool. Carlos stripped off his robe and stretched out naked on his stomach on the massage table, relaxing with a groan of contentment as he set his face into the round face cradle.

The sprawling ranch house and its secluded ninety acres of land in the southern Sinaloa region had been beautiful when he'd bought it last year, but he'd made certain improvements and added things like the waterfall currently splashing into the deep end of the swimming pool. The silvery sound of it soothed him, especially late at night when he lay in his bed in the master bedroom upstairs, the ever-present ache in his leg and his spinning mind about to drive him crazy.

His personal massage therapist adjusted the pillows beneath his shins and hips before covering his naked ass with a light sheet. He didn't care if she saw it, but she was a professional, not a whore, and so she insisted on proper "draping" whenever she worked on him.

"Still the left hip and lower back?" Juana asked him, one cool hand resting on the center of his bare back.

"Yes, and my calves, too."

He relaxed and closed his eyes at the familiar sound of her rubbing oil between her practiced hands. She smoothed it over the length of his back and across his hips with light strokes, then she leaned her weight into her hands and he couldn't hold back a deep groan of mingled pleasure and pain.

The woman might be seven inches shorter than him and slightly built, but she had magic hands, and she was worth double what he paid her. She came to his ranch at precisely nine o'clock each morning he was home, and worked on him for an hour. Her treatments, followed by a soak in his custom-built hot tub, were the best part of his day and the only thing that had helped him ease off the pain meds.

A firmer pressure dug into the side of his hip and he hissed in a breath, tensing.

"Breathe," she coaxed, maintaining the pressure.

He grunted and held back a retort that it was easy for her to tell him to breathe, since she was the one with an elbow in the side of his ass. But he trusted her, and knew this worked.

So he breathed through the pain, forcing his mind to clear and his body to relax. Soon enough the pain in his hip began to ebb. Juana continued to work out the knot with slow, sure strokes, switching back to her hands now, and it felt so damn good he growled low in his throat.

The sharp cry of a peacock brought his head up. Blinking in the glare of the overhead sun, he found Rex, his favorite peacock strutting his stuff along the strip of manicured grass beyond the deep end of the pool.

"Manuel," he hollered, annoyed that his massage had been interrupted.

A moment later a young boy of twelve shot out from around the corner of the main house. "*Sí, señor?*"

The boy was new to the job of helping take care of Carlos's menagerie, only a week into his routine. "Did you feed Rex his breakfast yet?" he asked in English. The boy's grandmother had asked Carlos to help him learn more English. Manuel understood far more than he could speak.

"*No, señor.*"

"Well, hurry up. He won't stop squawking until he gets fed." Damn bird was too haughty and demanding for his own good.

"*Sí, señor.*"

The boy scurried away, calling Rex, who ran after him like an eager puppy, his long, brilliant blue and green tail plumage trailing on the grass behind him.

Juana chuckled as Carlos lay back down and got settled again. "You spoil all your animals," she said in Spanish.

"I know." He couldn't help it. Though he didn't keep domestic pets, except for a few barn cats who helped keep the rodent population down in exchange for a cozy place to live and regular veterinary checks. He'd amassed quite a collection already: horses, a llama, three pot-bellied pigs, a camel, giraffe, and of course, Rex. The king of the ranch.

All rescues. That was deliberate.

Every creature he owned had been beaten, abused and

neglected, with no one to care for them until he had stepped in. Because after being raised by a single mother who didn't give two shits about him, or the two older brothers he'd lost to gang violence in their teens, he knew all too well how that felt.

He zoned out again when Juana began working on his lower back. Since being wounded in that shootout with the DEA, he was lucky to be walking at all, but his altered gait was pure hell on his body.

His cell rang a few minutes later. From the ringtone, he knew it was Antonio. Carlos ignored it, irritated that his head enforcer didn't know by now not to interrupt him during his massage from nine to ten.

He was half asleep a few minutes later when his brain recognized the long, gentle strokes that signaled his treatment was almost at an end. His muscles felt loose and pliable, but his dick was rock hard, trapped between his belly and the table.

He might have ordered Juana to take care of that too, but he respected her and her skills too much. Besides, he had an endless supply of whores to choose from. With a single phone call or text, he could have any one of them up here to the house and ready to go within half an hour.

"Will you be getting into the hot tub now?" she asked him.

"Later. You can go."

She left without a word, and only when he was alone did he return Antonio's call. His sixty-three-year-old and half-deaf housekeeper—Manuel's grandmother—was inside. Her hearing impairment a big reason why Carlos had hired her, since she wouldn't overhear anything she shouldn't, and therefore couldn't spill his secrets. She was the only staff he kept at the house, other than his two bodyguards, who patrolled the house and grounds at all times.

"Don't ever call me during my massage unless it's an

emergency," he snapped when Antonio answered.

"Right, sorry."

Whatever. "What did you call about?"

"The next delivery is scheduled for tonight, to Cartagena."

"How many girls?" He was one of the few *Veneno* lieutenants involved in the skin trade.

Women were weak and useless, except for three things: sex, providing children, and making money off of. *El Escorpion* didn't approve of human trafficking or sex slavery, per se, but he didn't do anything to stop it, either. As long as business continued to increase and their territory expanded, the head of the cartel overlooked everything else.

"Seven. Eight, if you want to include our special guest."

"How is our guest doing?" Carlos asked.

"Finally coming around to her training, I think. Close to breaking."

"No." Carlos didn't want her broken when she came to him. He wanted to do that himself. "Keep her there for now. Give her a while to rest up and regain her strength. You'll bring her to me in New Orleans next Friday night." He had a distributor there who owed him a favor and would be happy to arrange everything. "I'll text you the guy's number."

"All right. You sure you want her to regain her strength? She was a handful when we first got her."

"I'm sure. Text me when you've got it set up."

He ended the call, his dick throbbing like a damn toothache at the thought of what would happen between him and Victoria Gomez in that New Orleans hotel room. Once he was done with her, when she was broken in spirit and maybe in body as well, depending on how she behaved, he'd hand her over to a courier to be sold overseas.

Lust roared through him, the throb of his cock too delicious to waste on his own hand.

He texted one of his bodyguards posted out front of the house. "Call Teresa. Get her up here now."

Chapter Eight

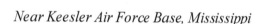

Near Keesler Air Force Base, Mississippi

"Six minutes!" the jumpmaster yelled over the drone of the C-130's turboprop engines. The tail ramp was open, revealing a sea of darkness below where the flat Mississippi swampland spread out several thousand feet beneath them.

"Six minutes!" Reid and the others shouted back.

Emerald Warrior was already into its fourth day, and the entire team was feeling the fatigue. Yesterday they'd spent nine hours out in the field covering procedure on how to call in close air support fire missions with an AFSOC combat controller named Ryan Wentworth, who they knew from their deployments to Bagram. Today they were doing a static line jump into "cartel territory" and linking up with another unit to search for drugs and hostages in a simulated village together.

Reid and his teammates climbed to their feet and hooked their lines onto the cable that ran toward the open tail ramp.

"Stand by!" the jumpmaster called out.

Ten seconds to go.

Third in line, Reid did the familiar airborne shuffle across the C-130's deck toward the tail ramp. Hamilton was in front of him, and Freeman was first in line, the former SEAL in his usual position of point man, since he was the most experienced operator on the team.

The jump light turned from red to green. "Go!" the jumpmaster yelled.

Freeman hopped off the ramp first, then Hamilton a second later. Reid was a step behind him. He launched himself off the back of the tail ramp, the sudden tension on the static line deploying his D-Bag.

He immediately started counting. Just before he hit three seconds, the canopy opened over his head in the dark night sky, and he caught sight of the remainder of his teammates exiting the aircraft above him in rapid succession. The Hercules was traveling at around 130 knots, so it was critical to stay as close together as possible. Any delay between jumpers caused big gaps that were hard to make up for on the ground.

The muggy Mississippi night air rushed around him as he descended toward the edge of the swamp that marked the boundary of the DZ. He toggled the chute to slow his fall at the end and executed a running landing, then quickly unstrapped and stashed his chute.

He spotted Hamilton and Freeman about thirty yards away. He waved his arm to signal that he was ready to rock, then brought his M-4 up into position and took a knee to scan his portion of the DZ.

Four more figures floated downward through the dark sky to land in various spots in the empty field. All around them, everything was silent.

When everyone was on the ground safely and ready to go, they moved toward the western tree line in a wedge formation, maintaining all around security. The mission plan called for them to rendezvous with another element on the northern edge of the swamp, one-point-three klicks away, before moving to the target.

Reid stayed on the left side of the formation with Maka. They picked their way through the trees and underbrush as they skirted the edge of the swamp, with Freeman and Hamilton in the lead. At the rendezvous point they formed a defensive perimeter and crouched down to await the other squad.

Six minutes later, Hamilton signaled that he'd seen something through his IR goggles. Had to be the other team making contact with an IR strobe.

Sure enough, a second later someone hidden in the trees called out the challenge word. Hamilton gave the predetermined response and waved Reid and the others forward.

A group of figures appeared through the trees in the distance. On a real op Reid and the others would have been on high alert in case it was a setup or ambush. Since this was a training exercise no one was going to shoot them, so while they would still act like professionals and keep their game faces on, they could afford to relax their guard a little.

The point man from the other team emerged out of the tree line and paused, the rest of his men waiting behind him. Hamilton stepped forward to meet them. "Fancy meeting you boys out here."

"Yeah, what're the odds of that?" the other man said in a southern drawl similar to Reid's. And when the other team's point man walked over to meet Hamilton, he had a big grin on his face. "How you doin', brother?"

"Tuck?" Hamilton said, astonishment as well as a smile clear in his voice. "I'll be goddamned."

Wait. Tuck, as in Brad Tucker? Team leader for the FBI's Hostage Rescue Blue Team? Reid knew him and a couple of the other guys from back in his SF days, and their teams sometimes crossed paths at Quantico for training. He hadn't known they were doing Emerald Warrior.

"Did you know it was us you were meeting out here?" Hamilton asked.

"They told us just before we loaded into the plane." Tuck slapped him once on the shoulder. "Good to see you."

"Yeah, it's like old home week." Hamilton half-turned and waved Reid forward. "Prentiss. Get over here."

Reid jogged over, unable to keep from grinning when he reached Tuck. "Hey," he said, grasping Tuck's outstretched hand. "Vance and Blackwell with you too?"

"Yep, the gang's all here." Tuck looked behind him and waved them over. "Vance. Blackwell. Come say hi."

The two men materialized out of the darkness, Vance's teeth seeming extra bright in his dark face as he grinned. "How's it going, my man?" he said in his deep baritone.

"Good to see you," Reid said, giving his old buddy a hug and a backslap. They'd served together on the same A-team for a while when Reid had first passed SF selection. Releasing Vance, he shook Blackwell's hand. "Heard you're a daddy now. Congrats." Blackwell and his wife had been to hell and back trying to have a baby. Reid was happy things had finally worked out for them.

"Thanks, man. It's been a long time coming, but it's awesome. How's Autumn?"

Reid shook his head. "Growing up way too fast. She's nine going on twenty-nine. I'm thinking of locking her in her room until she's thirty."

Blackwell laughed. "Yeah, not gonna lie, I'm glad we had a boy."

Hamilton gripped Reid's shoulder from behind and gave it a hard squeeze. "Prentiss is loving the hell out of this. Working down here in his old backyard."

"Yeah, it's good to be back home where we can get

real barbecue," Tuck said. As an Alabama native, the man knew good barbecue.

Oh, man. Now Reid's mouth was watering for smoked ribs and pulled pork. "We gotta hit up The Shed before we head back to Virginia."

"That's a deal," Tuck said, and pulled out his topo map to confer with Hamilton.

The rest of the guys mingled for a few minutes while their leaders went over the plan. One of the HRT members was a big sonofabitch named Bauer, damn near as big as Maka. A former SEAL, he knew Freeman. The SOF community was a small world.

Everybody was in high spirits when they finally started toward the objective village together. The HRT was responsible for neutralizing the drug runners and rescuing the two captives reported to be inside, while FAST Bravo would provide backup and then do a search for drugs, weapons and cash.

Each team started for the target village in a separate wedge formation, the tangled terrain and swampy conditions making the trek slow going. A half klick from their objective, they went into full op mode, staying silent and stealthy as they covered the remaining distance to where four dilapidated buildings sat in the middle of the bayou.

Old gnarled cypress trees gave them good concealment, the Spanish moss and vines swaying from their branches giving the place an eerie feel that made Reid all nostalgic. Damn, he loved it down here. He'd been hunting in this neck of the woods since he was a kid, so being out here in the swamp at night made him feel right at home.

Hidden behind the thick trunk of a cypress, Reid hunkered down to wait, the rest of his team fanned out amongst the trees as the HRT started toward the small group of wood-framed houses.

The enemy force didn't put up much resistance. Things went so smoothly—way more smoothly than it ever did in real life—it was all over in a matter of minutes. The HRT swept in hard and fast, catching the "cartel members" off guard, neutralizing the tangos and securing the captives. Reid and his teammates helped secure the village and conducted the search for contraband, while Rodriguez helped question a few of the prisoners.

When everything was done the teams fanned out in two semi-circles to await the incoming helos. The HRT guys and the rescued "hostages" boarded the first, and FAST Bravo with their captured "cartel soldiers" and contraband the second. Reid tried to see if Tess was at the controls of one of them, but he couldn't get a good look at the cockpit of either aircraft.

He jumped aboard the second one and chatted with Colebrook during the flight back to base, but he was distracted by thoughts of Tess. They'd talked every day since that scorching makeout session at her hotel nine days ago, but it felt like forever since he'd seen her. He was crazy about her.

She made him laugh. Made him feel comfortable. With her kindness and positive outlook on life, she was a balm to his cynical soul. She was stealing her way into his heart and he was too enthralled to stop it.

Also huge for him was her job. She'd served overseas in combat, had flown his team during a mission. She understood firsthand what he did for a living, the dangers and the commitment his place on the team demanded. That right there set her apart from any other woman he'd ever been with.

He needed to see her again, as soon as possible.

Once on the tarmac about fifteen minutes later, Reid was one of the last to hop out of the aircraft, and stopped to peer through the cockpit windows. A male pilot sat in the left hand seat, but when Reid's gaze slid over to the right one, his heart stuttered when he made out Tess's profile.

He stood there grinning like an idiot, raising his hand to acknowledge his teammates when someone called to him, but he didn't look away from Tess. Couldn't.

Come on, sweetheart, look at me.

Moments later she turned her head slightly and their gazes connected. A startled smile broke over her face and she waved once. He waved back and motioned toward the hangar with his eyebrows raised, asking her whether she and her crew were calling it a night after this. She gave a thumbs up in affirmation, one more little grin, and went back to her shutdown procedure.

A minute ago, he'd been tired and looking forward to a hot shower, some chow, and his bunk. Now, he was energized at the thought of spending even a few minutes with Tess. Getting any time with her at all was better than none.

Because the rules were relaxed due to the training atmosphere, both teams' commanders allowed them all to shower up and grab a bite to eat before the joint post-op meeting that lasted the better part of an hour.

FAST Bravo was bunking at a dorm just off base, a short bus ride away. Reid slung his duffel over one shoulder and rounded the corner of the command building, in the act of fishing out his phone to text Tess and see if they could meet up somewhere. The guys were heading to the bar with the HRT, but Reid wanted no part of it—he just wanted Tess.

His feet stuck to the concrete when he saw Tess waiting for him at the side of the building in jeans and a snug T-shirt that hugged the curve of her round breasts, her honey-blond hair down around her shoulders.

"Hey, stranger," she said with a smile.

Reid unstuck his feet and rushed straight for her. "Hey." He dropped his bag onto the sidewalk and grabbed her, wrapping her up in a fierce, tight hug. Her hair smelled like pears. "Damn, I've missed you."

Tess slipped her arms around his back and squeezed him in return, her face nestled into the side of his neck. "Mmm, me too. I'd almost forgotten how good you feel."

The husky edge to her voice sent a torrent of blood between his legs. "Well I haven't forgotten how good *you* feel." The memory had been torturing him for over a week now.

She gave a soft laugh and pulled her head back to peer up at him. Reid stroked the hair away from her face, getting lost in the pale green of her eyes. "Did you know it was my team you were picking up out there?"

"Yes, but I'm guessing you didn't see me until we got back here. You looked pretty surprised."

"Excited is the word you're looking for," he corrected her.

"Okay, then. Excited."

The pride swelling his chest was fierce. "I love it that you were at the controls tonight."

Her eyes lit up at his praise. "Thanks. How many more days are you here for?"

"Two. You?"

Her smile fell. "I leave tomorrow afternoon."

"Back to Fort Worth?"

She nodded, searching his eyes. "Any chance you'll get a few days off after this? Maybe you could come to Texas?"

He groaned. "No. We're headed straight back to D.C. and then I've got Autumn overnight on Saturday." He was glad he wouldn't be alone on the anniversary of Jason's death.

After that, he wasn't sure what his schedule would be. It changed constantly, depending on what was happening at the agency or whatever target they were sent after.

"Oh. When are you scheduled to have some time off

next? Because I'm not off until the end of June."

He'd failed at making his marriage work because of his job, and he and Sarah had lived in the same damn house. What were he and Tess going to do when *both* of them had demanding schedules they couldn't change, and they lived in different states? "I'll see what I can do." He'd find a way. Call in a favor or pull some strings to get time to visit her. Whatever it took.

A slow, soft smile curved her mouth. "Good. Because as much as I swore to myself that I'd never be with another military man, I've missed you like hell this past week."

"I've missed you too." Way more than he'd expected to. She'd triggered something inside him, revived a part of him that he'd thought was long dead.

Unable to stand the temptation she posed a moment longer, he brushed his thumb across her lower lip, and lowered his mouth to hers. Tess slid one hand to the back of his neck and raised her head to meet him. Her lips were soft and warm beneath his own, and he tasted toothpaste when he slipped his tongue inside her mouth.

Someone cleared their throat behind him.

Reid whipped around, automatically blocking Tess with his body. Maka stood there at the front doors, his huge silhouette all but blocking the light coming from the front of the building. "Problem?" Reid asked, feeling ultra-protective of Tess.

"Trip to the bar's been cancelled. Taggart's called us and the HRT guys in for a meeting."

Now? It was so late. He frowned. "About what?"

Maka shrugged, his face impassive. "Dunno, but it must be something big. Everybody's heading back inside."

Hell. "Okay. Be there in a minute." He waited until Maka left before turning back to Tess. Damn, he wished they could have more time together. "Sorry."

Her lips curved upward and she gave a little shrug. "It's okay, I know how it is."

Yeah, she did. He took her face in his hands. "I know you do." And that made a potential relationship between them a hell of a lot easier for them both, even with all their other challenges. With a sigh, Reid pulled her back into his arms. He loved the way she fit against him, her body soft yet firm, all her curves nestled into him.

"You be safe," she murmured, correctly assuming that he and his team were about to be deployed somewhere. Likely sent after a *Veneno* target.

"I will. I'll call you as soon as I get a chance. See if I can get a few days off and come to Texas."

"I'd love that."

"Me too." He kissed the top of her head, then she tipped her face up to his and he claimed that soft, sexy mouth once more. One last hug, and he was forced to leave her there, the feel and taste of her imprinted in his brain.

Inside the briefing room, both teams were already assembled when Reid walked in. A silent tension filled the air. Commander Taggart was up front with some guys wearing FBI windbreakers who Reid didn't recognize.

Taking the empty seat between Lockhart and Colebrook, Reid settled in.

"Okay, let's get to it," Taggart said in his booming voice. "All remaining exercises that you were scheduled to participate in within Emerald Warrior have hereby been cancelled. Because we just got a viable lead on Carlos Ruiz."

Absolute silence greeted the words, every operator riveted to what Taggart was saying.

"He's reputed to be close, southwest of New Orleans out in the swamp someplace, which is why we've been tasked with executing the warrant. We're closest, we're ready, so we've got the green light."

Ruiz's picture came up on screen for everyone to see.

"Couple of kids were out in the woods earlier tonight, and heard a woman screaming so they went to investigate and found more than they'd bargained for. They got pictures with a phone and sent them to local cops, who contacted the FBI. The reason we've called the HRT to this meeting is because we have reason to believe that the missing reporter Victoria Gomez is being held hostage at this place, and recent chatter suggests Ruiz is planning to ship female hostages along with his dope. Gomez being one of them."

Reid squeezed his hands into fists. Few things got him as riled up as people profiting off the skin trade, where women and sometimes girls not even in their teens were sold as sex slaves. As a man, it sickened him. As a father, it enraged him.

He stared up at Ruiz's picture, jaw tensing. *Fucking pathetic piece of shit.*

"HRT's Commander DeLuca is aware of the situation and monitoring it from Quantico," Taggart continued. "Ruiz and his men like to move around a lot, never staying in one place for long, so we're moving fast on this one. We'll give you the intel we have, then you'll decide how you want to do this," he said to both teams.

Reid and the others listened carefully while Taggart and the FBI folks laid out what they knew of the suspect property, Ruiz's enforcers, what to expect in terms of resistance, weapons, drug cache and possible other hostages as well. As soon as they wrapped up, Hamilton and the HRT team leader, Tucker, took over and organized a general plan of attack.

Once they had a general roadmap in mind, the individual team members got involved, giving feedback and suggestions. Taggart listened in, offering his opinion on a few points while HRT Commander DeLuca did the same via Skype.

In the end, they decided on a plan similar to what they had just conducted a few hours before, with certain modifications. FAST Bravo would go in support of the HRT, who would clear the buildings, eliminate any hostiles and free whatever hostages they found. Then Reid and his guys would take over the search for drugs, weapons, and question any prisoners—hopefully Ruiz himself—while the FBI and DEA support personnel and investigators finished processing the scene.

"All right, we're looking at a tight turn around on this one," Taggart announced to the whole room once the plan was agreed upon. "Everybody go kit up. Let's get ready to crash Ruiz's party."

Chapter Nine

"Blue Team in position," Tucker murmured through Reid's earpiece in the darkness. "Stand by for breach."

Reid kept watch with his teammates from their position behind some trees thirty yards from the wood-framed house ahead of them. All seven members of HRT Blue team were lined up alongside the east wall of the house, NVGs on and M4s up, ready to storm the place.

Overhead, tree branches swayed slightly in the breeze, blowing the draped moss hanging from them. The steady chirp of cicadas and crickets filled the night in a continual hum, and somewhere in the distance, an owl hooted in the darkness.

The scent of decaying vegetation and stagnant water hung in the muggy air. As far as they could tell, there was no perimeter security out here in the bayou. But without a doubt, as soon as the HRT breached the door, Ruiz and his men would come out fighting.

"Execute."

At Tuck's quiet command, one of his men blew the

locks off the door. A couple flashbangs lit up the stygian doorway a moment later, for a brief instant making it bright as daylight inside. The point man rushed inside, followed by the rest of the HRT.

"Go," Hamilton ordered FAST Bravo, just as shouts and shots rang out from inside.

Reid and three of his teammates rushed out of the trees to cover the east and south sides of the target house, while another four took the north and west sides and Hamilton stayed in between to monitor the situation.

Charging into position, Reid sighted down the barrel of his weapon and swept the side of the house, watching for anyone who might try and make a run for it.

It only took ninety seconds for the HRT to clear the house.

"House secure. Moving to outbuildings now."

"Move in," Hamilton ordered.

Reid led the way into the dilapidated house, his NVGs allowing him to see clearly in the darkness. The stench of the place was like a slap in the face—urine, garbage, pot and body odor all mixing with the sickly-sweet smell of rancid booze.

Inside the room on the left, a male body lay facedown on the floor. In the kitchen, two more lay sprawled out near the table. The HRT guys had already stripped them of weapons.

Reid motioned at Maka, Khan and Colebrook, and together they continued through the rear of the house and out into the backyard. They found the HRT boys already heading back from the rear of the property with three prisoners in tow.

Hamilton joined them on the damp overgrown grass. "Find what we were looking for?" he asked Tucker, who was in the lead.

"Nope, but we got one prisoner and two female hostages. The females need medical attention."

Reid took in the two half-naked women, who were hunched over with their arms crossed over their bare breasts, both of them crying softly. He turned his angry stare to the male prisoner who had his chin up, his expression one of defiance.

Hamilton nodded and spoke to Reid and the others. "Get started in there."

Reid and his teammates made short work of searching the place. "Small stash here," he called out from one of the bedrooms, the restraints still fastened to the bed turning his stomach. No way the females tied down in here had been restrained by choice.

Khan stuck his head in, noted the pile of pistols and rifles Reid had just found under a floorboard that had been thinly disguised beneath an old rug.

"Wad of cash, too," Reid added.

"Granger and Lockhart got a bunch of coke in the kitchen," Khan said, hunkering down to pry the board free and toss it aside.

By the time they finished they'd found another two caches of weapons, along with enough weed and coke to meet the arrest threshold for the prisoner the HRT had taken.

Hamilton stopped in the doorway. "Forensics team's here. You guys go check out the outbuildings while we process all this."

Reid got up and stepped out into the hallway. Beyond the open front door, FBI agents and some of the HRT guys were talking with the two female hostages, who now had blankets draped around them. Both were standing up on their own power and seemed to be moving okay, but neither were the reporter, Victoria Gomez. Had she even been here?

He turned sideways to let a few support personnel past him, and strode back through the kitchen and living room to the back door. From the sagging rear porch, he could just make out the shadowy shape of the shed near the back fence.

The boards creaked as Khan joined him on the stoop. "Ready?"

"Yeah." Together they crossed the yard. As he neared the fence, Reid noticed a gap where some of the old boards had been broken, as though someone had smashed through it in their haste to escape. A K9 unit was already back there checking it out.

Reid aimed the high-powered beam of his tactical flashlight through the shed's open doorway. A thin, badly stained bare mattress lay on the wood floor, along with a short, rusty length of chain attached to a bolt in the floorboards.

Reid's jaw tightened, knowing what it signified. They'd kept one of the female hostages chained up out here like a fucking animal.

"Jesus Christ," he muttered under his breath, and stepped inside.

Khan stopped next to him, taking it all in. "Damn."

Reid pushed out a breath and glanced around. "I'll look at the back, you check the front." He searched the floors and walls of the dismal prison, shifted the mattress aside to search beneath it, but there was nothing except that goddamn rusty chain and bolt. "Nothin'."

"Front's clear too," Khan said. "I'll start checking outside."

Reid joined him, a deep-seated anger roiling inside him. He was the father of a little girl. The thought of a man treating a woman like that, knowing the sick fucks had planned to sell them into the skin trade afterward, made him want to smash the bastards' faces in.

Again, he and Khan found nothing.

Reid reported their findings to Hamilton, who sent them out front to talk to the investigators. An ambulance was on scene now, treating the female hostages. He didn't even want to think about what kinds of injuries they might have sustained being held captive here by these animals.

As for his team, their work was done here. He and Khan started back through the woods together, heading for the spot where they'd left the van. "Think Ruiz was here?"

"If he was, the dogs will pick up his scent."

Reid hoped they did, but he doubted anything would come of it. Ruiz had eluded U.S. authorities for a long time, and he was smart. Too smart to be caught holed up here with his enforcers and human cargo.

He stepped over a fallen log, the beam of his flashlight cutting like a laser through the darkness. Then a branch snapped somewhere to his right.

He froze and whipped around, aiming the beam there. A branch in the distance swayed at waist level, having been disturbed by something.

Or someone.

Without a word, Khan was right next to him, weapon up. Reid shut off his flashlight and lowered his NVGs into place, allowing them to hunt without the light giving them away.

Khan squeezed Reid's right shoulder, signaling that he was ready to move. Reid crept forward, scanning the dense undergrowth, his pulse kicking up a notch. Was it Ruiz, or one of his men?

Something moved beyond the screen of leafy branches, right next to a path worn into the earth, making the surrounding brush quiver.

"Freeze," Reid called out in a hard voice. He had his rifle to his shoulder, finger on the trigger guard, Khan locked and loaded behind him and to his right.

The brush stopped moving.

Reid zeroed in on the spot, every one of his senses on alert. "Stand up and put your hands in the air," he commanded.

Nothing.

"Show yourself, *now*," he yelled, taking a few gliding steps forward. He hated that he couldn't see his target, or tell whether they were armed—

A figure stepped out onto the path, hands raised.

A woman. Naked.

Reid stopped. "Stay right there and don't move," he warned, approaching her slowly. She had something in her hand, but it didn't look like a gun. Too bulky, and not the right shape.

Leaving Khan to cover him, Reid pulled his flashlight out and aimed it at her. The woman flinched as the light blinded her, and when she raised her arms in a gesture of self-defense, Reid finally saw what she was holding.

A big stick.

And she had a goddamn rusty collar and chain dangling from her neck.

Oh, Jesus.

He immediately lowered and slung his weapon, and gentled his demeanor. "Put the stick down and get onto your knees for me." He needed to be certain she wasn't armed with something else. His and Khan's safety took precedence.

The woman seemed to weave on her feet for a moment, blinking at him with one bruised eye, the other swollen shut. Her face was too badly distorted to see her features clearly. They'd beaten the shit out of her, and it twisted Reid's stomach.

"It's okay," he said in a softer tone, holding one hand toward her, palm-out. "We're not gonna hurt you. We're with the DEA."

She stared back at him for a moment, her long, dark hair partially shielding her naked breasts. She was trembling all over.

"Put the stick down," Reid said again. "We're going to help you."

The woman swallowed. Her hand twitched on the stick, then she opened her fist and it fell to the ground with a soft thud.

Okay, he wasn't going to make her kneel before him while she was naked and wearing that goddamn collar, fresh from whatever those motherfuckers had done to her. "Cap," he said to Hamilton over their comms. "We found another hostage. Meet us on the road."

"Roger that."

The woman took what appeared to be an involuntary step back as Reid continued to approach her. He stopped, tried to look as non-threatening as he could with his size while armed and wearing tactical gear. He motioned to Khan, who was beside him now. "I'm Special Agent Reid Prentiss. This is my teammate, Zaid. He's our medic. Will you let him help you?" For starters, Reid wanted that fucking collar and chain off her, *asap*.

Her one-eyed gaze flicked over to Khan, her stiff posture and stance telling Reid that she was an instant from fleeing through the woods like a wounded doe. She had no reason to trust him, or believe that he and Khan were with the DEA. For all she knew they were more of Ruiz's men, or someone else from the cartel.

"What's your name?" he asked, not daring to move in case it triggered her flight response.

She didn't answer, her chest and shoulders rising and falling with her rapid, harsh breaths. Blood trickled down from where the chain had bitten into her neck, and her wrists and ankles were raw from whatever they'd bound her with. The rest of her was a mass of bruises and other marks. Fucking hell, he wanted to cover her up and carry her out of here.

"Okay, I'm here," Hamilton said through his earpiece.

Reid pointed a finger over her shoulder. "There's a road just up ahead. My team leader is there waiting for us. We can get you help."

The woman stared at him a few seconds longer, then glanced briefly over her shoulder and fixed her gaze back on him once more. Weighing her options. Realizing that there was nowhere for her to go. That she was trapped.

She crossed her arms over her breasts in a purely self-conscious move, seemed to hunch into herself as she dropped her chin. Reid lowered the beam of the flashlight, aiming it at the trail instead of her. Then she took a halting step back, instinctively moving away from him and Khan. Maybe not believing that there was someone actually waiting out on the road for them.

Reid bit back a sigh and reined in his frustration. She'd been through hell and back. He didn't blame her for being scared and distrustful. "Okay, we'll follow you. Go ahead and watch your step."

She kept going, her body angled away from them, too afraid to give them her back.

"Moving to you, Cap," Reid told him.

"Okay. Does she need medical attention?"

"Yeah."

Khan stayed silent, but Reid knew damn good and well his buddy was sickened by what had happened to her, and as a medic the urge to help her had to be burning a hole inside him right now.

A few yards from the dirt road, the woman stopped, having spotted Hamilton standing there near the van.

"Cap, is there a blanket in the van?" Reid asked.

"Gimme a sec."

Reid and Khan both waited in place while their team leader went to look, and the woman stood frozen in place as though she was afraid to move.

"Yeah, got one," Hamilton said a moment later.

"It's okay," Reid said to the woman. "It's our team leader. He's got a blanket for you. Let's get you covered up, and then Zaid can take a look at you." *And I'll get that fucking collar off you.*

The woman's breathing grew even shorter, the rapid rhythm of it telling Reid that she was a second away from either freaking out or bolting. Maybe she thought they were going to kidnap her again.

She'd been through too much already. He couldn't put her through any more fear.

"Cap," he murmured into his mic, keeping his gaze pinned to her. "Gonna need a hand here. She's too scared." He shifted his weight onto the balls of his feet, ready to spring into action if she bolted.

"Hang on." Seconds later Hamilton materialized through the trees, the blanket already spread open in his hands.

The woman gasped and whirled, and in the edge of the flashlight's beam Reid caught the abject shock on his team leader's face for a split second as Hamilton saw her and the state she was in. She whirled to flee, and Hamilton reacted instantly, leaping forward to capture her with the blanket, wrapping its folds around her as he lifted her off her feet.

Reid cursed silently and burst toward them. She let out a shrill scream and tried to fight her way free, but Hamilton had his arms locked around her, holding her to his chest. "Shhh, shhh, it's okay," he said gently. "Hey, no. I won't hurt you. Shhh."

Reid and Khan stopped a few feet from them and stood there. Reid's heart squeezed as the woman stilled and finally curled into a ball, the blanket swallowing everything but the top half of her face and head.

Hamilton gently sank to the ground on his knees and pulled her into his lap. "It's all right. Just breathe. Nobody's ever going to hurt you again. I'm going to carry you to the van and—"

"N-no," she said sharply.

Hamilton glanced up at them. Maybe the bastards had taken her that same way. Thrown her into a van before bringing her out here. "Okay, no van. I'll carry you out to the road and my guys will call an ambulance up. Because you need medical attention. All right?"

She hesitated a moment, then managed a nod, and Reid let out a sigh of relief before asking for an ambulance to be sent around.

"Here we go." Hamilton stood and started for the road. Reid stayed behind them to light the way with his flashlight while Khan loped ahead. When Reid emerged from the trees behind Hamilton, Khan was already bringing the van up. He popped out and slid the side door open for them.

The woman made a sound of protest and tried to twist away.

"I'm just going to sit you on the edge of the floor, not put you in it," Hamilton said to her, never breaking his stride. Reaching the van, he gently set her inside the open doorway, and straightened. He turned his head and met Reid's gaze, those steel gray eyes were so full of rage they all but glowed in the half-light. "Get that fucking collar off her," he snarled under his breath.

Reid didn't have to be told twice. He waited until Hamilton moved aside before approaching the woman, taking his helmet off so she could see him better in the moonlight. "Let's get this chain off you, okay?" he said, reaching for it.

She tensed and drew away slightly, but otherwise didn't move, her one functioning eye darting back and forth between the three of them.

Khan aimed the flashlight for him. Reid moved in close to get a good look at the collar. Some asshole had locked it with a padlock, giving her only a fraction of an inch breathing room between her skin and the rusted metal. It had worn a raw strip around her entire neck and throat, and he could tell with one look that the bloody wound was infected.

God dammit.

"I need a lockpick kit."

"Try this," Khan said, handing him a multi-tool.

Reid got to work. He tried his best not to tug on the collar, but he had to when he gave the multi-tool a final savage twist. "Sorry," he murmured, but the metal hook on the padlock sprang free. He pulled it off and tossed it into the dirt, then carefully pried the stiff halves of the collar apart, the rusted links of the chain clanking dully on the van floor.

She hissed in a breath as it pulled away from her raw skin, and when Reid saw how deep it had cut into the sides of her neck, he clenched his back teeth together to suppress a growl of pure rage.

"There we go," he said, finally pulling it free. He wanted to hurl the goddamn thing into the woods, but they'd need it for evidence, so he tossed it inside the van.

Hamilton moved in to crouch in front of her. "Can my medic take a look at you now?"

She looked from him to Khan, and Reid thought she was about to give her consent when the ambulance turned onto the road and headed for them. Her hand shot out from the blanket and latched onto Hamilton's in pure reflex, seeking reassurance. Or protection.

With them, she had both.

Hamilton curled his fingers around her slender hand. "It's all right. They'll help you. Give you something for the pain."

Her throat worked convulsively as she swallowed, her gaze trained on the approaching ambulance.

"What's your name?" Hamilton asked gently.

Her head turned, her one open eye focusing on him. "Victoria," she said, her voice hoarse either from disuse...or screaming. "Victoria Gomez."

Chapter Ten

Tess felt much calmer by the time she arrived at the hospital. When she'd received Reid's text that he was there, she'd been afraid he or one of the other guys had been injured or worse during the op. But he'd assured her he was fine, and she'd agreed to meet him here.

The automatic doors to the emergency department swooshed open before her. She rounded the corner and let out a relieved breath when she saw Reid standing with his back to her down the hallway, speaking to Khan and Hamilton, all of them still in their tactical uniforms.

The latter two glanced over at her, and when Reid turned around, the slight smile he flashed her filled her with warmth. He said something to the others, then headed her way, and she had to hold herself back from rushing up and throwing her arms around him.

She searched his eyes as he approached. "You okay?" she asked when he was a few steps from her. The anniversary of his friend's suicide was coming up next weekend, and she knew it was on his mind a lot. Whatever had happened tonight might have exacerbated it.

"Yeah. Let's go outside." And to her surprise, he wrapped a proprietary arm around her shoulders as they headed back toward the main doors, all but staking his claim in front of whoever was watching. "Were you at base the whole time?"

She slid her arm around his waist, enjoying the flex of taut muscle beneath her palm. "Yes. We were on standby, in case we needed to insert another unit or extract some of you guys." The night air was warm and without the humidity that made being outside in the daytime at this time of year so uncomfortable.

"You take a cab here?"

"No, a rental." She fished the keys from her pocket and hit the keyfob to unlock it, blinking the lights on the SUV's mirrors and taillights. "Want me to drop you back at base, or where you're staying?" It was after two in the morning and he looked exhausted.

Reid turned her to face him and backed her gently up against the driver's side door, taking her face in his hands. He held her gaze for a moment, but before she could ask him what had happened and whether he was okay, his mouth was on hers. Slow. Firm. Shockingly tender. Her insides melted and she slid her hands up his chest to his shoulders, savoring the hard planes of muscle before easing upward to slide into his short hair.

All too soon he stopped and lifted his head, leaving her heart reeling and her body heavy with arousal.

Tess licked her lips, tasting him. "So what happened out there?"

He stroked the fingers of one hand through her hair, seemed to hesitate before answering. "Ruiz wasn't there. HRT took out three of his guys and arrested another. They found two female hostages. Then Khan and I found another one on our way back to our vehicle."

The way he said the last part had her insides tensing.

"They'd…" He stopped, looked away.

"You can tell me."

He exhaled a breath, focused on his fingers as he drew them through her hair. "Do you remember the story about a female reporter who was kidnapped a while back? Her family was killed during Sunday dinner, and she was taken."

She remembered. "Victoria something."

He nodded. "It was her."

"Oh! Was she alright?"

"No, not even close. They'd chained her to the floor of a shed out back. When we found her in the woods, she was naked, with just this rusted metal collar and chain hanging from her neck. They fucking chained her there so she couldn't get away, Tess."

She winced, horrified. "Oh my God."

He shook his head, almost in disbelief. "They beat the hell out of her, all over. So bad I didn't recognize her. The damn collar had rubbed the skin off her neck, and her wrists and ankles were raw from where they'd tied her."

Tess narrowed her eyes and shook her head in silent disgust. Animals.

"I don't know what else they did to her, but I can imagine." He drew in a deep breath, let it out slowly. "At least I got the collar off her before the paramedics took over."

She reached up to curl her fingers around his wrist, stroked her thumb over the inside of it. "You freed her."

Reid's gaze slid to hers, full of torment. "She freed herself, somehow." He traced his fingers along her cheek, her jaw. "Hamilton stayed with her in the ambulance and while the medical team worked on her. The agency and FBI are hoping she'll be able to give them something that will help them capture Ruiz. She said he was there a week or so ago. Apparently, they were getting ready to ship her to him in New Orleans so he could do what he wanted with her before selling her to a skin trafficker."

God, it made Tess sick to think of what would have happened to her. "But she's safe now."

"Yeah." His gaze dropped to where his fingers stroked over her chin. "I've never seen anything like that before. Not that bad, and definitely not that up close. I kept thinking about you, and Autumn, and what I'd do if any man who…" He stopped, a muscle bunching in his jaw.

Tess turned her face to press a kiss into the center of his palm. "I understand." That had to have been so hard, to see a woman treated with such sickening cruelty. The *Veneno* cartel and others like it were a cancer, metastasizing at a faster rate than the DEA or any other government agency could kill the diseased cells. Something more had to be done to end them and their reign of terror.

He dropped another gentle kiss on her mouth and eased back. "It's late. You must be tired."

Not as tired as him, she bet. "I'm okay. What time do you have to report back at base?"

"Oh-seven-hundred. Taggart decided to give us a few hours off before the post-action briefing. Hopefully by then we'll have more intel and maybe a lead on Ruiz."

She pulled the driver's side door open. "Come on. I'll drive you back."

Reid slid into the front passenger seat and shut the door. Tess started the engine and reached for the gearshift to put it in reverse, but Reid grabbed her hand, making her look over at him questioningly. In the parking lot lights streaming through the windshield, his expression was somber. "I want to go back to your hotel with you."

The emotion in his eyes wrenched her heart. "Okay."

Thirteen minutes later they stepped out of the elevator on her floor. Twenty seconds after that, they were at her room. This time her hand was completely steady as she slipped the key card into the slot and unlocked the door.

She knew what she wanted, and it was Reid.

She kicked off her shoes and turned to face him as he finished unlacing his last boot. Anticipation buzzed in the pit of her stomach, but she wasn't afraid that this might be a mistake. She wanted him, and they had something special she intended to explore.

Tess met him as he was straightening, sliding both hands into his hair as she leaned up to kiss him. Reid let out a low groan and wrapped both arms around her, one about her hips and the other around her shoulders, lifting her easily off the ground as he started walking her backward. She wound her legs around his waist and held on tight as he carried her to the queen-size bed and laid her down on her back.

Pulling the sheets down beneath her, she reached for the hem of his tactical shirt but he stopped her with a low negative sound and stretched out on top of her. A moan bubbled out of her at the feel of his hard, hot body pressing her into the bed. She slid her hands down to grab the bottom of his shirt, impatient to feel his bare skin.

"No." Reid blocked her hand.

Confused, she stilled and stared up at him.

Gazing down at her, he came up on his forearms, one hand smoothing the hair back from her face. His eyes were so intense, simmering with something she couldn't name. "I just need to…" He seemed to struggle for the words, then gave up and leaned down to cover her mouth with his.

She'd expected him to unleash all the pent-up hunger and sexual tension inside him. Instead his fingers bunched into her hair, holding her gently in place as he made love to her mouth. And that's exactly what it was.

Unsure what to do other than follow his cues, Tess sighed and let herself get lost in the feel and taste of him, her entire body relaxing and heating as arousal flowed like sun-warmed honey through her veins. He sucked at her lower lip, then the upper before easing his tongue into her mouth and caressing hers in a languid, erotic dance.

God, he knew how to kiss. Time was elastic, stretching and extending until she was floating in a haze of arousal and need.

Tess squirmed beneath him, this slow, sensual exploration driving her crazy. She let go of his head and grabbed the hem of her shirt, pulling upward. This time he lifted up enough to help her, and the low growl that came out of him when he saw the cobalt blue pushup bra she wore made her tingle all over. He slipped one hand beneath her to deftly undo the hooks, and she pulled it off, his hot stare devouring the sight of her naked breasts.

She'd just dropped the bra over the side of the bed and was reaching for him when he cupped her left breast in his hand, squeezing gently. She sucked in a quick breath and bit her lower lip as her nipple tightened to the point of pain. Reid's expression was one of total absorption as he stared down at the tender flesh he cradled, fingers caressing her skin before he brushed his thumb over the straining peak.

Tess made an unintelligible sound and grabbed the back of his neck, wanting his mouth there.

He lifted his deep blue gaze to hers, his thumb drawing lazy circles around the taut bud, sending streamers of pleasure across her nerve endings. "I need to touch you. Stroke you all over. And I want you to just lie back and enjoy."

Through the haze of arousal, it hit her. What was driving him to make this all about her.

This was because of tonight, and what he'd seen. How helpless he'd felt when Victoria Gomez had stumbled across their path in the woods. He couldn't erase that memory or wipe it clean, but he could replace it with this—a man giving a woman pleasure and lavishing her with tenderness.

He didn't just want this. He *needed* it.

Tess's heart squeezed in understanding. She set a hand on the side of his face and held his gaze for a moment before nodding.

Reid closed his eyes and nipped gently at the heel of her hand before bending down to her breast. He rubbed his scruff against the tender skin, then flicked his tongue across her straining nipple.

Sparks of pleasure radiated outward, sizzling along her skin. She arched her back and closed her eyes, her heart thudding in her chest.

Those big, gorgeous hands began smoothing over her bare skin, starting with her neck and shoulders, pausing to tease her breasts before moving lower, tracing the shape of her ribcage and the indent of her waist, leaving trails of heat in their wake. She shivered and swallowed a moan when he undid the button at the top of her jeans and slid the zipper down, the slight metallic rasp sharp in the tension-laden quiet.

Lifting her hips, she allowed him to ease the denim over her hips and down her thighs, the anticipation building to a fever pitch. She was already wet and aching, more than ready for him.

Tossing her jeans aside, Reid rolled to his side, cupped one breast and leaned down to take the sensitive center between his lips.

"Ohh," she moaned, lifting upward, her hand disappearing into his hair to hold him close. She shuddered as lightning raced through her body, each pull of his lips and stroke of his tongue intensifying the throb between her legs.

He kept tormenting her breasts, first one, then the other, his right hand gliding over her ribs and stomach to her upper thigh. Tess clenched her fingers in his hair and held her breath, dying for the moment when he finally made contact where she needed it the most.

Rather than giving it to her, he made her wait. He was totally focused, riveted as he mapped every one of her curves with his hands. A glide of his callused palm over the bare skin of her lower thighs made her shiver. The light graze of his fingertips over the sensitive skin of her inner thighs made her toes curl.

"Reid," she finally whispered when she couldn't stand the burn anymore.

He slid his left hand into her hair and covered her mouth with his, pushing his tongue between her lips just as his right hand slid between her legs to cup her slick center. Tess moaned and raised her hips, needing more pressure, more friction. His fingers glided over her folds, spreading the wetness upward until he swirled a fingertip over the top of her swollen clit.

Tess gasped and squirmed beneath him, trying to get closer. Reid made a soothing sound and sucked at her lower lip, then repeated the feather-light caress.

"Oh, God, I'm begging you—" Her words died in her throat as he increased the pressure for an instant, then slid his fingers down to push inside her. Something very close to a whimper escaped her lips. She dropped her head back onto the pillow and closed her eyes as sparks exploded inside her.

"You're so soft and beautiful," he whispered against her chin, his teeth nipping gently while his fingers rubbed at the swelling spot inside her.

All she could do was grip his head with both hands as he dipped back down to suck her nipple. His fingers worked her gently, patiently, sliding over that beautiful glow inside her, and then settling his thumb on her clit.

Oh... Oh, God...

He made another low sound, his tongue flicking over her captive nipple as he sucked and drove her out of her damn mind with his hand. Her muscles were rigid, little tremors racing through her as she gasped for air. The sweet pleasure changed, transforming into something far more powerful, a dark, gathering wave of sensation growing inside her.

She whimpered as it loomed there, hovering just on the edge of the horizon.

"Wanna feel you come for me, darlin'," he whispered against her breast. "Wanna hear you, feel you clench around my fingers."

The words, the sensations, but most of all the single-minded focus behind them, shot her right to the edge. Her inner walls squeezed around his sliding fingers, the added pressure against the side of her clit making her eyes roll back.

"Oh, yeah," he groaned between sucks. "Just like that, sweetheart. Let me make you fly."

That's exactly what it felt like. Flying. Except he was the one at the controls, not her. She was helpless to do anything but float higher and higher, carried along on the tide of sensation he created in her body. It was mind-blowing.

It was also a little terrifying.

Reid held her like that, suspended in ecstasy until finally, she was there.

Tess cried out as her orgasm hit, pulses of pleasure streaking through her entire body until they gradually faded away, leaving her gasping and spent.

He released her nipple and immediately claimed her mouth in a slow, loving kiss that made the backs of her eyes sting. How? How could she not fall for him after what he'd just done—and the *way* he'd just done it? She hadn't been prepared for that kind of shattering emotional and physical intimacy. Reid made her feel like her soul was about to be torn in two.

She squeezed her eyes shut, then sucked in a breath when he eased his hand from between her legs. Opening her eyes, she blinked slowly, focusing on his gorgeous face.

"C'mere," Reid murmured, sliding both arms beneath her and drawing her into his body, dragging the covers over them both as he did.

She cuddled into him as close as she could get, finally sliding her hands up under his shirt to rest her palms against the hot, smooth skin of his back. The bulge of his erection pressed against her lower abdomen through his tactical pants, and part of her felt guilty. He'd been so giving and attentive with her, he deserved the same. Especially after what he'd seen tonight.

He reached back to turn off the bedside lamp, plunging them into darkness. The quiet surrounded them, his strong arms enfolding her in a cocoon of security as his hands stroked languorously up and down her spine.

She was warm, sated and drowsy. She'd let herself drift for a few minutes, then give him the same comfort he'd given her. If he'd let her.

Her eyes snapped open sometime later when he shifted next to her in the darkness. Her heart jolted. Crap! She'd fallen asleep.

Tess raised her head, trying to see the bedside clock. "What time is it?" she mumbled.

"Six."

Already?

"I gotta get back to the dorm and shower before we head in for the briefing." He started to sit up.

She tossed the covers back and threw her legs over the side of the bed. "I'll drive you."

Strong hands grasped her shoulders and pressed her back against the bed. In the faint light coming through the gap at the bottom of the window blinds, Tess stared up at him. "Stay right where you are," he said softly. "I'll grab a cab."

"But—"

He cut off her argument with a tender, melting kiss.

"No buts." He stroked a hand over her hair, his fingers combing through it lightly, a sensual tug against her scalp. God, the man could drug her with that move alone. "Get some more sleep."

But you're leaving. And I didn't get to return the favor last night. She wanted to, a heady pulse of arousal spreading through her body at the thought. "Well what…" She bit back the rest of the words, not wanting to sound needy.

His lips curved upward. "I'll call you as soon as I know what's going on. It's only a ninety-minute flight from here to Fort Worth. I plan to be on the first flight I can make."

The building pressure in her chest eased, and she smiled back at him. "You haven't even left yet, and I already miss you and can't wait to see you again."

He laughed softly. "That's my plan, darlin'. Making you crazy for me."

Oh, she *really* liked it when he called her that in his Mississippi drawl. "Well it's working." She was so hooked, it wasn't even funny. Reaching up to slip a hand around his nape, she squeezed gently. "You be safe, and I'll see you soon."

"Yeah, you will. Now go back to sleep," he whispered, dropping one last kiss on her lips and pulling the covers up over her.

Tess curled onto her side and watched while he laced up his boots, murmured goodbye when he paused at the door.

"See you soon," he said, then slipped out into the hall.

The door closed and the lock clicked into place. Tess rolled to her back and stared up at the ceiling, the heaviness in her chest growing with each imagined step he took down the hall. Falling for another man with a dangerous profession was probably asking for heartbreak, but it was too late for that to stop her now.

All she could do was keep going and see what happened, and pray that the combined weight of time, distance and his baggage wouldn't crush her in the end.

Chapter Eleven

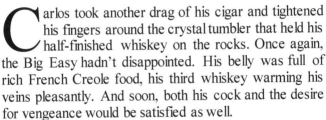

Carlos took another drag of his cigar and tightened his fingers around the crystal tumbler that held his half-finished whiskey on the rocks. Once again, the Big Easy hadn't disappointed. His belly was full of rich French Creole food, his third whiskey warming his veins pleasantly. And soon, both his cock and the desire for vengeance would be satisfied as well.

Exhaling a stream of smoke toward the ceiling, he glanced around the decadently furnished room. This place had been a brothel back in the day, and the velvet and leather used in the décor had a sensuous, erotic feel. The perfect setting for what would transpire here as soon as they brought the reporter whore in. She'd had almost a week to heal up now, enough time for her face and body to recover sufficiently, with a little help from some skillfully applied makeup from the salon people he'd hired to make her presentable for him.

He glanced at his watch, irritated that she was late. A soft knock drew his attention to the door. "What is it?" he asked in annoyance.

Antonio stepped into the room and shut the door behind him. Even cleaned up and dressed in a suit with his black hair slicked back, he still looked exactly like what he was. A killer.

One look at his chief enforcer's face, and Carlos knew something was wrong. "Well?" he demanded.

"She's gone."

Not believing his ears, Carlos set his drink down on the mirrored side table next to him, his fingers all but crushing the cigar as he clenched it. "What?" Two enforcers were supposed to have escorted her here an hour ago.

Antonio shifted his weight and drew in a breath, seemed to struggle to meet Carlos's gaze. "Manny just called me. There was a sting at the bayou house."

The cigar and drink forgotten, Carlos shot to his feet and advanced on Antonio, too angry to take any kind of satisfaction in the way the other man paled and took a step back. "What kind of sting?" he snapped.

"He said it was the FBI and the DEA working together. They stormed the house, killed some guys, took one prisoner and took the women. Manny was the only one who escaped."

Carlos curled his upper lip into a sneer. Manny had run rather than protect Carlos's investment. "Fucking coward. Where is he?"

"Outside Baton Rouge. Or so he says."

"And that reporter bitch, they took her too?" He'd made it crystal clear that two of his men should guard her at all times.

Antonio nodded in confirmation.

Rage exploded inside him, dark and deadly. With a snarl he swept an arm out, clearing the top of the antique sideboard with one vicious swipe. Crystal decanters and glassware exploded against the wall and floor, covering the marble tiles in glittering shards and puddles of liquor.

It did nothing to cool his temper. "How the fuck could they let this happen?" he roared, rounding on Antonio, who stood there unmoving, his face impassive, still a little pale. Because he knew exactly what could happen when Carlos was in a rage. "She was supposed to be here an hour ago, and I'm just finding out about all this now?"

"He didn't think it was safe to call it in until now."

"Because he's more worried about saving his own pathetic skin instead of protecting my business," Carlos scoffed. Manny would pay for that. Dearly.

The whore was gone. Out of reach now. Carlos ran a hand through his hair, fighting to get a grip on his temper. He forced himself to take a deep breath, then another, his mind whirling, a red haze clouding his thoughts.

The loss of the female cargo hurt his pride more than his bank account, but that bitch reporter... She knew exactly who he was, would tell the U.S. authorities that he'd been at the property a week ago.

And she was fucking smart. Smart enough to have put pieces of his operation together during her captivity, no matter how isolated they'd kept her. He wasn't stupid enough to think his men hadn't let something slip in front of her, having mistakenly assumed she wasn't a security threat since she was bound hand and foot and would be sold off soon enough.

And now, because of their incompetence and unforgivable cowardice, he would never get the chance to punish her personally for what she'd done to him.

The ache in his leg and hip transformed to a searing pain, as though his body was screaming its outrage. But there was no way to get her back now. No way to get the retribution he'd planned out so carefully and dreamed of for so long.

His chance was gone. The only remaining viable targets to focus on now were the agencies and units involved in tonight's operation.

Resolve hardened inside him. Going after a federal agent was a risk, but he couldn't afford to appear weak and powerless against anyone, and he was sure to catch hell from *El Escorpion* for bringing undue attention to himself and the cartel as a whole.

So be it. Carlos was sick of playing the faithful lap dog to the head of the cartel. Someday soon, he was going to be head of the organization. All he needed was the right opportunity to crush his rivals…and *El Escorpion* himself.

In his world, ruthlessness was the key. And it was something he had in large supply.

So he would identify the men who had done this to him. He would find them and figure out a way to make them pay, make a statement to show the whole world that he was untouchable. That he could get to anyone who posed a threat to his business.

Calmer now in spite of the residual anger simmering inside him, he faced Antonio again. "Call Manny. If he wants to live, he'll work all his contacts and find out who was there tonight. Have everyone in our network talk to whoever they need to in order to ID those men. I want faces and names. Personal information." He'd still kill Manny for running tonight, after he'd taken care of this. A real man would have stood his ground and died in a hail of bullets rather than run off into the woods like a scared fucking rabbit.

Antonio nodded and started to turn away, but Carlos stopped him with an upraised hand. "Do whatever it takes to make this happen in the next forty-eight hours. Pay off whoever you need to. I don't care how much it costs." Two days would give him more than enough time to slip back into Mexico undetected and wait for news from the safety of his ranch, where he was hidden and protected by the local population. "Tell them to find a weakness I can exploit."

Because *no one* fucked with Carlos Ruiz. Not even the United States government.

****

Lying on a rolling board beneath the Mustang's engine in the garage of his building, Reid finished emptying the oil pan and wiped his hands with a clean rag before replacing the bolt. He'd had a hell of a week, but at least he'd stayed busy, a blessing when Jason's anniversary was coming up on Sunday. On the last turn of the wrench, his cell rang in his pocket, the specific notes putting an instant smile on his face.

Tess.

It had been almost a week since he'd left her in that hotel room in Biloxi. His plans to fly to see her had fallen through because Taggart had ordered the team back to Virginia that same day.

They'd spoken on the phone every day since, sometimes several times a day, but it wasn't enough and he still planned to head down there the first chance he got, maybe even next weekend since Autumn was supposed to go away with her mom and Max right after school let out for the summer. He didn't want to say anything to Tess until he knew for sure, though, and maybe not even then, because surprising her and just showing up at her door would be a hell of a fun thing to do.

Rolling out from beneath the vehicle, he sat up and answered. "Hey, gorgeous."

"Hey yourself. What are you up to?"

"Just finishing up an oil change."

"Mmm, I love that you're so good with your hands."

He went rock hard in his jeans at the husky edge to her voice. "I love that you appreciate it."

Her soft laugh was sultry, sexy as hell. "And after the oil change, what plans have you got? It's Friday night."

"I'm gonna wax this baby up. Rub her all over and stroke her curves until she purrs for me like a kitten."

"That's so unfair. Making me jealous of a damn car."

He chuckled. "I'd rather be stroking your curves, believe me."

He'd replayed everything about those few hours in bed with her a thousand times over this past week. How she'd felt underneath him, her curves and hollows nestled into his body. How silky soft her skin was. How responsive she'd been to every single touch and caress. The sweet sounds she'd made as she clung to him, the way she'd clenched around his fingers when she came.

He'd recalled every single detail of it in his mind when he stroked himself in the shower, his entire body aching for her.

"Well that's good. What are you waxing your baby up for, anyway? Hot date or something?"

"Yep. I'm taking Autumn for dinner after her softball game tomorrow afternoon, then bringing her back here for a sleepover."

"Aww. Maybe take her to that dessert place we saw after dinner?"

"I was thinking about it." He wiped his palm over the rag on his thigh. "Wish you could be with us."

"Me too. But I'll be with you in spirit, if that counts."

"It totally counts." She was one of the most grounded people he'd ever met. Just hearing her voice soothed him. "What are you up to?"

"I've got a hot date with my TV and a slice of strawberry cheesecake I bought on the way home."

"My night sounds more fun."

"Depends on your point of view. Been a busy week, and I'm cool with curling up by myself for the night."

"Been flying a lot?"

"Not as much as I'd like. Mostly meetings due to some reorganization in our department. And paperwork, which

I hate."

"Don't we all."

"What about you, any updates on the Ruiz case?"

"Still no lock on him. They think he's back in Mexico now, and down there because of his money, connections and reputation, he's pretty much untouchable."

She grunted. "It's so damn frustrating that we can't operate down there."

"Tell me about it." Although the time was coming where the Mexican government was going to have to relax its policy on that and allow them in.

Nothing the Mexican officials had done so far had been the least bit effective in curtailing, let alone destroying, narcotic production or smuggling down there. The cartels pretty much owned and ran everything, and so much of the country outside their control was corrupt anyway, the only solution Reid could see was to bring an outside force down to help clean the country out.

"The analysis of the dope we seized came back a few days ago." He had no problem sharing this information with her because she was a fellow agent involved with the case and had the same security clearance he did.

"And? Anything interesting?"

"The lab identified it as coming from a region about a hundred miles southeast of where the agency previously thought the *Venenos* operated. So their territory is expanding instead of shrinking."

She sighed. "Figures. What about that reporter? How is she doing?"

"Still in the hospital, last I heard. Hamilton's been in to talk to her a couple times. She's been giving the agency valuable information about Ruiz and his crew."

"I'm glad she's getting better. I can only imagine how badly she wants Ruiz captured."

Wasn't that the truth. He climbed to his feet, picturing Tess curled up on a couch with her golden-blond hair down loose around her shoulders. "I miss you." It amazed him how much. He thought about her constantly.

A tiny pause followed the announcement. "I miss you too." He could hear the pleasure in her voice.

He blew out a breath, aware of an aching pressure blooming in the center of his chest. "So, what are you going to watch while you eat your cheesecake?"

"The first Harry Potter movie, I think. Autumn would like that."

He smiled. "Yeah, she would." They talked about movies and favorite shows for a while, and when he heard her yawn for the third time, he took pity on her. "You go curl up and relax. I've gotta finish this up and grab something to eat before I starve to death."

"Okay. Have fun tomorrow. Say hi to Autumn for me."

"I'll do you one better. We'll call you from the car when we leave the park, and you guys can talk about the movie."

"Deal."

Reid smiled, determined to get down there and surprise her. Maybe Autumn could help him come up with a unique way to do it. "G'night, darlin'."

"G'night, handsome."

He slipped the phone back into his pocket and picked up the first quart of oil sitting on the foldable workbench, that damn ache between his ribs growing sharper.

****

Twilight was Carlos's favorite time of night. The air was soft and warm, filled with the hum of insects, and the breeze was cool. Here on this little piece of paradise that he'd carved out of his portion of the cartel's massive territory, he was free.

And completely alone.

He sighed, pushing away the loneliness he tried so

hard to ignore. It bothered him less and less these days, but sometimes…

His gaze strayed over his shoulder to the sprawling hacienda he'd built. For some reason, ordering a whore up here to the main house didn't appeal to him tonight. He'd given up the idea of finding someone to love who would love him back when he was eighteen. He'd loved once and only once, back then when he was young and stupid, and all he'd gotten in return was his heart stomped on when she'd left him, complaining that he was too poor to waste her life on.

That ultimate betrayal, after his worthless slut of a mother had ditched him and his brothers, had changed him. Now women were nothing more than objects for him to control, buy or sell as he pleased.

If the girl who'd crushed his heart could only see him now, that bitch would be sorry. But that *other* bitch escaping him last week still burned like a hot coal in the bottom of his gut.

Seven days he'd waited for news, either about her or one of the agents involved in the sting that had taken her from him. A lead. A tip. Something. Anything that might allow him to strike back at the people who had humiliated him with that raid last weekend.

Carlos stopped at the corral fence and set the sole of his cowboy boot on the lower rail as he held out a handful of cornhusks to the giraffe watching him from the far corner. At least his animals made him happy. Animals were simple. Loyal, once he earned their trust. Unlike their human counterparts.

This young female was exceptionally wary of humans, however. Fearful of approaching lest she be beaten with sticks the moment she got close, as the men from the circus had done to her when she'd foraged for food in their tent. They'd nearly killed her.

"Come on, I brought this out just for you," he crooned,

tossing some over the top rail and scooping out another big handful from the bucket he'd brought from the kitchen.

The animal twitched its ears and stared back at him with those huge brown eyes surrounded by insanely long eyelashes. Such a pretty girl.

Whatever it took, he was determined to get this one to eat from his hand.

He waited there, unmoving for God only knew how long. His upper arm rested on the top rail, his hand long since having fallen asleep because of the awkward position, the cornhusks still in his fist. Then the giraffe took a step toward him.

Carlos held his breath, waiting. He'd spent hours doing exactly this, standing at the fence and letting her get used to his scent. Making sure he stayed still, never doing anything that might startle her. Showing her he wasn't to be feared. Was the effort finally paying off?

She took another halting step. Then another. And another. Until she was close enough to stretch out her long, spotted neck to sniff at the offering while still leaving a foot of space between her muzzle and his hand.

He didn't dare move, enthralled, willing her to come that last few inches and take from him. He wasn't a patient man, never had been, and his money and power meant he didn't have to rectify that character flaw. But he had patience enough for this. To offer another lost soul who'd known only fear and deprivation a chance for something better. The shot at a better life.

The giraffe's nostrils flared and her long purple tongue darted out to curl around the husks, snatching them from his hand without making contact.

"Cheater," he told her, and reached down for another handful from the bucket.

The crunch of footsteps over the gravel path that connected the corral with the back lawn sounded behind him. Startled, the giraffe jerked her head up and whirled around to lope away back to the safety of the far side of the corral.

Madre de Cristo. Carlos spun around to find Antonio striding toward him, and threw his hands up. "What the fuck are you doing? She was almost ready to take from my hand!"

Antonio stopped, looking uncharacteristically uncertain as he stood there staring at Carlos.

Carlos heaved out an irritated sigh and set his hands on his hips. "What?"

"I just thought I should tell you… One of our contacts has ID'd some of the men on the DEA team from last week."

"How many?"

"Two."

They'd been working this angle for a week, and only managed to identify two members? Pathetic. "And?"

"And…there might be a weakness we can exploit."

"Might?" He stared at Antonio, incredulous, not even caring about what kind of weakness he meant. "You come out here and interrupt me about this with a *might*?" Maybe it was time to open up the spot of head enforcer. Or clean his ranks entirely. How was he ever going to take over the cartel with a bunch of incompetent idiots under him?

Antonio cleared his throat. "We're looking at targeting one of the agent's family members. I was going to send one of the guys up there tonight. To D.C."

"Just get it done." Beyond annoyed, impatient for results that might actually get him somewhere, Carlos flapped a hand at him. "Go. And don't tell me again until you have something solid."

"Sure, boss."

He turned back to face the giraffe as Antonio's footsteps faded away behind him. She'd been spooked and wouldn't approach him now. He was back at square one.

Muttering under his breath, Carlos picked up the bucket, dumped the husks over the fence for her and trudged back toward the house. His night was ruined. The only thing that could save it was getting word of a firm target to strike at.

Chapter Twelve

Autumn's stomach grumbled as she and her mom stopped at a red light not far from their house. She reached out to turn on the radio and switched to her favorite pop station, pre-game jitters dancing around in her belly, adding to the hunger. "Can we stop somewhere on the way to the park? I'm starving."

From behind the wheel, her mom shot her an irritated look. "Why didn't you eat before we left the house?"

"There was nothing to eat."

Her mom made a frustrated sound before focusing back on the road and proceeding through the intersection now that the light was green. "Right. There weren't three different kinds of yogurt in the fridge that you asked me to buy the other day, or five different kinds of fruit, or bread, cheese and cereal. Or a big jar of peanut butter in the pantry. You know what that's called? Laziness."

Autumn stemmed the urge to roll her eyes and didn't say anything. Her mom had eyes in the back of her head, so Autumn knew better than to try it.

"There's a Subway on the way," her mom finally said

in a ticked-off tone that rang with annoyance. "I'll stop this time. But don't make a habit of this. From now on you can take ten minutes and make yourself something before we leave the house. You're old enough to feed yourself a snack, at least."

"Fine," Autumn said on a dramatic sigh, secretly pleased that she'd gotten a Subway out of the deal. Then she changed the subject. "Is Dad coming to the game?"

Her mom's mouth pinched, just like it did every time Autumn brought him up. It was weird to think they'd ever been married, because Autumn sure couldn't remember them being together. Even now when they talked, all they did was argue, though usually by text or email. "I would imagine so. And Max said he'd try to come by if his meeting finished up in time, too."

Autumn didn't care whether Max showed up or not, she only cared whether her dad did. Her mom's boyfriend was nice enough, and so was his house, but the truth was, Autumn resented having to share her mom with anyone. She didn't like having to follow all the rules he set just because she and her mom were living in his house. Though again, she didn't say it aloud. Her mom was really protective of him. "So I'll go with Dad straight after the game's over?"

"Yes."

Awesome. She was super excited about him coming to watch this afternoon. He was gone so much for work, and that meant he missed a lot of the games.

Practices, she didn't care about him not being there, but for games she did. Her fielding was still iffy because she wasn't that good with her new glove yet, but her arm was getting better each game and last time she'd even gotten a base hit. She loved it when he was sitting there in the stands, cheering her on. On the opposite side of the field from where her mom sat, but Autumn didn't mind that. Plus, she had the sleepover to look forward to after.

She loved hanging out with her dad, just the two of them. He'd take her out to eat right after the game, then they'd go home to his place and watch a movie together or play cards or a board game. Sometimes he'd make them popcorn or root beer floats, and he didn't make her take a shower or bath until the morning. She also loved her bedroom there. He'd let her pick out the paint color and comforter set, and let her arrange all the furniture the way she wanted. At Max's house, everything had been picked out for her, and she had to keep it perfectly clean or she got in trouble.

Autumn smiled to herself, already looking forward to tonight. Maybe her dad would make her chocolate chip pancakes for breakfast. He barely ever burned them anymore. And he'd totally be up for going to the park tomorrow for a game of catch, help her break in her glove more.

The traffic was bad, making her mom uptight, but Autumn didn't mind the delay because it gave her more time to listen to the music. A few minutes later her mom slowed the Lexus and pulled into the turning lane next to a strip mall. Autumn spotted the Subway sign immediately, over in the corner.

Her mom steered into the lot and parked out front of the shop. "What do you want?" Her tone was a little short, but that was probably because they were running behind with the traffic, and this unexpected stop had added time her mother hadn't been anticipating. Her mom hated being late, said it was rude.

Autumn was quick with her order. "Six inch turkey on whole wheat, with mustard and mayo. A little lettuce, *no* tomato." Disgusting things. "And a chocolate milk. Please," she added politely.

Her mom's expression softened at the show of manners and appreciation. "Okay, wait here." She shut off the engine and started to pull the keys out of the ignition, which would kill the radio.

Autumn shot out a hand to stop her. "No, wait! This is my favorite song."

"Ugh, fine." Her mom dropped her hand from the keys and left them in the ignition. "I'll be right back, but lock the doors when I get out."

Don't roll your eyes. Her mom was so insanely overprotective sometimes. "*Okay*, Mom." Autumn waited until her mom shut the driver's side door before hitting the automatic lock button. Safe inside the cool interior, she tapped her foot and started singing along with her favorite artist, her nerves about the game forgotten.

The driver's side door handle jiggled.

Autumn glanced over, expecting to see her mom, but her heart stuttered when she saw the strange man standing there instead. He had a hard, tanned face with a mean expression and tattoos on the front of his neck.

He was a bad man. She could tell just by the look on his face. And the way he was staring at her made prickles crawl up her arms.

He yanked on the door handle again.

Her insides shriveled and she froze in her seat, staring into those dark, evil eyes. She only had a moment to process that he was trying to break into the car, when he raised his arm and smashed something against the window. Glass crunched and tiny bits of it flew inside as he kept bashing at it.

Autumn screamed and undid her seatbelt to scramble away, flattening herself against her door, but the man didn't stop. In the blink of an eye he reached in, unlocked the driver's door and was sliding behind the wheel before she could draw another breath to scream.

"Don't you fucking move," he snarled at her in an accented voice as he started the engine.

Her throat squeezed shut and her heart pounded in her ears as the car came to life, spurring her into action.

She reached for the door lock, trying to pull it up so she could get out of the car and run. So he couldn't take her.

A hard, cruel hand locked around the back of her neck. It squeezed, the painful pressure making her cry out.

"I said, don't *move*," he snapped, his fingers crushing the back of her neck as he shot the car backward out of the parking spot.

No! He was kidnapping her!

Unable to break free of his grip, Autumn's eyes darted around frantically, searching for help. Two people were gaping at them from the sidewalk out front of the stores, their eyes wide with horror. "Help!" she screamed at them. Why weren't they doing anything?

One woman lunged forward as if to grab at Autumn's door handle. "Hey!" the lady yelled at the man, her voice muffled under the music coming from the radio.

The bad man shifted into drive, hit the gas and floored it.

Autumn grabbed his wrist to pull his hand from her neck and fought to turn around, but he was too strong, and even digging her nails into his skin didn't do anything. He grabbed the base of her ponytail, sticking through the opening at the back of her ball cap, and yanked, wrenching her head to the side.

Terrified, Autumn caught a glimpse of her mother as she raced out of the sandwich shop. Her face was stricken, eyes bulging as she stared at the moving car.

Tears flooded Autumn's eyes as their gazes locked through the shattered window for an instant, fear clogging her throat, twisting her stomach until she almost threw up. "Mom, *help* me!"

"Shut up," the man muttered, yanking on her hair again, never easing up on his grip as he sped through the parking lot and out onto the busy street.

****

Reid was in the shower, washing away all the sweat from his recent workout at the gym with Maka when he heard his phone ring in his adjoining bedroom. He had it set to go to voicemail after four rings, so he took his time scrubbing his hair and rinsing all the soap off. The phone rang again a few seconds later. He killed the water.

The phone rang a third time as he was wrapping a towel around his waist. Whoever it was, it must be important.

Hustling out of the bathroom, he headed straight for the dresser where he'd left the phone. All three calls were from Sarah's number. Reid frowned. She never called him, only texted or emailed. Maybe it was Autumn calling from Sarah's phone.

He called back, putting the phone to his ear as he strode back to the bathroom to get dressed.

"*Reid*!"

A split-second's shock hit him at the sound of his ex's voice on the other end of the line, instantly covered by alarm at the sheer panic in it. His entire body tensed. "Sarah, what's wrong?"

"Autumn's gone! Some asshole just broke into the car when I ran into Subway, and drove off with her!"

"*What*?" The blood drained from his face with a hot, prickling sensation.

She let out a broken sob. "Oh my God, I don't know where he took her, I—"

"Did you call the cops?"

Another sob, this one so full of anguish the hair on Reid's nape stood on end. "They're out looking for her right now."

Calm down. You need to calm the hell down. Think. But it was fucking impossible when his baby girl had just been kidnapped. His heart beat triple time, a sickening thud against his ribs. "Where are you?" He ran back to the dresser, yanked out a pair of jeans and a T-shirt.

"I'm still at the strip m-mall," she quavered.

"Give me the address. I'm on my way." He kept talking to her as he dressed, grabbed his keys and shoes and ran out of the condo. The blood roared in his ears as he raced for his car, terror and helplessness racing through him in a chaotic, unstoppable tide. The cops would find Autumn. He couldn't handle the alternative.

The Mustang's tires squealed as he turned out of the parking garage onto the street and gunned it. He kept Sarah talking to him, trying to get as much information as possible out of her despite her hysteria. Why the hell had she left the damn keys in the ignition in the first place? He bit the accusing question back. Sarah and he might have their problems, but she was a great mother and would never do anything that would put their daughter in jeopardy. This had been a horrible tragedy, plain and simple.

"Have to go. The d-detective wants to t-talk to me," Sarah gasped out.

"I'll be there in under ten minutes. Just stay put and don't leave until I get there." He hung up and immediately dialed Hamilton, started talking as soon as the man answered. "Someone just broke into Sarah's car and took Autumn from a strip mall in town. I'm heading there now." He could barely get the words out, his hands shaking on the wheel.

"*Fuck*," his team leader barked. "Aw, Jesus, Reid—is there anything we can do?"

His eyes stung. "I'll let you know. But I'll be unavailable for…until we get her back."

"Of course, man. Understood. You need *anything*, you let one of us know. I'll alert the guys. We'll all be praying for her."

"Thanks," Reid said hoarsely and hung up, his throat

too tight to get any more words out. He was fucking sick with apprehension, his stomach a roiling mass of terror.

It seemed to take forever for him to reach the mall. Half a dozen cop cars were already on scene, and he picked out Sarah immediately standing on the curb out front of the sandwich shop.

Reid jerked the Mustang to a stop just outside the police tape and leaped out, barely remembering to slam his door shut. A cop came at him, hand upraised in warning. "I'm Autumn's father," Reid called out, holding open his wallet to show his agency ID as he shoved his way past. His eyes locked with Sarah's, and the terror grew sharper.

Sarah's face crumpled and she launched herself at him. Reid caught her, crushing her close to his chest while she lost it. "She's gone," she sobbed out, shaking so hard it made Reid's teeth rattle. "My baby's gone and it's all my fault!"

"No, don't say that," he managed, his own eyes burning as he looked to the detective, a middle-aged Hispanic man dressed in a suit standing a few feet away. He needed fucking answers. "What've you guys got so far?"

"Several eyewitness accounts, and we're running the surveillance video now. We've already put out an amber alert for her."

Good, because Sarah's Lexus was probably their best hope of finding them. With that many people alerted to look out for the car during daylight hours in this populated an area, chances were good someone would spot it. He just prayed someone did before the asshole who'd taken Autumn could hurt her. "What did the perp look like?"

"Hispanic. Mid-twenties. Tats on his neck. Possibly a gang member."

Fuuuuck. Reid swallowed hard, his blood pressure nose diving.

"Our forensics people are trying to see if they can get a match to anyone in our database. The tats should help."

Reid's brain spun. Every second that ticked by was its own separate agony. Autumn had just been abducted by some gangbanger asshole and there was not a goddamn thing Reid could do to help her. When he thought of how scared she must be and what could happen to her… Christ, it killed him to not be able to protect her. "What about the FBI?" he grated out.

"They're monitoring the case and will send agents to us to assist, but for the time being, it's our investigation."

Sarah took a long, shuddering breath and went limp against his chest, exhausted. Reid scooped her up before she could fall and carried her to a bench out front of the sandwich shop. "We're gonna find her," he vowed, fighting back the grief and terror ripping at his insides. "We'll find her and she'll be okay. The asshole probably just wanted the car. He's probably already ditched Autumn a few blocks from here. She's smart, Sarah. Real smart. She'll get to a phone and call us."

The words had just left his mouth when his phone vibrated in his pocket. Reid all but dumped Sarah off his lap and yanked his phone out, his heart plummeting when he saw Maka's number. Reid shoved it back into his pocket and wrapped an arm around Sarah's shuddering shoulders. He didn't want to talk to anyone right now except Autumn.

Sarah didn't say anything, just leaned her body into his and hitched in jerky breaths, her acceptance of his embrace testament to how distraught she was. "Have you called Max?" he asked her.

She nodded. "He's c-coming."

Reid didn't exactly love the guy, but right now they needed all the help they could get, so it was all hands on deck. Sitting here doing nothing was slowly eating a hole through his gut, but what else could he do? Jumping back in his car and driving around like a madman looking for Sarah's Lexus, was pointless.

His phone vibrated again. He snatched it up, clenched his jaw when he saw Khan's number. He appreciated his teammates worrying about Autumn, but there was no way he was talking to anyone right now.

Unless Tess called him. God, he wanted to hear her voice so bad, tell her what happened, but he didn't think he'd be able to hold it together if he did. He'd never been this raw and afraid, not even during combat or when he'd found Jason hanging in that shower.

He swallowed hard, struggling against the rise of tears that burned the back of his eyes. Losing it wouldn't change anything, and it wouldn't help find Autumn. He had to hold it together, be the strong one.

Max finally arrived and took Sarah from him. Reid talked to the lead detective some more, then agreed to go down to the station with him. The asshole should have dumped Autumn by now if he'd only been interested in the car. Why hadn't she gotten to a phone and called him yet?

Maybe he wanted more than just the car.

The idea scared the living shit out of him.

Sarah and Max met him at the police station a few minutes later. Because of his position as a DEA agent and his security clearance, the detective allowed Reid to view the security footage with him in his office.

Reid's stomach clamped tight as he watched the thug approach the Lexus and smash in the driver's window before climbing in. And the asshole was armed, the butt of a pistol sticking out of the back of his waistband.

Arms folded across his chest, Reid squeezed his hands into fists, wanting to punch something. To scream. His little girl had no chance against that motherfucker.

The detective stopped the video feed and studied Reid. "Maybe you should sit down for a bit."

"No." He was barely containing the need to pace around the room as it was. Planting his ass in a chair would make him crack wide open.

"Okay, then how about—" He stopped when his cell rang. Pulling it from his belt, he checked the display, then answered. When he glanced at Reid with a somber expression a moment later, every muscle in Reid's body tensed in denial.

No. Autumn had to be okay. They had to find her.

His heart thudded in his ears as the detective hung up. "What?" Reid demanded.

The detective's expression didn't change. "Citizen just reported finding Sarah's car."

Oh, God... "And?"

"Suspect ditched it in an alley a few miles from here. It was empty. Cop showed up on scene right after and looked around but there was no sign of your daughter."

Reid's shoulders sagged and he closed his eyes. So the bastard had dragged Autumn from the car and taken her somewhere. Bile burned the back of his throat.

"Forensics team is on their way there now. Someone might have seen where they went."

The next few hours passed in a slow, life-sucking blur. Reid demanded to go to the scene with the lead detective. Forensics were dusting for prints when they arrived, and searching for any clues that might point them to where the suspect had gone with Autumn. None of the residents living along the alley had seen anything.

The investigation had hit a dead end.

Alternately panicked and numb, he waited hours more back at the station, briefly speaking to Commander Taggart, and waiting for news. None came.

By midnight, when it was clear they wouldn't allow him to help with the investigation further, and there was nothing more he could do but wait, he reluctantly left. His phone had a dozen text messages on it. Every single one of his teammates had reached out, offering their support and urging him to call if he needed anything. Much as he appreciated the offers, he didn't return any of the calls.

Climbing back into his car, he froze when he saw the German Shepherd pom-pom puppy sitting there on his dash, staring back at him with its plastic googly eyes.

Completely hollow inside, he shut the door and sat there staring at it while a razor-sharp blade slashed through his heart. Tears blurred his vision and he sucked in a deep breath, gripping the steering wheel so tight his bones hurt. His baby was missing, and he couldn't bear the thought of what might have happened to her.

Tess. He needed to call Tess. He had to tell her, but dammit, he just needed to hear her voice.

His hand shook as he pulled out his phone. After three rings he was about to hang up, unwilling to leave a message right now. Then she picked up.

"Hey, I was just thinking about you."

The sound of her chipper voice made the tears burn hotter. "Tess," he croaked out, barely clinging to the last shred of his control.

"What's the matter?" she blurted, voice tense. "Reid?" she prompted when he didn't answer. "What's wrong?"

He swallowed, struggled to breathe. "Someone broke into Sarah's car a few hours ago and took off with Autumn."

"*What*? Oh my God."

His throat spasmed. "The cops can't find her. It's been hours and there's no sign of her, and I…" His voice broke. He lowered the phone to his shoulder and bowed his head as a sob tried to rip free. The burn in his chest spread into his throat, agonizing, unbearable.

"Reid, oh, God, I'm so sorry," she breathed, sounding as stricken as he felt. "Is there anything I can do?" With the phone resting on his shoulder her voice was faint, far away. Just like she was. And he was here alone, not knowing how he was supposed to cope with this.

He shook his head, battling his emotions even though she couldn't see him. He dragged in a ragged breath and exhaled slowly, but it still felt as if his lungs might explode. "No. Just needed to hear your voice." He wished she were here, needed to feel her arms around him so badly.

"Oh, baby…"

The endearment, the tormented note in her voice, undid him. "I gotta go," he blurted, a second away from losing it and unmanning himself.

"Reid, wait—"

He ended the call, unable to continue. The phone fell from his numb fingers into his lap as the crushing weight of despair crashed down on him. Suffocating. Compressing his chest cavity until he couldn't breathe, crushing his heart.

The phone rang almost immediately. Tess. But he couldn't bring himself to answer.

Reeling, he started the ignition and somehow drove home, though he didn't remember getting there. His phone rang twice more during the drive, both times Tess, and both times he ignored them. He felt a hundred years old as he climbed out of the car and headed for the elevator in the underground garage.

A few paces from his door, he got a text. Out of habit he glanced down, expecting to see a message from Tess begging him to call her back.

Autumn's frightened face looked back at him instead.

He jerked to a halt, staring at the screen, for a moment wondering if his eyes were playing tricks on him. She was dressed in her ball uniform, her cap covering her hair, her deep blue eyes wide and her expression pinched.

Before he could react, a message appeared below it.
Missing something?
Reid's heart slammed into overdrive, the surge of

adrenaline making him shake all over. What the *fuck*?

Another message appeared.

Nobody fucks with Carlos Ruiz. We're going to do exactly the same thing to her as we did to the reporter you rescued.

His stomach pitched at the threat, a thousand horrific images bombarding his brain. He'd seen the state Victoria Gomez had been in. Could guess what they'd done to her, and what would have happened if she hadn't escaped that night.

By sheer force of will, he stopped picturing those animals raping and torturing his daughter. He called the person back, his chest heaving as he waited for whoever it was to pick up, white-hot rage burning inside him.

No answer. No voicemail. Just that ring droning in his ear.

He hung up and dialed the detective, wanting to scream. "It's Carlos Ruiz, a *Veneno* lieutenant my team's been after," he ground out. "Someone just texted me Autumn's picture and threatened her using his name."

"Hell," the detective muttered. "Where are you?"

"My place." Fuck, he was gonna puke. Right out here in the hall. He couldn't move, all his muscles locked tight. Carlos fucking Ruiz or someone affiliated with him had Autumn.

"Sit tight. We'll be there in a few minutes."

Reid lowered the phone and brought up Autumn's picture again. Acid churned in the pit of his stomach as he stared at her frightened little face. She was all alone with that monster, praying for a miracle. Probably hoping her daddy would come rescue her.

A strangled sound wrenched from his throat as he stared down into those terrified blue eyes. *I'm coming, baby girl. Daddy's coming.*

Except he couldn't do shit, because he didn't know where she was.

What he did know was what Ruiz and his sickening excuses for men were capable of doing to a woman. To do that to a nine-year-old girl?

His knees gave way.

Angling his body so that his back bumped against the wall to keep him from pitching over, he allowed himself to slide to the carpeted floor, the phone clutched tightly in his hand. As the scalding hot tears burst free at last, he covered his head with his arms and sobbed as he succumbed to the overpowering tide of grief.

Chapter Thirteen

———◦◇◦◇◦———

"**Y**ou did what?" Carlos stood in the hotel room with his encrypted phone to his ear, his entire body stiff, hardly able to believe what he'd just heard.

"You wanted me to find an opportunity. So I found one and acted on it," Javier answered, his tone both defiant and a little annoyed, as though Carlos should be more grateful for what he'd done.

Carlos dragged a hand over his face. "How old is she?"

"I dunno. Young. Elementary school age."

Madre de Cristo. Taking a federal agent's daughter in broad daylight, in front of the fucking mother. It was a miracle they hadn't already found Javier and killed him. "And you're going to do what with her?"

"Make a statement."

He pulled in a calming breath before responding. "You've just put us in the crosshairs of every federal agency. Do you even realize that?" He needed to do some damage control and shore up security. Fast.

"Don't worry. I'm well clear now. I've switched cars four times already. She's tied up in the trunk. It's all good. And I've got a potential buyer lined up to take a look at her when I get into North Carolina."

Carlos frowned. He'd never sold a kid before. Wasn't sure he was comfortable with it. "How do you know it's not a setup, asshole?"

"It's not. He's a regular of mine."

Carlos still didn't like it. Well, he liked that they'd put the fear of God into at least one FAST agent, but he didn't like all the rest of the bullshit Javier had just rained down on them. "Take her someplace and lie low until you hear from me. I need to figure this out."

"Don't worry, boss. I'll keep her well entertained."

Carlos hung up without responding and called Antonio. "We need to get to North Carolina. Tonight."

****

Reid didn't even remember driving to the police station, fear for his daughter eating away at his insides like acid.

When he walked in and saw Sarah and Max already sitting in the detective's office, the look on his ex-wife's face made Reid's heart constrict. Before he could utter a single word, Sarah shot out of her seat, her eyes spewing pure venom as she came at Reid.

"You bastard!" she shouted, slamming her fists against his chest, hard enough to knock him back a half-step. "They took our baby because of you!"

Reid's entire body went cold as the truth behind the accusation hit him like a sledgehammer to the solar plexus. He didn't even try to stop her hitting him. He deserved this and more, and part of him wanted the punishment. "I—" He shut his mouth because there was nothing he could say in his defense.

She was right. And fuck, he was dying inside because of it.

"Sarah." Max had an arm around her chest as he tried to pull her away. "Stop it. This isn't going to help."

"It's fucking helping *me*," she snarled, fighting Max off to stand rigidly in front of Reid, the accusation and rage in her eyes flaying him alive. "Your damn job already destroyed our family, and now it's destroyed our daughter too," she choked out, and shoved him hard in the center of his chest.

Reid rocked back on his heels to absorb the blow and clenched his jaw, battling the urge to turn and drive his fist through the wall. "There was a leak," he said roughly.

"A *leak*," she spat, her voice dripping bitterness. "The *Veneno* cartel has Autumn, Reid. That's more than a goddamn *leak*." She clenched both hands in her hair, her expression distraught as she shook her head. "I can't handle this. I just can't..." Her shoulders jerked and a ragged sob burst free. Max cursed, caught her shoulders and pulled her to him, and this time she didn't fight.

Reid stood there staring at the floor while Max consoled her, his whole world coming apart at the seams as the sound of her grief and terror sliced at the raw, gaping wound in the middle of his chest.

Rapid footsteps sounded in the hallway, then the detective appeared in the doorway. His gaze swung from Sarah to Reid and back, his face tightening as he shut the door behind him. "Mrs. Prentiss, have a seat." He pulled out a chair and tugged Sarah into it before facing them all, hands on hips. "I realize this is hard on all of you, but blaming and accusing aren't going to get your daughter back. If you can't refrain from attacking one another, I'm gonna kick you all out. Is that clear?"

Sarah and Max only stayed another ten minutes before she couldn't take it anymore, and they left. Reid was left alone with the detective as he went over everything he knew about Ruiz and his network. A lot of it was classified but he'd be damned if he'd keep it to himself if it might help get Autumn back.

An hour later he was sitting there alone in the office, having been told to go home. He'd given everything he could, and there was nothing more that could be done. Reid didn't like it, but he had no choice but to accept it. A crushing pressure filled his chest as he dragged his ass into his car, his ribcage compressing until it felt like his heart and lungs would implode. He was cut off from the investigation now, unable to help the police any more, and no one wanted him to do anything.

Useless as a one-legged man at an ass-kicking.

He spotted the liquor store on the left when he stopped at a red light a few miles from his building. Without even realizing it, he'd already made the decision and was turning into the parking lot. He walked straight to the whiskey aisle and stood there staring at the neatly stacked row of bottles, hands clenched into fists at his sides.

Fuck it.

He grabbed one, the weight and feel of the bottle a familiar comfort.

Back at his place, he dropped his ass onto the couch and uncapped the bottle, his hand shaking as he poured himself a tumbler full. He sat there staring at it for a long moment before taking one step closer to the abyss and lifting it to his nose.

The moment he inhaled that familiar scent, every pleasure center in his brain lit up, like Christmas and the Fourth of July combined. His whole body groaned at the sweet temptation in his hand, craving it so much his heart pounded and his mouth watered.

The reaction scared him so much he set it back down on the table. He forced his fingers to release it, his mind in chaos as he fought his oldest and most feared adversary.

He wanted the oblivion the booze offered. A respite from the pain and sheer helplessness that was shredding his insides, even if it was only for a few hours. But if he did this, he wouldn't be able to stop at one glass. Or one bottle.

No. Autumn still needed him. He had to be sober if she was found.

His gaze strayed to the mantel, to all the pictures of him and Autumn lined up there in the frames. Grief punched through him so hard it stole his breath.

She's gone. She's gone and it's my fault.

His hand shot out and grabbed the tumbler.

****

Tess hitched the strap of her hastily-packed overnight bag higher up on her shoulder and jogged through the half-empty terminal at Dulles. After Reid basically hung up on her and wouldn't answer her calls, she'd pulled some strings at headquarters and hopped a transport from Fort Worth within the hour.

Maybe coming to D.C. was a giant mistake, but right now she didn't care. This thing between her and Reid might be new and fragile—and she didn't even know what "it" was—but there was no way she could have stayed in Texas while he was going through hell alone here. If she'd overstepped her bounds by flying here to be with him, well… She'd deal with the repercussions later.

She pulled her phone out to try Reid again and saw there were no messages. The phone rang in her ear, then Reid's voicemail picked up.

Frustrated and sick at heart for what he must be going through, she dodged around the slower-moving passengers on their way to baggage claim and exited onto the sidewalk.

She jumped in a cab and went straight to Reid's

place. The sidewalk outside his building was deserted, not surprising since it was one in the morning. At the front door, she buzzed his unit and waited.

No answer.

She buzzed again, and waited another minute.

Nothing.

Was he at the police station? At headquarters? Maybe at Sarah's place?

She walked back to the sidewalk and around the side of the building to stare up at his unit. The blinds were pulled over the sliding glass doors that led out onto his patio, but she could see lines of light around the edges. Was he in there? With him refusing to answer her calls, she had no way of knowing where he was.

Discouraged, she strode back around front, ready to buzz his unit one last time and then find a hotel nearby.

"Tess?"

Surprised, she spun around to find two of Reid's teammates walking up the front walkway from the street. The big one, Agent Maka, and the one Reid was closest to, Agent Khan, the team medic. "Hi."

"You just fly in?" Khan asked.

She nodded. "Hopped a transport right after Reid called to tell me Autumn had been taken, then hung up on me. You guys know where he is?"

Khan frowned. "He's not home?"

"If he is, he's not answering the buzzer. And he won't pick up when I call."

"Sonofabitch," Maka muttered, striding toward her alongside his teammate. "You got the code?" he asked Khan.

"Yeah." Khan dug out his phone and fixed his gaze on Tess when he got close. "I'm Zaid, by the way. And this is Kai."

"Hi." She quickly shook their hands and followed them up to the front door, anxiety eating at her. Reid wouldn't do anything crazy, would he? "Have you guys heard from him?"

"No," Khan answered. "We've been getting sporadic updates from Commander Taggart. But after the last one, we told our team leader we would come check on Reid in person."

She zeroed in on the first part of that sentence. "Why, what was the last update?"

Zaid met her gaze, the overhead lights illuminating his hazel eyes, startling against his bronze skin. "They found out who took her."

Tess's heart started to pound. "Who?"

"One of Carlos Ruiz's enforcers."

She gasped and blanched, put both hands to her mouth. "Oh, sweet Jesus."

"In retaliation for a raid we conducted against some of his guys last week. Apparently, Reid got a text from the asshole around nine," Kai said as Zaid punched in the code to open the front door. "We didn't find out until about forty-five minutes ago. Taggart went to meet him at the police station and stayed there until Reid left. That's when we got the update from Hamilton."

Tess lowered her hands and faced the door, her heart sinking. *Oh, Reid.* Her eyes stung at the thought of Autumn so scared and alone with a monster from Ruiz's crew. "How the hell did one of Ruiz's guys find Autumn, and how did he get Reid's cell number?"

"Good questions," Zaid said, his voice flat, hard. The door buzzed and he pulled it open. "The agency and FBI are looking into it now."

If Ruiz or anyone else from the cartel had that much info on Reid, then it stood to reason they'd found more about the other team members. "What about you guys?" She slipped past Zaid as he held the door open for her.

"We're not sure yet. Analysts are trying to figure out how bad the breach is," Zaid said.

She followed them to the elevator and stepped inside, feeling tiny sandwiched between the two big men, especially Kai. "I can't even imagine what he's going through right now," she said quietly.

"I know," Zaid said with a shake of his head as they rode up to Reid's floor. "It's gotta be hell, because I know how sick the rest of us feel. She's a sweet little girl and we just want her found safe."

If one of Ruiz's men had taken Autumn, then the chances of that happening were practically nil. They knew it as well as she did, but none of them would admit it because they all wanted to cling to the hope that Autumn still had a chance.

Tess swallowed and frantically tried to think of what she could say or do to help Reid right now. There couldn't be anything so agonizing as the pain of a parent losing a child.

Her insides grabbed tight when the elevator stopped and the doors slid open. She followed the others down the carpeted hallway to Reid's door, their steps hushed by the carpet. Zaid tried the doorbell and they all waited for a minute.

Apparently too impatient to try the bell again, Kai reached over his buddy's shoulder and pounded a big fist on the door. Tess cringed at the level of noise at this time of the morning, but Reid's neighbors would just have to understand given the circumstances.

When Reid still didn't answer, Tess got really worried.

Kai pounded again, harder this time, the door vibrating against the frame. "Prentiss. Open up," he called out, his deep voice echoing up and down the hallway in the thick silence.

Someone a few units down yanked their door open to glare at them. Kai and Zaid ignored the man, so Tess pulled her agency ID out of her back pocket and flashed it toward him. The man quickly disappeared back into his unit and shut the door.

When she faced the others once more, Kai's dark eyebrows were drawn into an imposing scowl. He made an irritated sound in the back of his throat and pulled his fist back to begin pounding again, but Zaid held up a hand to stop him and tried a different approach.

"Come on, buddy, open the door," he called out.

Still nothing. Fear trickled through Tess. It was Sunday, May nineteenth. The anniversary of Reid finding Jason hanging in the bathroom. Given that Autumn had just been kidnapped by ruthless cartel members, would he… She shook the thought away. No. No, he wouldn't. Couldn't.

"Reid," Zaid said with tried patience.

Finally, a familiar drawl came from inside. "Not up for company right now, boys."

Tess closed her eyes in silent thanks and let out a deep breath. *Thank God he's okay.* But was it her imagination, or had his voice sounded a little slurred? Tess glanced at the others in question, and the two men exchanged a meaningful, worried glance, their faces turning grim.

"You know what?" Kai finally threatened. "Either you open this door, or I'll break the goddamn thing in—"

Zaid held up a hand and cut Kai off. "We've got Tess out here with us. She flew in to see you."

They all waited in tense silence for a response, Tess holding her breath. Ten seconds later, footsteps sounded from inside. The lock turned, and the door opened.

Reid stood there in the opening in jeans and a rumpled T-shirt, his face haggard.

"Hey, brother," Zaid said quietly.

Reid didn't answer. His bloodshot, red-rimmed eyes went right to Tess. Their gazes locked for an instant, then his face crumpled and he shoved past his teammates to reach for her.

Tess's heart almost exploded when he dragged her close and crushed her to his chest, holding her so tight she couldn't breathe. She started to wind her arms around him, but stopped as a terrible suspicion hit her.

Oh, no... Had he been drinking? She didn't smell it on him, but his disheveled state and the look Zaid and Kai had just shared worried her. "Reid," she breathed, unsure what else to say. Of course he was gutted, but he wouldn't hit the bottle now, would he? She flattened her hands on his broad back and sought Kai and Zaid's gazes over the top of his shoulder.

Reid made a strangled sound and tightened his hold, his face buried in the side of her neck. "I don't know what the hell to do," he moaned.

"Let's get you back inside," she said to him.

"I'll get some coffee going," Kai said, stepping past them into the apartment.

Reid stayed glued to her, his face pressed into the crook of her neck as he shook his head. "It was Ruiz. One of his guys took her," he said, his voice cracking.

"I heard," Tess murmured, meeting Zaid's eyes.

Zaid reached for Reid's shoulder, pulled him up and spun him around to steer him back into the apartment. "Come on, man."

Reid sucked in a shaky breath and shoved the heels of his hands into his eye sockets as Zaid walked him through the kitchen to the living room and sat him on the couch. Her heart sank when she saw the open bottle of Jack Daniels and the glass on the coffee table. It still had liquor in it. How much had he had?

Without looking at her, Zaid picked up both the bottle and glass and handed them to her. Tess took them, catching the shame that flashed in Reid's eyes.

"I didn't drink it. I shouldn't have bought it in the first place, but... Fuck, I just didn't know what the hell else to do," Reid said, his voice breaking on the last word as he dragged a hand through his hair.

"You should have called one of us," Zaid said, a hard edge to his voice.

Tess carried the bottle and glass straight to the kitchen and poured every last drop of the whiskey down the sink. Without pause, she checked the cupboards and drawers in the kitchen, the bathrooms and his bedroom for good measure. She found nothing.

Zaid met her gaze as she walked around the corner with empty hands and she shook her head to let him know she hadn't found anything. He was perched on the edge of the wooden coffee table facing Reid, his forearms braced on his splayed thighs.

In the quiet, the sound and scent of brewing coffee came from the kitchen while Kai rummaged through the cupboards gathering mugs. Tess stood still and focused on Reid and Zaid as they stared at each other from two feet apart.

"Talk to me," Zaid said.

Reid drew in a deep breath and collapsed back against the couch cushions with a soft groan, not meeting his teammate's eyes. Tess walked over and sank down beside him, wrapped an arm around his shoulders and snuggled into his side, offering what comfort and support she could. He didn't return the embrace, but he didn't stiffen or push her away, either.

"Look, I don't need a goddamn lecture about my drinking," Reid began in a warning tone.

Zaid raised a dark eyebrow and stared him down. "You sure as shit do, my friend. Not only did you almost fall off the wagon tonight after years of fighting to stay sober, you were about to do it when you could get a call at any moment that an actionable tip's come in, and then you'd be too out of commission to act on it."

"I know," he muttered, looking away, anguish and

self-disgust etched into his face. "That's why I didn't drink it."

"But you wanted to."

"Yeah, I wanted to."

This was uncomfortable as hell, but there was no getting around it, and under the circumstances Tess agreed with Zaid's tough love approach. They had to be clear with Reid right here, right now. "No more alcohol, Reid," she said in a firm tone. "Promise us. It's only going to put a temporary Band Aid on this, and make it a hell of a lot worse for everyone after." Wanting to soften the harsh words, Tess rubbed his upper arm with her palm. "Autumn needs you to stay sober." *I need you to stay sober.*

He closed his eyes, his head sagging forward as though it was just too heavy to hold up any longer. "God dammit, if anything happens to her, then I don't wanna be here," he rasped out, and Tess's chest constricted.

"You can't give up on her," Zaid said, his voice hard. "You fucking *can't*. Understand? Giving up is not an option. Not for any of us."

Reid turned his head and shot Zaid a lethal glare. "You think I'm giving up on her? Fuck you, Zaid. You were right next to me the night we found Victoria Gomez. You saw what they'd done to her. And now that sick fuck's threatened to do all that to my baby—" His voice shredded and he glanced away, his jaw flexed so tight Tess could all but hear his back teeth grinding.

"Still not giving up," Zaid said, his voice level but firm.

"Me neither," Kai said, carrying a mug of coffee in and thrusting it at Reid. "So drink up, brother. You gotta be ready when they find her."

Reid shot him a searching look. He snatched the mug without saying anything and brought it to his lips.

Zaid got up and walked around the coffee table to

take the easy chair opposite Reid, easing the tension in the room. Kai brought her and Zaid mugs of coffee before seating himself on the loveseat arranged perpendicular to the couch, his big frame making the heavy piece of leather furniture look almost dainty.

"Who sent you guys, Taggart or Hamilton?" Reid said dully.

"Taggart talked to Hamilton, and Hamilton texted all of us," Kai answered. "We volunteered to come over. So yeah, we all know the gist of it."

Reid grimaced and lowered his mug. "Yeah? Well you didn't hear the part where Sarah started screaming and hitting me when she heard the news about Ruiz." His fingers flexed around the mug handle, a restless motion that screamed his agitation. "Said it's my fault. That my job had not only destroyed our family, but now it's destroyed our daughter, too."

Tess winced and squeezed his shoulder, the muscles iron hard beneath her hand. "She was upset. I'm sure she didn't mean that."

Those deep blue eyes drilled into hers like a laser. "That's *exactly* what she meant. And you know what? She was right."

Tess shut up. And God, no wonder he'd been about to hit the bottle after that on top of everything else.

"How the hell did they get your personal information?" Kai demanded.

"No fucking idea. As of right now there are two-dozen agents in various agencies scrambling around trying to get answers. And you guys better beef up your personal security until we know how far the leak's gone."

"I'd say it's gone way too fucking far already," Zaid said from the easy chair, his expression dark.

Reid set the coffee mug on the table, ran his hands over his face. "I just want her back."

"We all do," Kai said. "And we're all here for you.

If we get a lead on where this asshole's hiding, we all want a piece of him. But most of all, we want Autumn back safe and sound. We'll all do whatever it takes to make that happen."

Reid nodded and lowered his hands. "Yeah. Christ, yeah, I just want her to be safe."

Oh, God, please let her still be alive, Tess prayed. The alternative was straight up horrific and unthinkable.

After a few minutes of silence, Reid finally began to open up to them. She stayed beside him as he outlined the sequence of events that had led them to now. An hour later he seemed to sort of shut down, and there was nothing more his teammates could do for him. He was restless and hurting and clearly not in the mood for company.

"Look, I appreciate you guys coming over, but you don't need to keep vigil with me," he said to his teammates. "Both of you go on home and get some sleep. If I hear anything else, I'll let you know."

Kai and Zaid exchanged a look, then Zaid focused on her. "You staying with him?"

"Yes." She sought Reid's gaze. "Unless you don't want me to?"

"I want you to," he said, his bloodshot eyes holding hers.

"Okay. You guys call us if you need anything, you hear?" Zaid said as he got to his feet.

Tess stayed on the couch while Reid saw his teammates out. When he locked up and turned back to her, he sighed and let his shoulders slump, exhaustion clear in every line of his face and body.

Aching for him, she got up and closed the distance between them, sliding her arms around his waist and leaning into his body as he embraced her. "You've got good friends, Reid. They love you and Autumn."

"Yeah, I know." He pressed his cheek to her hair. "I didn't expect you to fly up here."

"I couldn't stay there while you were going through this."

He was quiet for a long moment, then nuzzled the top of her head. "He sent me a picture of her."

She stiffened. "What?"

"He took it in the car after he'd taken her. She was in her ball uniform. And her face...she was so damn scared, Tess. It just killed me to look into her eyes and not be able to help her."

The level of cruelty necessary to not only target a federal agent's family in revenge, but to attack an innocent child and then send taunting texts to her father was testimony of the depraved animals the *Veneno* cartel had in its ranks. "I hope he doesn't surrender when they find him," she said, her voice cold. "I want him dead."

"You and me both."

Tess ran her hands up and down his tense back, hoping to soothe him, wishing there was something more she could do to help him bear this. "Are you hungry?"

"No, can't eat right now."

"Think you could get some sleep?"

"No."

She understood.

"It's Jason's anniversary today."

She lifted her head from his shoulder to look into his tortured face. "I know." God, how much pain could a man bear before he broke?

"That, on top of everything else and what happened with Sarah after she heard the news about Ruiz... It's no excuse, but I drove past a liquor store on the way home and I just thought, 'fuck it'. So I stopped and went in." Shame flickered in his eyes.

"I poured everything down the sink," she said, not sorry but bracing for his anger anyway.

"Thank you," he said instead.

She relaxed and rested her cheek against his shoulder

again, glad he'd allowed her to stay and that he wanted her here at such an emotional time. "Welcome."

He was silent for a minute before speaking again. "You know, when I first quit drinking I thought cold turkey was too hard so I switched to a non-alcoholic beer. Then I had to quit even that because it tasted too close to the real thing. I was doing pretty well by the time Autumn was old enough to understand what alcoholism meant. I never hid it from her. When she was about five or so I told her exactly what it was and that I was doing my best to stay sober. She looked up at me, cocked her head and said I should try root beer instead."

Tess smiled, picturing it easily in her mind. "That's adorable."

"Yeah. I always make sure I've got some of our favorite brand on hand. There's some in the fridge right now." His grip on her tightened and Tess squeezed her eyes shut, his pain slicing through her. "They're gonna find her, right? The cops or the feds. Hell, even a citizen, I don't care."

The desperation in his voice shredded her inside. "Yes." There was no question that Autumn would be found. Tess just hoped they found her in *time*.

They stood holding each other for a while before Reid spoke once more. "You've gotta be exhausted," he murmured against her hair.

She shook her head. "I'm fine."

"You should sleep."

"I'm not sleeping if you're not." That wasn't right. She'd come here so he wouldn't have to bear this alone.

He kissed the top of her head. "How about we lie down together for a while then, and if you fall asleep, I won't hold it against you."

"Okay."

Lacing his fingers through hers, he led her past Autumn's closed bedroom door to the master bedroom.

The lights were off, but there was enough coming through the open doorway from the kitchen for her to see the big king-size bed she hadn't paid attention to before while she'd been looking for bottles.

Reid laid his phone on the bedside table, then pulled the covers down. Tess took off her shoes. Fully dressed, they both climbed in, and he immediately pulled her into his arms. She settled against his hard frame with a sigh and slipped an arm around his waist, surrounded by his heat and scent, willing him to take the comfort she offered.

He curled one thick arm around her back, and sifted his free hand through her hair. "I'm so damn glad you're here," he whispered hoarsely.

"Me too," she whispered back.

They lay together in the silence, listening to the sound of each other's breathing, each of them hoping his phone would ring with good news.

Praying for a miracle.

Chapter Fourteen

Autumn jolted awake in complete darkness. Fear surged through her, making her body go rigid, her heart swelling painfully in her chest. Her arms and legs ached from being bound together behind her. Her mouth was dry, the piece of tape over her lips. She was still locked in the trunk, but it wasn't as hot as it had been. Where had the man taken her?

The car stopped.

Her pulse pounded sickeningly in her ears when a door opened and shut. Footsteps came toward the back of the car.

Autumn tensed, a film of cold sweat coating her skin as she waited.

The trunk popped open. She squeezed her eyes shut, but no light penetrated her eyelids so she opened them. It was dark out. The bad man from before leaned over her, a light somewhere in the background illuminating half of his face. Fear slithered through her when he grinned, the light gleaming on his gold front tooth.

"It's time, little angel," he said in an accented voice

169

that sounded almost excited. He held up a phone, the bright flash of light blinding her as he took a picture.

By the time she opened her eyes again he was reaching for her. She bit back a cry of fear, tried to scurry backward away from him but with her limbs bound she couldn't move. The man grabbed her, roughly jerked her out of the trunk and tossed her over his shoulder. Bone dug into her belly and she gritted her teeth, determined not to cry in front of him.

But inside she was shaking with terror.

He carried her a short distance to another vehicle, where a different man waited. "You fed her?" the new one asked.

"Nah. What's the point?"

Autumn couldn't help but struggle as the first man passed her over to the second. He carried her to the new car and lowered her into the trunk. She tried to scream for help but the tape muffled her voice. No matter how she kicked and screamed, the man's grip didn't loosen. He didn't say a word to her as he closed the lid, locking her inside. She thrashed and wiggled around, tears streaming down her cheeks, but it was no use. The first man had tied her too tightly.

Then a door shut and the engine started. A moment later the car began moving. Taking her farther away from her parents, and anyone else that might help her.

Autumn sagged on the musty carpet inside the trunk and cried, wishing with all her might that her daddy would come with his team and rescue her. Shoot the bad man who had her and get her out of this trunk.

Daddy, where are you? Please find me.

****

Reid hadn't expected to doze off, but he must have, because the next thing he knew his eyes snapped open in the semi-darkness of his bedroom, his heart in his throat and his pulse pounding out of control in his ears.

Autumn. He'd dreamed of her trapped in a dark place, alone, crying out for him.

Fuck.

He swallowed hard and rolled away from Tess, who was curled on her side next to him, sound asleep. He'd lain awake for a long time, staring at the ceiling with her warm weight settled against him while her breathing slowed and she slipped into a deep sleep. Feeling guilty as hell for being safe and warm in the face of what his daughter was going through at that same moment, and yet pitifully grateful for Tess's soothing presence.

Sitting up, he swung his legs over the side of the bed and ran a shaky hand over his face. Was his daughter still alive? Had the dream meant something? A glance at the clock showed he'd only been asleep for about twenty minutes.

"Reid?"

He stiffened, didn't speak as Tess shifted over and set a hand on his back.

"You okay?" she murmured.

No, he was the furthest thing from okay. He was going out of his mind.

Without a word, Tess scooted closer and pressed her soft body against his back. She wound her arms around his chest, resting her cheek on the top of his spine. He was so keyed up he almost shrugged her off and shoved from the bed, but she didn't deserve his anger and frustration. She was just trying to help.

Right now, though, he was walking a dangerous line. A volatile mix of emotions churned inside him, a raging storm he couldn't escape. And in that moment, that's exactly what he craved—an escape. A distraction. More than he'd ever craved alcohol. And Tess was unwittingly placing herself directly in the line of fire.

"Can I do anything?" she asked, gently rubbing one hand over his chest in comforting little circles. But instead of calming him, her touch blended with the chaotic rush of adrenaline and fear roaring through his veins. The darkness was a living thing inside him, searching for an outlet.

Not trusting his ability to contain it, Reid reached up and locked his hand around her wrist, stilling the gentle movement, trying to think of an answer to her question. *Yes. Make me forget. Get me out of my head, even if it's just for a little while. Please.*

The desperate plea was like a scream in his head, filling his throat, his mouth, until he all but choked on it.

Tess cuddled in even closer, turned her face into his nape and pressed a kiss to his overheated skin.

Reid closed his eyes and forced air into his aching lungs, banishing the hellish image of Autumn's frightened face and focusing instead on the dark undercurrent of desire heating his blood. Tess was soft and warm along his back, her clean, pear scent wrapping around him. Easing the constriction in his ribcage even as she made the fire burn hotter.

The weight of her breasts nestled against his back as she shifted, her lips brushing along the oversensitive skin at the side of his neck. He sucked in a breath as heat exploded throughout his body, pooling between his legs. His cock surged, swelling until it strained the front of his jeans. Aching for her touch.

"Tess," he choked out, his voice a warning rasp. She had no idea what she was doing to him. How on edge he was.

"I'm right here," she whispered back, gliding her lips up to his jaw, to the edge of his mouth. Willingly offering herself to him. A sacrificial lamb to slake the hunger of the beast raging inside him.

The beast snapped its chain.

Releasing her wrist, Reid spun around and captured her face in his hands. In the faint light coming into the bedroom from the hallway, he caught the flare of surprise in her eyes, and the darkening of desire.

And when she lowered her lashes and leaned forward to press her lips to his, he was lost.

Reid gripped handfuls of her silky hair and slanted his mouth across hers, unleashing his inner demons, desperation driving him.

Tess gasped softly at his ravenous hunger but didn't pull away, pushing the softness of her breasts to his chest as he plundered her mouth with his tongue. His body was like an exposed high voltage line, every single brush of her against him sending electricity racing along his nerve endings.

He pushed her backward, turning them so he could pin her beneath him on the mattress, starving for the feel and taste of her, the chance at oblivion she offered.

Wedging his hips between her thighs, he settled the ridge of his erect cock against her center and gripped the bottom of her shirt to peel it over her head. She raised her arms to help him, undid her bra as he tossed the shirt aside, revealing the plump mounds of her breasts, her nipples erect.

Pushing them together with his hands, he dove down to capture one straining center in his mouth. Tess moaned and arched her back, her fingers clenching in his hair for a moment before running down his back to pull his shirt up.

Reid released her captive nipple only long enough to shrug out of his shirt, then went back to sucking and nipping at her tender flesh, his hands going straight for the fly of his jeans. Tess wrapped her arms around his shoulders, one hand holding his head to her breasts while he shucked his jeans and underwear and kicked them off.

She made a hungry, approving sound and reached for

his hips, her fingers like fire against his skin, stroking over his ass, the backs of his thighs, tracing the line of his hipbones until finally, finally, she gripped his heavy, swollen cock.

Reid froze for a second and shuddered at the feel of her gripping him, a guttural growl tearing from his throat. Her lips were hot against his chest, kissing, sucking, a lash on his already frayed control.

Breathing hard, he fumbled with the fastening of her jeans. Her fist stroking his raging hot flesh, making him shudder, she raised her hips so he could drag the denim down her smooth legs, leaving her in just a scrap of black lace.

She slid her fist up the length of his cock, making a swirling motion around the swollen head. Pleasure punched through him, a greedy, voracious need he was frantic to satisfy.

Hooking his hands in the waistband of her panties, he yanked sharply, ripping the fabric apart. Tess gasped at the barely leashed violence of it, but sat up to grab the back of his head with her free hand and fuse their mouths together once more.

Reid groaned into her mouth and shoved her flat beneath him, overwhelming her with his strength and size. There was no finesse, no seduction in his touch, his kisses, only raging hunger. The ache in his cock was almost unbearable, the need to plunge into her slick, soft heat making him shake.

He nipped at her chin, scraped his teeth along the side of her neck as she flung her head back, offering her breasts to him. He cupped them in unsteady hands, pausing only a moment to suck at each distended nipple before moving lower, fixated on the tender flesh between her splayed thighs.

Reid grabbed her wrist and pried her hand free of his cock as he shifted lower, pressing his teeth into her belly while he gripped her upper thighs and pushed them wider apart. The sight of her shadowed folds opening up to him, the scent of her arousal hit him like a sledgehammer to the chest.

With a low growl, he clamped his fingers around her thighs to hold her still and buried his mouth against her core. Tess cried out and tensed at the contact, but Reid held her fast as he tasted her, swirling his tongue around the hard bud of her clit, sucking it before plunging his tongue inside her.

Her fingers grabbed at his hair, her hips rising to press into his face. "God, Reid…"

He couldn't think. He was all instinct, driven by the need to take, claim, ease the ache between his legs even if it couldn't ease the ache in his heart. Driving his tongue into her core one last time, he reveled in her helpless cry as he rose to his knees and leaned across her to grab a condom from his nightstand drawer.

She reached for his cock but he pushed her hands away and rolled the condom on, his fingers shaking, his breath rattling in his lungs, heart pounding out of control. As soon as he had it on, he grabbed Tess's long legs and set them over his shoulders. Her hands flew to his chest as he lined the head of his cock up against her entrance, the position making her completely vulnerable to him.

The single part of his brain that was still functioning warned him that he was being too rough, going too fast, but he couldn't slow down. The best he could do was stare down into her eyes, let her see his need, the raging hunger inside him as he clamped a hand around her hip and pushed the head of his cock into her.

Slick heat enveloped him, sending fire racing up from the base of his spine. Tess's fingers curled around the tops of his shoulders, her eyes clinging to his as he stayed like that for a heartbeat, two.

Then she lifted a hand and traced her fingertips down

the side of his face in a gesture so tender it broke him. He flexed his hips, sinking into her as deep as he could go in one inexorable thrust.

Tess grabbed hold of his nape, her eyes squeezing shut as a choked cry came from her throat. Reid stilled, every muscle in his body trembling at the feel of her clenching around him. "Tess," he rasped out, his heart about to burst. He didn't want to hurt her.

Her eyes fluttered open and met his, and the fingers dug into his nape relaxed slightly. She shifted a little, the small motion sending agonizing pleasure blazing through him.

The selfish part of him wanted to pull back and then thrust, fuck her as deep and hard as he could until the orgasm buzzing at the base of his spine exploded. With the last of his restraint he slid his thumb into his mouth and reached down between their bodies to settle it over the swollen bud of her clit.

A soft, startled moan spilled from her lips and her eyes closed, a look of raw pleasure transforming her features. And he couldn't stay still a moment longer.

Adding pressure with his thumb, he rode her, slowly at first, then faster as she moaned and twisted in his hold, her thighs trembling on his shoulders. She was slick, hot perfection, her body gripping him like a fist as he drove in and out of her.

His vision hazed over as the pleasure magnified, looming like a huge wave at the edge of his consciousness. "Aw, Tess," he grated out, unable to stop now, every slide into her body better than the last. Gritting his teeth to hold his release back, he slid his thumb over her clit and angled his hips to hit her sweet spot with his cock on every sliding stroke.

Her fingers dug into his skin, every breathless moan and cry pushing him higher. Just when he couldn't hold back a second more her core clenched around him, rhythmic squeezes as her sounds of pleasure turned into a wild sob and she arched, coming.

Reid leaned forward to bury his face in her hair and pumped faster, faster, letting the hunger rule him. Ecstasy spiraled up, up, his cock swelling even more until he drove forward one last time and held there, locked as deep inside her as he could get. The orgasm slammed into him like a blast wave, so intense it wrenched a guttural shout from him as he threw his head back and came.

Gasping, his skin slick and muscles trembling, he sagged into her embrace. Tess stiffened a little and he dimly realized he essentially had her folded in half with her legs still over his shoulders.

Grasping one ankle at a time, he gently eased her legs off him, groaning in relief and contentment when she pulled him tighter to her and wound her legs around his thighs, holding him close. She smoothed one hand up and down his damp spine and stroked his hair with the other while their thundering heartbeats slowed.

He allowed her to cradle his full weight, sinking deeper into the solace she offered as the wall of exhaustion finally slammed into him. Sleep enveloped him in a warm, weightless cocoon that sucked him straight into the oblivion he'd so desperately craved.

****

When the call came in, *El Escorpion* left the family dining table where everyone was eating breakfast together, and strode to the second-floor office in the main house.

The special phone on the polished mahogany desk was encrypted not only to scramble the signal and make it impossible for anyone to trace its location; it also digitally disguised the voice of whoever answered it. "*¿Sí?*"

"It's Ramon."

"Ramon. What can I do for you?" They'd met in person several times. Not that Ramon knew it. Only a handful of people knew who *El Escorpion* truly was.

"It's Ruiz."

Ah. This wasn't going to be good, then. "What about him?"

"He's kidnapped a DEA agent's daughter. One of the FAST members who conducted the raid on Ruiz's...recreational property in Louisiana."

More like his whore farm. *El Escorpion's* hand tightened around the phone. "Did he. How old?"

"Nine."

Hijo de puta. "When?"

"Last night. In Virginia. I've sent you a picture."

The phone buzzed, and an image of a dark-haired little girl popped up on the screen, her deep blue eyes full of terror. She was stretched out on her side, staring at whoever had taken the picture. Someone had slapped a piece of silver duct tape across her mouth, and her hands and feet appeared to be bound behind her.

This is what one of the organization's top lieutenants was up to? Terrorizing a little girl? Bringing the wrath of the DEA and a dozen other federal agencies down on the cartel? "He did this personally?" Seemed ballsy for Ruiz. And of all the violent and extreme things he had done in the past, this one was the most repugnant.

"One of his men. Javier."

El Escorpion's lip curled. *That piece of shit.* The things those men were capable of doing to that little one... "Is she still alive?"

"I think so, but I'm not sure."

The lack of information was annoying, to say the least. "And Antonio?" Ruiz's dimwitted head enforcer. His former one had been excellent. The start of this entire downward spiral had begun right after Dillon Wainright had been killed.

"Was waiting for the girl to be delivered to him, last I heard."

"Where?"

"Somewhere close to the Virginia/North Carolina border. I don't know the exact location."

"*Find out.*"

"Yes, boss."

"Don't call again until you have the location." The back lawn was visible from the office window. It was far too long, and some weeds were showing. Why the hell couldn't the landscaper see it? "Now. Was there anything else?"

"No."

"Then this conversation is over." *El Escorpion* ended the call and placed the phone back on the desk before turning to stare out at the overgrown lawn. So messy. This situation. This business.

So. Over the past week alone, Ruiz's overinflated sense of importance and power had resulted not only in the near exposure of the inner workings of the cartel the night of the raid when his female playthings had been rescued, but he'd also just brought the fury of half the U.S. government down on them by kidnapping a FAST agent's innocent child.

Well. That would not do.

No, that would not do at *all*.

Chapter Fifteen

Tess's eyes snapped open when Reid shifted beside her in his bed. They'd fallen asleep spooned together but at some point, they'd both wanted space because they were sprawled apart as far as they could get while still staying on the mattress.

Disquiet buzzed in her belly as the memory of what they'd done a few hours ago came back to her. Carefully climbing out of the bed, she gathered her fallen clothing from the floor and tiptoed out of the bedroom.

The moment she eased the door shut without waking him, she took a deep, relieved breath. Sleep was the best thing for him right now, and she needed to think.

She showered in the guest bathroom, trying to make sense of what was going on inside her as the hot water rushed over her head and body. Sleeping with Reid during such an emotional crisis probably hadn't been her best idea, but she'd wanted to comfort him so badly.

As for whether or not she was prepared to take on everything that came with him…how could she not? The simple truth was, she was in danger of losing her heart to him—and his daughter—and she couldn't turn away now. Not when he needed her, and not when she knew exactly what it was to feel that helpless and scared, as she had when the men from Brian's regiment had shown up at her door to tell her he was gone.

She'd realized two important things. Keeping him at arm's length wasn't going to make her happy. And becoming a widow at such a young age had taught her that life was far too short to spend it holding back out of fear that something else bad might happen.

By the time she'd finished the shower and dried off, her mind was made up. She stared at her reflection in the steamed-up mirror above the sink, gearing up for the battle ahead. She was a soldier at heart, and she would see this through to the end, supporting him however she could. However much he would let her. If it all blew up in her face later on… She'd deal with it then.

After dressing, brushing her teeth and running a comb through her wet hair, she went to the kitchen and made coffee as quietly as she could. She opened the fridge to see what he had that she could cook up for breakfast, and a lump formed in her throat when she saw the bottles of root beer and girly-packaged yogurt containers sitting on the top shelf.

Autumn was supposed to have stayed overnight last night. She should have been there right now instead of Tess, rummaging in the fridge for something to eat and waiting for Reid to wake up so they could get on with whatever adventures they had planned for the day together.

Instead she was God-only-knew where, probably terrified, maybe in pain. Or maybe…

Tess shut the fridge, suddenly sick to her stomach.

"You're up early," a deep voice drawled from behind her.

She spun around to find Reid walking toward her from

the bedroom wearing only a pair of jeans. Her heart skipped and her mouth went dry at the sight of his bare torso on display mere feet from her.

In the darkness last night, she'd explored every dip and hollow of that muscular body. She'd held him as close as she could. Held him *inside* her.

For her, that kind of intimacy wasn't casual. Not at all. But she wasn't sure whether it was for him or not.

She licked her lips. "Thought I'd put on some coffee and make us something to eat. Toast sound good?"

Reid closed the distance between them and drew her into a hug, one big hand sliding into the back of her hair to hold her head against his shoulder. "I'm not hungry."

Settling into his hold, she scented the toothpaste he must have just used. "You still need to eat something."

Instead of arguing, he eased her head back and searched her eyes, his thumb tracing along her jaw. "I was too rough last night."

Blood rushed to her face and she lowered her gaze, uncomfortable. "No, I'm fine."

"Tess. Look at me."

The quiet command had her lifting her gaze immediately.

"I was rough and selfish, and I'm sorry."

She couldn't look at him. "Reid, you weren't selfish—"

"Yeah I was." He tipped her head back and kissed her softly. Slowly. Igniting sparks of heat low in her belly. "I'm glad you're still here. When I woke up I thought you were gone until I smelled the coffee."

"I wouldn't have taken off without saying goodbye." She settled her hands on his waist, taking in the circles beneath his eyes. "Did you get much sleep?"

Pain shadowed his deep blue eyes. "No. I keep waiting for the phone to ring. I feel like I should be *doing* something."

"I know." The helplessness and lack of action was awful. "Maybe we should head down to the police station and wait there."

Reid took her face in his hands. "Thank you."

"Hey, it's noth—"

"I mean it," he said softly, staring deep into her eyes. "Thank you."

She cleared her throat and dropped her gaze to his throat. "You're welcome. I just wish I could find her for you."

He kissed the bridge of her nose, then released her and headed for the coffee pot. "Mind if we take these to go?"

"Not at all."

Within twenty minutes they were seated in the lead detective's office. Given the early hour, only a handful of officers were at the station. Seated behind his desk, Detective Espinosa had bags under his eyes as well, and his shirt was rumpled. As though he'd pulled an all-nighter trying to get a lead on Autumn.

"I wish I could tell you we have something more to go on," he told them, "but I don't. I've talked to the lead FBI agent helping with the case and there's no update to pass along."

Reid sat next to her like a granite statue, his hands fisted on his thighs. Tess reached out and took one of them. He uncurled his fingers and wrapped them around hers, squeezed in silent acknowledgment.

Espinosa spoke to him. "As a father I can appreciate just how hard this must be on you. There's really nothing more you can do here, though. Go home and—"

"All due respect, Detective, but I can't do that." Reid's voice was hard. Unwavering.

Espinosa released a deep breath and nodded. "I understand. Just know that we're doing everything we can to locate your daughter."

Out in the lobby, Reid dropped her hand and started

pacing from one side to the other, and her own stomach coiled in sympathy. "I need to *do* something," he told her, his eyes tortured. "I can't just sit here doing sweet fuck all when she's out there somewhere, needing me."

Tess crossed to him and took both his hands in hers, looking into his tortured eyes. "They're going to find her, Reid. I promise. And she's going to be okay." They had to believe that. Hope was the only thing keeping him going.

Reid's jaw clenched as he stared at her, emotion swirling in his eyes. Then he grabbed her and hauled her up against him, his strong arms holding on for dear life as he buried his face in her neck.

His phone chimed.

He released her so fast she stumbled, her heart shooting into her throat when she saw the tension in his face as he looked at the screen. She held her breath, waiting, praying.

"*Fuck.*"

Her stomach dropped like a concrete block. For a moment, it felt like the room spun around her. *She can't be dead. Can't be.* "What?" she whispered, afraid of what he would say.

"Another goddamn head fuck," he snarled, stalking back toward Espinosa's office.

Without looking at her, he handed her the phone. It showed a picture of Autumn, a piece of duct tape covering her mouth, her wide eyes staring at the camera. The bastards had tied her hands and feet behind her.

Below it was another message from the kidnapper.

Waiting for the fun to start.

****

Reid was barely holding it together as he and his teammates gathered with the HRT guys at their headquarters at Quantico. Three hours had passed since he'd received the text from whoever had sent it.

The picture of Autumn wasn't proof of life, but he had to believe she was still alive. Why bother transporting her at all if the kidnapper was planning to kill her? It made no sense.

Now everyone was assembled, but everything was moving too slowly. That text had originated from a phone nearby in the southern mountains of North Carolina. Analysts within the DEA, FBI and NSA were working as fast as they could to pinpoint the location, and working all their contacts to try and find a possible target. Once they got that, they could pull the trigger and go get Autumn back.

Because of his highly personal and emotional involvement in the case, Taggart had removed Reid from the op. Disciplined as he was, no matter the outcome of the rescue op, he was going to be too emotional to stay objective, and that could get someone killed. So he was sidelined for the time being, and this joint mission was going to go ahead without him.

The HRT would rescue Autumn, and his teammates would insert with them to go after Ruiz and his thugs, along with whatever drugs, money and weapons they could find. But he was damn well going to be there when it happened, as close as he could get to the action. That was the deal, and Taggart was allowing it because he trusted Reid. They'd monitor the situation from the mobile command center together, with DeLuca and the FBI support staff.

Reid looked up from the satellite image of an isolated North Carolina mountain community they were studying when Tess walked into the room. She was dressed in her flight suit, her crew and one other following her into the room. Their gazes met and she gave him a reassuring smile, silently conveying her faith in Autumn being alive.

A little of the tension inside him eased. His girl and the men he considered his brothers were going to get his baby back today, and once captured, that motherfucker Ruiz would pay for what he'd done.

For now, revenge could wait. All Reid cared about for the moment was getting his daughter back safely. Then he could worry about the rest of it. And do whatever it took to ensure Ruiz rotted inside a U.S. prison for the rest of his natural life.

"All right, people." HRT Commander Matt DeLuca strode into the room, all business in his tactical uniform, and Taggart on his heels. "Our analysts have come up with a target location."

Yes.

Reid's heart thudded in his throat as DeLuca walked over and set his finger on a point on the map in front of Reid and the others. "Best we can tell, the cell that call originated from is now here. And satellite images show a private log home hidden in the trees. It's a rental property."

When DeLuca turned his attention to the screen at the back of the room, Reid followed his gaze and focused on the satellite image there.

"It's isolated. Only one road in and out. We got a tip saying Ruiz, or at least some of his men are there, and a wiretap confirms he made a call from that phone two hours ago. There was chatter about a girl, but we can't say for certain it was Autumn. Based on all that, however, we're going in. At this point we don't know what kind of manpower or resistance to expect, and that means we have to be ready for anything. So let's lay this thing out together."

SA Tucker immediately got to work with his team while Hamilton took charge of FAST Bravo's meeting. Reid hovered on the periphery, hyper-focused on every detail. Everything passed in a blur. Ideally, they would wait to execute the joint raid when it was dark, but with Autumn's life potentially hanging in the balance, they were going now.

He didn't see Tess again after the briefing, not even out at the flight line at the airport. He'd suited and kitted up with the rest of his teammates, but when they reached the tarmac, Reid headed left with Taggart, DeLuca and some other support staff rather than going right with the other operators. It chafed that he couldn't be the one to kick down the door on this op and rescue his daughter, but he understood and trusted his boys. That would have to be enough.

The taskforce touched down at a small, private airstrip several miles from the target house some fifty minutes later. As Reid hopped out behind Taggart, he studied the cockpits of the other two birds and thought he spotted Tess in the right hand seat of the last one but she didn't look his way as he climbed into the modified RV that was to serve as their mobile command unit.

Agents inside it were already monitoring satellite links and cell tower activity in the area. While the HRT and Reid's teammates met again to go over the details of the coming op, the RV rolled out toward the mountain town where the target location lay.

Reid stayed in his seat as they wound up the switchbacks, thinking of Autumn. Remembering all the little milestones in her short life. The day she'd been born. Taking her home from the hospital, terrified he might break her. The first time she'd smiled at him and it wasn't gas. Her first steps. That first time he'd picked her up from preschool and her face had lit up when she'd seen him, then raced over and launched herself into his arms.

Easter. Halloween. Birthdays and Christmas. Their trip to Orlando just over a month ago. That time she'd made the game-winning catch a few weeks back and she'd immediately looked for him in the stands…and the huge smile that had broken across her face when she realized he'd been there to see it.

And he also thought about all the milestones he'd missed, either because he was overseas or on a training mission somewhere.

His career had cost him a lot. He couldn't handle it if it cost him Autumn, too. Nothing was worth his baby girl's life, and he felt sick that his job had been responsible for this nightmare.

The RV stopped at a pullout on the side of the winding road, the tinted windows giving passersby no clue of what was actually going on inside. Support agents were waiting a few miles back in their vehicles, ready to arrive on scene once the HRT and FAST Bravo had secured the target location.

While the minutes ticked by, Reid was forced to sit there and do nothing as the hive of activity carried on around him. But when Taggart looked over at him and jerked his head in a silent order to come over, Reid was off his seat and beside his commander in the space of a single heartbeat.

"How you doing?" Taggart asked, scrutinizing him.

Reid already had his game face on. "Fine."

His commander's expression softened a fraction. "I know this is hard on you. Being stuck here instead of with the boys at a time like this."

"It's okay. I get it." And Taggart was a father too, so he understood on some level what Reid was going through.

Those pale aquamarine eyes focused on his. "We're going."

Reid expelled the breath he hadn't realized he'd been holding. *Thank God.* "When?"

"Two minutes." He handed Reid a headset. "You can listen in and watch as long as you stay out of everyone's way."

Reid snatched it and put it on without a word, his pulse accelerating. Taggart turned away and faced the wall of monitors set up on the inside of the RV, a group of analysts seated before their stations in front of him.

Commander DeLuca walked over from the front of the unit, the brim of his San Diego Chargers cap pulled low over his forehead. "You boys ready to do this?" He looked from Taggart to Reid and back, green eyes sharp.

"Yup," Taggart said. "Let's pull the trigger."

Reid glued his gaze to the monitors as both commanders issued the green light. It was weird to hear Hamilton's voice responding on the other end of the headset, weirder still to not be with his teammates on this critical of an op, but being able to monitor everything live from here was a thousand times better than having to sit back and wait for word at HQ in Virginia.

Within minutes both Blackhawks were in the air, Tess at the controls of one of them. The helos raced over the mountains turned brilliant green with their spring foliage, carrying the teams toward the target house and the unsuspecting narco terrorists hiding there.

If Autumn was there, she would be back in his arms within an hour or two.

Chapter Sixteen

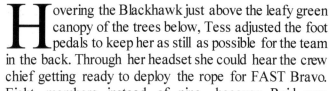

Hovering the Blackhawk just above the leafy green canopy of the trees below, Tess adjusted the foot pedals to keep her as still as possible for the team in the back. Through her headset she could hear the crew chief getting ready to deploy the rope for FAST Bravo. Eight members instead of nine, because Reid was somewhere still on the ground in the mobile command unit.

She watched out her cockpit window and down through the chin bubble, catching sight of the heavy braided rope as it snaked toward the forest floor. She kept the hover steady while each member slid to the ground.

"Team's on the ground and rope's secure," her crew chief reported a minute later.

"Copy that." She toggled the switch on her headset to speak to command. "Package delivered. Chalk two leaving DZ."

"Copy, Chalk two. Withdraw to assigned coordinates to await extraction."

"Roger." With one last glance at the team of men

fanned out beneath her aircraft, Tess eased the cyclic forward, nosing her bird forward as she pulled collective and began to climb.

"Ground team's taking fire, captain," her crew chief said as they hit five hundred feet.

Tess automatically looked out her window, trying to see them. A streak flashed by in her peripheral vision.

"RPG!" the crew chief yelled.

She didn't even have time to react. Another streak flashed by, and then a loud thump sounded over the noise of the rotors. The helo lurched.

Tess's gaze flew to the instrument panel.

"I've got a caution light," her copilot said beside her.

"Yeah, I see that," she muttered, pumping the pedals, but it was no use. Her pulse tripped. "Pedals are stiffened up." Shit, it had cut hydraulics to the tail rotor. "I've lost tail rotor authority."

The helo swung hard to the right, but there was nothing she could do to counteract the sudden yaw except pull collective and increase the angle of attack of the main rotor. Trying to pull them higher and buy them another minute.

But they were flying on borrowed time.

"We're going down." She anxiously scanned the terrain below for a possible place to put down. Up ahead she spotted what looked like an old logging road through a gap in the trees. It would have to do; she didn't have time to try and find a different option.

Tess's mind raced with all the emergency procedures she'd learned, fighting her body's natural reaction to the crisis as she focused on getting them down on that road. "Everybody brace," she commanded the crew, dropping the Blackhawk lower. The road was narrow, and coming up fast. She only had one shot at this.

They were still turning to the right, and going too fast. She had to slow them down enough to do a run-on landing on that road if they were going to have any chance of walking away from this. "I'm gonna drive it in," she said to the copilot, all her concentration on hitting that road. *And then hope we don't die.* "As soon as we stop, you pull the fire levers."

"I'm on it."

Tess eased the cyclic back to slow them, her eyes fixed on the rapidly approaching strip of dirt that would serve as their runway. The helo's nose came up but without the tail rotor to keep them straight, they were still moving to the right.

Dammit. She had to time this just right and land nose-first, otherwise they'd flip over and over and crush everybody on board.

Her muscles tensed, her body bracing for impact as the nose swung around to face forward once more. The narrow strip of road loomed nearer, rushing at them as she cleared the trees.

Now!

She drove them down hard into the ground. The wheels hit with such force it snapped them forward in their harnesses. Tess grunted and reached for the power levers as they shot off the ground for a second, then bounced again.

She buried the cyclic, but the trees ahead of them were coming up too fast. The Blackhawk skidded across the dirt surface, somehow staying right-side up. She half-turned in her seat as they screamed toward the far tree line, instinctively angling her body in an instinctive attempt to steer them, but it was no use.

The tip of the main rotor then the nose smashed into the trees with a bone-rattling thud. Glass and metal crunched around her.

Tess's four-point harness jerked taut over her shoulders. Her right collarbone snapped. She swallowed a scream, a thin cry escaping her as needles of agony shot out from her right shoulder.

Through the haze of pain, she was dimly aware of the main rotor slashing through the tree trunks, getting chewed to hell, bits of metal and debris flying through the cockpit. Something stung her left cheek like an angry hornet. She gasped, fighting for breath, her left hand still on the collective, her right arm hanging at her side.

Beside her, the copilot quickly pulled the fire levers, arming the onboard fire extinguishers and instantly shutting down the twin turbine engines.

Tess fought to clear her head, struggling to breathe through the pain. Smoke filled the cockpit, the acrid stench of hot oil heavy in the air. The windscreen and chin bubble were destroyed, the front end of the aircraft distorted around the tree trunks they'd slammed into.

Get out.

"Everyone out," she commanded through gritted teeth. She couldn't move her right arm. Her copilot seemed okay, but she wasn't sure about the guys in the back.

"Tess, you hurt?" the copilot asked.

"My collarbone," she gasped out, fumbling with her left hand to hit the single button quick release on her harness.

She hadn't realized how much of an angle the cockpit was bent forward until the harness released. Her body fell forward in the seat, and she threw out her left arm to keep from smashing into the control panel, the sudden movement wrenching another cry from her as white-hot needles ripped through her right shoulder.

The copilot leaned over her. "I've got you." Strong hands gripped her under the arms. Her pain-filled scream echoed through the ruined cockpit as he hauled her up and muscled her between the seats and into the back.

Agony engulfed her, stealing her breath, rendering her immobile. Someone else grabbed her around the waist. She forced her eyes open, stared up at her crew chief through the fog of pain.

"Got you, Tess," he said, quickly moving backward as they carried her together out the left side cabin door. Shredded trees covered the ground like sawdust, branches and bits of the chewed-up rotor blades strewn all over.

"The crew," she forced out, trying to counteract the pain and shock. She was pilot commander. She had to clear her head, look out for her crew.

"All accounted for. Banged up, one's got a leg injury, but not as bad off as you," the chief said.

She sagged in relief at the news, closed her eyes and clenched her teeth as every step they took jarred her injured shoulder.

They carried her a safe distance away from the ruined aircraft and set her down, leaning her back against a tree trunk. Her left cheek stung like hell, but it was nothing compared to the pain in her shoulder. She grabbed hold of her right upper arm, cradling it to her side to relieve the pressure on her broken bone.

The sharp, staccato beat of gunfire echoed in the distance, probably from near the target house. Tess's eyes snapped open, scanning through the trees for any sign of a threat. One or both teams must have engaged the enemy. Her copilot immediately got on the radio to contact command and let them know everyone had survived.

"Here. I'm gonna try and stop the bleeding," her crew chief said, putting a gauze pad to her left cheek and pressing hard.

She was shaking, sucking in choppy breaths while her heart raced, pins and needles in her hands and feet. Breathing way too fast. *Slow it down, Tess. Get control.*

"Where else hurts?"

"R-right collarbone," she forced out. "Can't m-move my arm."

He used an elastic bandage as a makeshift sling around her right arm and bound it to her body, then wrapped a thin thermal blanket around her. "Eat this," he said, pressing something to her lips.

Before she could protest or ask what it was, she smelled chocolate and obediently chewed it up, willing the sugar to counteract the shock a little. "Where the hell did that RPG come from?" she said after she swallowed, the pain a bit more bearable now that her arm was secured.

"Barely saw it before it hit," the crew chief said.

Shit, that had been close.

Her copilot was on the radio to someone back at command. He stopped in mid-sentence, his gaze swinging in the direction of the firefight. "Roger that." He set the radio down, his expression urgent as he faced Tess and the others. "Command says a handful of Ruiz's men are moving in our direction, and they're coming fast."

****

Reid stood frozen behind Taggart, his gaze glued in horror to the monitor in front of him, trying to process what he'd just seen.

He'd just watched Tess's aircraft fucking crash into the trees. The helo's wreckage was hidden from view by the thick canopy obscuring the satellite, and now both FAST Bravo and the HRT were engaged with the enemy force at the target property. The other Blackhawk was nearby, but there was no room for the crew to land to attempt a rescue.

Taggart put his hand over the bottom of the phone and half-turned to Reid. "They're all alive, but Dubrovski and one of the crew are hurt."

God, not Tess. Before Reid could ask how badly, Taggart resumed his conversation.

Then Reid's attention caught on a sat feed showing four men coming in and out of view through the trees, heading in the direction of the crash site. They were armed, and dressed in civvies rather than uniforms.

Ruiz's men.

Fear shot through Reid, but Taggart had already seen it. He alerted the person on the other end to the threat and told him to stand by. Then he called out in a loud voice so everyone in the RV could hear him. "I need volunteers to get in there and rescue the crew."

"I'll go," Reid said automatically, already turning for the door. There was nothing he could do for Autumn at the moment, but he sure as shit could get in there and protect Tess.

Taggart grabbed his upper arm to stop him, his pale aqua gaze intense. "I'm putting you in charge. Pick four agents and gear up, then get out there before Ruiz's men do."

Reid leapt into action. He rounded up four special agents providing perimeter security and found a ballistic vest, helmet and weapons. They didn't have much time, so after a brief rundown of the situation and a look at the map, they jumped in an agency SUV and roared off to a spot up the road that put them as close as they could get to the crash site.

He hopped out of the vehicle and took point as they entered the forest that stood between them and the downed helo crew, on alert for Ruiz's men. Seventy yards in, the distant crack of sporadic gunfire filtered through the trees.

"We've lost visual on you," Taggart's voice said in Reid's earpiece. "Be advised, enemy force is a hundred-twenty-yards east of crash site, and closing."

Reid moved faster. "Copy." The race was on to reach the crew before Ruiz's men did.

The dense trees and heavy underbrush made it impossible to maintain a straight path as he led them deeper into the woods, using a compass to keep his bearings. About a half mile in, the smell of oil-laden smoke reached them. Looking up, Reid spotted a plume of dark gray overhead, trailing west from the downed helo. An arrow pointing right to them, for both rescuer and foe.

They pushed faster, hurrying through the woods as the sound of the distant gunfire grew louder. Reid shifted his grip on his rifle, all his senses on alert as they neared the far side of the forested area. Pausing just inside the screen of trees that bordered the old logging road to look around, he spotted the smoking helo about fifty yards to the left, then swung his gaze right.

The moment he saw Tess conscious, propped against a tree and wrapped in the silver thermal blanket, his heart rate slowed and he pulled in a deep breath. They'd made it in time.

"Chalk two, we're moving toward you from your ten o'clock," he told the crewmember monitoring the radio frequency.

"We copy."

Reid signaled the others behind him to move forward, and emerged from the trees.

The crewmember hunched down beside Tess said something to her. She twisted her head around to look, her honey-blond hair fallen out of its normally neat bun and tangled around her face and shoulders. Blood smeared the lower half of her left cheek. When their gazes connected, the sheer relief on her pain-pinched face made his chest tighten.

Directing three of his men to maintain a perimeter, he and the fifth man started toward the crew. Reid hurried to Tess and crouched down beside her while the other man went to check out the other injured crewmember.

He set a hand on the uninjured side of her face, bringing her gaze to his. "Hey, sweetheart." He didn't care if it gave his feelings for her away to the others. He was just so damn glad she was alive after that harrowing crash. "Where are you hurt?"

She peered up at him with pain-glazed eyes. Her pupils were evenly dilated though. "Right collarbone," she muttered, grimacing as she shifted.

She was beyond pale, her skin having an almost grayish tinge. He was worried about internal injuries as well. He slid his fingers around her wrist, pressing the pads of his index and middle finger gently against her radial artery. Her pulse was rapid, but strong.

"I put a sling around it as best I could," her crewmember said to Reid.

Reid kept his gaze on Tess and released her left wrist to gently palpate her ribs and abdomen. She didn't even flinch. "Let me see that cut." He gently angled it toward him so he could see it better. Head and facial wounds bled like a mother. Something had sliced her skin open about an inch below her cheekbone, a couple inches long, but it didn't look too deep. "Can I take a look at your shoulder?"

She nodded, lips pressed together in a tight line that told him she was in a shitload of pain. As carefully as he could, he peeled the thermal blanket away from her upper body. They hadn't removed or cut the top half of her flight suit, and her right arm was bound across her chest.

Straddling her thighs, he balanced on the balls of his feet and pulled the collar of her flight suit aside. One look told him the clavicle was broken. Badly. A large lump lay beneath her skin at the edge of her shoulder, the amount of swelling and the bluish-purple color dead giveaways.

"Can you feel your right hand and fingers?" he asked.

She gave him a tight nod, her breaths choppy.

Good. "Anywhere else hurt?"

"No." She winced again and stilled, sucking in a sharp breath.

He was betting she was beat up in other places, but the amount of pain from her busted collarbone was masking everything else. But he was confident she didn't have any internal injuries. "Listen, we've got to move all of you out of here now. A few of Ruiz's men are headed this way."

Those pretty eyes focused on him and she nodded. "Okay."

Reid leaned down a bit to wrap an arm around her waist, careful to steer clear of her right shoulder. "Can you stand?" A glance to the right confirmed that the agents Reid had brought were standing guard while the crewmembers helped their injured comrade up onto his good leg.

"Yeah." She slipped her left arm around his waist, got to one knee and then pushed to her feet, hissing air between her teeth, eyes squeezed shut tightly.

He hated like hell to see her hurting but there was nothing he could do for it right now except get her to safety. "There you go," he said, shifting his grip on her. "You gonna be able to walk out of here?" They had to follow the same route he and the others had just taken. He'd carry her if necessary, but it would hurt her a hell of a lot more.

Her eyes opened and she gave a terse nod. He didn't blame her for not wanting to answer verbally when she was in that kind of pain.

"Okay then." He glanced at the others. "Let's get moving." He placed one of the agents out front, then moved in third in line with Tess and left the others to bring up the rear.

"How close are they?" Tess managed between breaths as they started through the woods. Every step would jar her shoulder, sending a fresh wave of pain through the broken bone. Reid would have spared her if he could have, but their safety dictated they move fast.

"Close enough that we can't stop. So if this gets to be too much for you, let me know and I'll carry you." He contacted Taggart using the two-way radio. "Crew's secured. We're heading back to the vehicle."

"Copy. Still no visual on you, or the tangos."

"Understood." He squeezed Tess's waist. "Let's get outta here."

She didn't answer, just tightened her grip around him and doggedly kept moving forward. It was quiet now, the distant gunfire silent.

Too quiet.

Fifty paces into the trees, a tingling in his gut had him tensing. He stopped and looked to the right, scanning the heavy underbrush. The others stopped too, followed his gaze.

A gunshot rang out through the trees, shattering the stillness. Bark flew off a tree trunk not eight feet from where Reid stood.

"Down," he snapped at Tess, pushing her to the ground and grabbing his rifle, ignoring her cry of pain. He stepped in front of her prone body and dropped to one knee, trying to get a bead on the shooter, or at least which direction the shot had come from.

A second shot pierced the air, hitting the foliage above him.

Then Reid spotted him. Screened by the leafy branches and undergrowth, half-hidden behind a tree trunk. "Four o'clock, thirty yards," he said to the others.

He didn't have to look back to know the agents were getting into firing position, all his focus on the threat in front of him. Reid searched for his target. Was this the asshole who'd taken Autumn? His finger was steady on the trigger guard, just waiting for the guy to give him an opening. Enough to bury a bullet in him.

"Give me your sidearm," Tess grated out behind him.

Keeping his eyes trained on the area where the shot had come from, Reid quickly slid his pistol from the holster on his thigh and passed it back to her.

"Prentiss."

The sound of Hamilton's voice in his earpiece startled

him. "Yeah, here," he said, sighting down the barrel of his rifle.

"What's your position?"

"Sixty yards northwest of the crash site, in the trees," he murmured, still watching for an opening. "We're taking fire."

"We can hear it. House is cleared, HRT's searching it, so we're headed your way."

Please let Autumn be there. "Music to my ears," he answered, his entire body coiled, ready as he scanned the trees.

Bring it, assholes.

A deep, pulsing rage built inside him, speeding up his breaths. He would take out every last one of these motherfuckers singlehandedly for what they'd put his baby girl through.

"Hang tight, we're coming to you."

"Copy."

"Eleven o'clock," Tess cried behind him.

Reid's gaze shot to the place she'd indicated, and he caught a flash of movement through the trees. The hair on the back of his neck stood up as he realized what it meant. The bastards were trying to surround them.

He used hand signals and quiet commands to alert the others, and locked on the target area, watching for more movement, poised to fire.

Three shots cracked through the air in rapid succession. The bullets hit a tree not ten feet from where Reid crouched.

But the shooter had just given away his position. Reid honed in on it, waited a heartbeat, and the moment he saw movement, squeezed the trigger.

A strangled yell mixed with the rifle's report. Then the rest of the enemy opened up.

Rounds peppered their position, shredding leaves and branches around them, above them. Reid cursed and spun around to dive on top of Tess, but she'd already flattened herself on the ground, making as small a target as possible, her expression strained, eyes locked on the distant trees as she aimed the pistol with her left hand.

Her bravery in the face of danger while badly injured touched him on the deepest level.

Reid dove to the ground in front of her, shielding her with his body while he settled the butt of his weapon against his shoulder and took aim. Several of his team began returning fire. A round hit the ground so close to him he heard its whine. Dirt sprayed into his face. He blinked it from his eyes and searched for a target, fired the second he locked on something moving in the underbrush.

A hidden enemy fired from the right. The rounds sprayed torn-up leaves and earth a yard from where Tess lay stretched out on her belly. She flinched and flattened her cheek against the ground, covering her head with her good arm.

Fuck. Reid swung his body around, putting himself between her and the new shooter to return fire, not even bothering to wait for a target.

Shots cracked from behind them.

One of Reid's men cried out and fell, clutching his side.

Shit, they've surrounded us.

Reid swung the barrel of his rifle around to face the new threat and fired, hoping to make the shooter take cover. But how many were there? He and the others couldn't stay here pinned down and be picked off one by one, it was suicidal.

He rolled to his side, was just reaching out to grab Tess by the back of the flight suit to haul her to her feet so they could make a run for it through the woods. Suddenly measured semi-auto fire sounded to Reid's left. He recognized the sound of the M4s immediately.

Cavalry's here.

The shooter now in front of Reid made a break for it. Reid tracked him, firing just as the man emerged between two trees. He fell and disappeared from view. Reid waited a few heartbeats, searching for another target.

Hamilton's voice sounded in his ear. "Five tangos down. Moving to you from the southeast."

"Hold your fire," Reid commanded everyone. "Friendlies incoming from our southeast."

Moments later, familiar figures appeared through the thick screen of leafy branches. Reid expelled a deep breath as Freeman's dark face appeared in a gap between the trees. The point man stepped out into the open, Hamilton and the other six members of FAST Bravo right behind him. Reid pushed to his feet, still on alert.

Hamilton strode past Freeman, headed straight for him as two agents began treating the wounded one. "Any other tangos?" Hamilton asked, his gaze moving back and forth as he stared into the surrounding underbrush.

"Not sure. We hit a few, but I can't tell how many there were in total. They'd surrounded us."

Hamilton's steel-gray gaze scanned the trees for a moment, then he waved the rest of the team forward. "Let's get the injured to the vehicles."

Reid grabbed his arm. "Wait. What's going on at the target house? Did they find Autumn?"

"Not yet."

Reid bit back a sigh of disappointment and frustration.

Hamilton clapped him on the shoulder once. "HRT's still searching the place. As soon as we're sure you guys are in the clear, we'll head back and do our own sweep. If we find her, I'll contact you personally."

Reid clenched his jaw and nodded once.

"Ambulances are already waiting where you left the SUV," Hamilton said to Reid.

"Good." He stepped over to help Tess up, who had managed to push to her knees by herself. She was pale, her face glistening with sweat, still holding his pistol. When Reid took her left wrist, it was ice cold. *Shock.* God, she'd been through so damn much today.

He pulled her into a gentle hug, careful of her right arm. "Okay, sweetheart. Let's get you the hell out of here." He grasped her left wrist.

"Autumn," she said, her fingers trembling slightly in his. "Is she there?"

"Don't know." It was tearing him apart to not be in there searching for her right now. But there was no way he was leaving Tess to make the remainder of this hike alone in her condition. "Let's get moving, huh?"

Tess managed a nod and leaned into him while he steadied her with an arm around her waist.

"Not too far now," he told her, shortening his strides so she could keep up, watching the underbrush for any further sign of a threat. "Almost there."

With his teammates surrounding them and providing added protection, he relaxed his guard a little. His mind shifted back to Autumn. Was she at the target house? Had someone tried to whisk her away when the assault had begun?

Tess didn't say anything as they walked at a fast clip, her mouth compressed into a grim line and his pistol still in her left hand. Reid led her through the forest, retracing the path they'd taken on the way in.

Finally, they reached the edge of the road where they'd parked the SUV. Three ambulance crews were waiting for them.

Reid ushered Tess to the closest ambulance and sat her down on the rear of the deck. She closed her eyes, swallowed and sucked in a deep breath, looking as though she was fighting the urge to puke.

"Okay, brother, we're outta here," Hamilton said from behind him.

Reid straightened and turned to face his team leader, a

sudden lump clogging his throat. He closed the distance between them in three strides and grabbed Hamilton's wrist, hard. "You go find my daughter," he rasped out, desperation making his heart pound.

Hamilton's face hardened, his eyes turning to pure steel. "If she's there, we'll get her out and bring her to you. I give you my word." He gripped Reid's forearm, squeezed tight. An unspoken vow to back up the words.

It would have to do.

Keyed up and powerless to charge to his daughter's rescue, Reid stood there dragging in deep, unsteady lungfuls of air as his teammates were swallowed up by the dense trees. Go get her, guys. *I can't lose her. I just can't.*

Only when he was sure he had control over himself did he turn back around to face Tess. The paramedics were trying to get her to lie down on a stretcher inside the ambulance.

Hopping up into the back, Reid approached her and forced a reassuring smile. "You won't be needing this anymore," he said, gently easing the pistol from her grip before winding his fingers through hers.

This woman had dropped everything and come running when he'd needed her most, then put herself in harm's way to help find Autumn. For those things, she would always have his undying gratitude. Along with his cynical, banged-up heart.

"You're one tough cookie, Agent Dubrovski," he told her.

"I don't feel very tough at the moment," she muttered through clenched teeth as the paramedic began probing at the fracture site. Her fingers tightened around Reid's and she looked up into his eyes. "Any word on Autumn?"

It touched him that she was still thinking about his daughter even after everything she'd just gone through. "No."

She squeezed his hand, giving him strength. "Go to the

house."

"No, I can't leave y—"

"Reid. *Go*." She flinched when the male paramedic shifted her right arm. "You need to be there. Go."

The naked emotion in her voice made his heart pound. "Thank you," he whispered, bending to brush a swift kiss across her lips. He took a backward step toward the open doors, holding her gaze. "I'll come see you as soon as I can."

Tess gave him a brave smile in answer. "Just go get her and give her a hug from me."

"That's a promise, darlin'." Reid jumped down from the ambulance and ran to catch up with his teammates.

Chapter Seventeen

Tess came to slowly, blinking heavy eyelids as consciousness returned. She squinted against the bright light overhead, made out the curtains surrounding her bed and the quiet beeping of a machine nearby. Bits and pieces of the time between Reid leaving and the ambulance bringing her here returned.

They'd drugged her on the way and she only vaguely remembered lying on the operating room table staring up at the bright overhead lights and breathing through the mask placed over her nose and mouth a few seconds before she'd gone under.

Angling her chin, she tugged aside the neckline of her hospital gown with her left hand. A sterile bandage covered her right shoulder, and they'd bound her arm to her chest. The pain wasn't too bad, way less than before the surgery, more like a bad toothache that pulsed with every beat of her heart.

The slice on her face throbbed a little too and her mouth and tongue were dry. She ran it over her teeth, aware of the rawness in the back of her throat from where they'd intubated her. Damn, it was hard to believe she'd survived being shot down a few hours ago.

The curtain around her bed swept aside to reveal a middle-aged nurse in cotton candy pink scrubs. She smiled at Tess. "Agent Dubrovski. How are you feeling?"

"Tess," she corrected. "Thirsty. And groggy."

"I would imagine so," she said, efficiently checking Tess's vitals. "I can give you some ice chips, but no water just yet."

"What time is it?"

"Just after six. A.M.," she added.

"How did the surgery go?"

"It was perfect. Your clavicle is all pinned back together again. You'll have a nice bump there to remind you of today for the rest of your life, but after six to eight weeks you should be almost back to normal."

Six to eight weeks seemed like a damn long time before she could use her right arm properly again.

"Agent Prentiss is waiting to see you, if you're up to it."

Her heart leapt. "Reid's here?"

The nurse's lips twitched in a quick smile. "Been waiting out in the hallway for over an hour now. I told him I'd ask you before letting him in here."

"Sure, he can come in." Had they found Autumn? Nailed Ruiz? She looked around for the remote to raise the head of the bed.

The nurse helped her and handed her a glass of ice chips. "Try a couple and see how they settle before you eat too many," she warned with the shake of a finger. "If they stay down, we'll go from there."

Tess didn't argue, already crunching on the ice chips. The nurse left the room, and a minute later Reid walked in. Her chest squeezed tight at the sight of him there in his tactical uniform, tall and strong. He gave her a tired smile and strode toward her.

"How you feeling?" he asked, taking her left hand.

"Did you find her?" she blurted, unable to stand it.

His expression froze, and she caught the desolation in his eyes. For one instant, her heart seemed to stop beating, an icy wave sweeping through her. "She wasn't there," he said.

Tess searched his eyes, her heart beating once more, but she needed clarification. "Ever?"

He shook his head. "They don't think so." He glanced around to make sure no one else could overhear them before continuing. "There were adult female hostages inside. Kept in cages."

Tess winced and shook her head. Goddamn animals all deserved to be gut shot. And they'd taken Autumn. Distress flowed through her, making her pulse pound.

Reid rubbed his thumb over the back of her hand. "None of them had seen a little girl."

That was both good and bad. "And Ruiz?"

His deep blue eyes hardened into glacial chips of ice. "He was never there either."

She frowned. "But all the intel said he…" She trailed off, since her words would just make the situation worse. Reid was dealing with too much already.

He blew out a harsh breath. "Yeah. I know." Another tired smile, the shadows beneath his eyes dark as bruises. "But at least you're safe and sound and on the mend now."

She swallowed, dropped her gaze to their joined hands. "Thank you. For coming in to get me."

"Are you kidding me, Tess?" he said, sounding offended. "You think I wouldn't come for you at a time like that?"

She squirmed inside. "I just meant that I realize you could have stayed behind to wait for word on Autumn." She lifted her eyes to his. "But I'm really glad you didn't."

He gave her a hard look. "I'd do it all over again in a heartbeat if it meant protecting you."

Why did that make her all teary? She blinked and dropped her attention back to their joined hands.

His strong fingers stayed locked around hers. "The doc said everything went well. If everything looks good they're discharging you today, and your boss said the agency is flying you back to D.C. with your crew soon after that."

She looked at him. "What about you?"

"I'll stay down here with the guys. The analysts are chasing down other leads on Autumn and Ruiz. If they were in the area, we may get another tip that pans out next time."

"That makes sense." She blew out a breath. "I just hate not being here with you for the rest of this."

Reid leaned forward and kissed her forehead. "I know, sweetheart. But even when you leave, you'll still be with me here." Raising her left hand, he unfolded her fingers and pressed her palm against the center of his chest.

And right then and there, Tess lost the last remaining pieces of her heart to him.

****

Reid stayed with Tess while they transferred her to a room on the surgical floor, and waited until she was fast asleep before leaving her around two in the afternoon. He took a cab back to the hotel where the taskforce was meeting, exhausted, his heart heavy. Would this nightmare ever end?

Maka and Khan were standing in the lobby when he walked in.

"How's Tess?" Khan asked, his expression concerned.

"Resting. Surgery went well, and they think she'll have normal function of her arm after she heals up."

"That's good news."

He nodded. The only good news he'd had in days.

"Anything new come in while I was gone?"

Maka shook his head. "Sorry, brother. Nothing."

The frustration and adrenaline had long since drained away now, replaced by a slow sinking sensation in the pit of his stomach. Every hour that passed without a tip on Autumn reduced the chance that she'd be found alive. He wasn't ready to allow himself to think that she might be dead already, but it was there at the back of his mind, held at bay only by sheer will.

Khan eyed him. "When's the last time you ate something?"

"I dunno." He honestly couldn't remember, or tell anymore whether the grinding pain in his stomach was due to hunger or despair.

"Come on." Khan grabbed his arm and towed him into a conference room off the lobby. The rest of FAST Bravo was there with the HRT guys, gathered around the table laden with sandwich platters and other snacks. One of the HRT sniper teams must have been called in to assist as well, because Colebrook was talking with his brother Brody on the far side of the room.

"Eat," Khan commanded, giving him a little shove toward the table.

Reid grimaced. The thought of food right now wasn't appetizing in the least but his body needed the fuel, so he reached for a turkey sandwich and started chewing, the bread and meat sticking to the roof of his mouth.

While he ate, the guys asked him about Tess, then they filled him in on more details about the op. They turned his already touchy stomach.

"How many women were there?" he asked after he forced the last bite of his second sandwich down his throat.

"Nine. All in the basement, all in cages," Granger answered, his expression full of buried rage as he polished off an iced tea.

"Assholes treated them worse than stray dogs," Lockhart added with a shake of his head. He was the quietest one of the whole team, so him offering the comment was testimony of just how upset he was about it. "Made me sick, to see them like that."

Reid understood that completely. Victoria Gomez had been chained to the floor by a collar around her neck. He'd seen the marks on her. Welts from whatever they'd hit her with, and little round burn marks probably made by cigarettes. Were they doing that to Autumn too? She was only nine, but that didn't mean shit to savage animals like Ruiz and his men. He was terrified they'd abused her, sexually as well as physically.

The sandwich congealed in his belly, threatened to come right back up again. He swallowed hard.

A sharp whistle rent the air.

Reid swung around to find Taggart standing in the conference room doorway and HRT Commander DeLuca striding to the rear of the room. "Listen up, boys," Taggart called out.

Silence descended as all eyes swung to DeLuca in his trademark San Diego Chargers ball cap. "Just received a tip on Ruiz saying he got spooked and took off for Florida. We think one of his men alerted him during our assault. Word is he's trying to arrange a flight out of the country. We need to find him before that happens. We're monitoring our channels to see if we can pinpoint a certain area, but if the cartel is helping him that's gonna make it hard for us to get a lock on him unless we get another tip or some insider help."

"God dammit," Reid muttered, shoving a hand through his hair. Was Autumn with Ruiz? Was she even in North Carolina? Where the hell *was* she?

Across from Reid, Colebrook's phone chirped. He grabbed it, showed it to his brother, their heads together as they started talking, their expressions intent. Then

Brody Colebrook pulled out his own phone, checked it, and nodded as his brother put up a hand. "Commander, could we talk to for you a sec?"

DeLuca raised his eyebrows, appearing as surprised by the interruption as everyone else. "What's that?"

"Check your phone. I think we might have a possible solution to our problem."

We? Who did he mean by "we"?

A charged silence followed as DeLuca checked his phone. What, had they all gotten the same message from someone?

DeLuca frowned, then his head jerked up and he locked gazes with Colebrook. After a tense second, he swung his gaze to Taggart and beckoned him forward. "Commander."

Reid had no idea what the hell was going on, but it was annoying as hell to be left in the dark. A low buzz of conversation filled the room as the Colebrook brothers and both commanders met over in the corner.

"Any idea what they're talking about?" Reid asked the teammates standing near him.

"Nope," Rodriguez said. "But it must be good, and DeLuca, Brody and Easton all seem to be on the same page."

God, this was driving Reid insane. What the hell was going on? He battled his impatience as the four men talked, and Taggart's fascinated expression as he listened to the others made him curious as hell.

An analyst rushed into the room and went directly to speak with the two commanders. She handed DeLuca a slip of paper and rushed out again. DeLuca read it and nodded, his expression tightening.

Brody Colebrook said something to him. DeLuca took off his Chargers cap and ran his hand over his head in clear agitation before putting it back. Whatever they were discussing, he didn't look happy about it. DeLuca said something back to Brody, who answered, and then all four men swung their attention to Reid.

Every muscle in his body tensed.

Autumn. They knew something about her.

Without even being conscious of moving, Reid was pushing his way through the wall of bodies to get to the four men in the far corner. "What?" he demanded when he got close, not giving a rat's ass about chain of command or protocol or any other bullshit. "Is it about Autumn?"

Whatever it was, he needed to know. He aimed a hard look at his commander. Fuck this, he wasn't going to be kept in the dark if they knew something, and didn't want them withholding intel in an effort to spare him.

His heart clattered against his ribs as he waited for a response.

Taggart's gaze cut to DeLuca, then focused back on Reid. "I don't want to get your hopes up in case we're wrong."

The pressure around his ribs eased slightly. "Just tell me. I'm dying here."

"We think she's still alive."

All the air rushed out of his lungs and he slumped forward. Easton grabbed him around the ribs, as though afraid Reid would keel over.

Over the rush of blood in his ears Reid was aware of the stark, brittle silence in the room, of all the eyes on him as everyone stared. "How do you know?" he forced out, his throat tight.

"The tip we just got says she is," DeLuca said. "Seems like a credible source. We're trying to find out who sent it, but whoever it was, they're an insider."

"What else did the source say?" He wanted proof. A location.

"No location for your daughter, but the person said they'd be in touch with more details soon, including proof of life."

The backs of his eyes burned and he had to blink a couple times as he dragged in a ragged breath. His baby was still alive and he was going to find her. Bring her home.

Then DeLuca's eyes shifted to Taggart.

"And?" Reid prompted. There was something more they weren't telling him.

Taggart's pale turquoise gaze was steady on his. "We don't know whether it's authentic or not, but if it is… Someone in the *Veneno* cartel just offered up Ruiz to a contact of ours on a silver platter."

Reid frowned. That made no sense. Except that the cartel world was as fucked up and cutthroat as they came, so he was just glad for the tip. "What are you planning to do?"

"If we do this, we've got five hours at most. Not enough time to get us all down there and stage a full-scale op. So we'd have to go with a plan B that involves a single agent and a…" He glanced at the Colebrooks before continuing. "Certain source we're thinking of bringing in. For an off-the-books stab at Ruiz," DeLuca said.

"A private contractor?" Reid asked.

"More like a consultant," DeLuca said, sharing another loaded look with the Colebrook brothers. Reid glanced at his teammate, Easton, who didn't say anything. What the hell? Why weren't they letting him in on the details?

Impatience pulsed through him. "Whatever it is, whoever it is, I want in." They needed an agent; he was it. And he wouldn't take no for an answer.

Taggart folded his arms across his chest and stared at him. "You sure about that? You don't even know what we're thinking about yet."

"Hundred percent." If it meant getting his daughter back, he'd do fucking anything. Including giving his own life.

His commander nodded once, not seeming the least bit surprised, then turned to DeLuca, the hint of a grim smile Reid recognized all too well on his face. It meant serious shit was about to go down. The kind that resulted in captured or dead tangos.

And a recovered little girl.

"And there's your answer, DeLuca," Taggart said. "Make the call."

Chapter Eighteen

Carlos undid the top button of his shirt as the hired car sped toward the private airstrip outside Orlando. The sun was low in the sky. In another hour it would sink below the horizon. He'd made good time getting down here, but he wasn't in the clear yet.

Even in the comfortable, air-conditioned interior, he was sweating, the humidity like a blanket of moisture on his skin. A cartel plane was waiting for him at the airstrip, the crew already aboard and ready to take off for Mexico the moment he boarded.

Not that he was happy about having to run back there with his tail between his legs, about to be hauled up on the carpet by his master like a fucking dog that had shit on the kitchen floor. That was mostly the cause of his inability to stop sweating.

El Escorpion had taken the unusual step of calling him to a face-to-face meeting at the leader's compound near the Mexican Riviera. Powerful and feared as Carlos was within the cartel world, even he didn't have the balls to disregard that summons.

Either the meeting was because of today's raid at the North Carolina compound, that bitch Victoria Gomez, or the little girl. Fucking women, they were nothing but trouble. At least he'd been able to offload the girl, giving him one less problem to worry about.

The driver turned onto the access road and the runway came into view as they cleared the trees. A sleek Learjet waited on the tarmac. Carlos's men were there standing by, their weapons concealed as they maintained security for him. Others would be hidden out of sight to keep watch and alert him to any potential threats.

Carlos didn't anticipate any. He'd kept a low profile during his stay in the States, and was glad he'd listened to his gut and not gone to see the little girl or inspect the new shipment of women in North Carolina.

Unfortunately, his men hadn't ended up killing any DEA or other federal agents during the assault today. But his point had been made.

He could get to them and the people they cared about whenever he chose. One more reason people would be too scared to cross him.

Now it was time to cut his losses, be smart, and retreat back to the safety of his home country where he could hide out of sight and gain protection from the locals. He'd have to kiss ass during the meeting with *El Escorpion*, but he would survive it.

When the car stopped, Antonio hopped out of the front and came around to open Carlos's door, one hand on the butt of the pistol holstered on his thigh, eyes hidden behind his sunglasses. "Everything's clear," he said to Carlos, scanning the area.

Carlos slid on his own shades before grabbing his small suitcase and stepping out onto the tarmac. A stiff breeze swept across the airstrip, tugging at his linen suit and bringing a blessed measure of relief from the humidity he hated so much. He didn't know how people stood living in the South during spring and summer.

Without a word, he headed for the plane, Antonio following him. Two more of his men stood guard at the bottom of the stairs leading into the cabin. They nodded at him. "Everything's ready. Have a good flight, boss," one of them said.

Carlos ignored them and climbed into the spacious cabin, already feeling more relaxed. He was under the protection of the cartel now. The interior was the most luxurious money could buy, with plush, top-grain leather seats and polished oak trim.

Tossing his bag onto the aisle seat, he sank into the one next to the window with a satisfied sigh. As always, a crystal decanter and tumbler sat ready for him. He poured himself three fingers of whiskey and settled back into the seat as Antonio closed the cabin door and secured it.

Even with all his usual security measures in place, he kept an eye on what was happening outside his window as the pilots turned the aircraft and taxied to the end of the runway. His men all stood near the hangar doors now, and there were no other people or vehicles around.

The aircraft paused at the end of the runway for a moment, then the engines powered up. As they sped down the strip of asphalt, Carlos allowed his guard to drop completely. Leaning his head back against the plush leather seat, he sipped at his drink and allowed his mind to go blank. God, he needed some downtime.

A subtle upward tilt of the nose, and they were airborne. Seconds later the landing gear tucked away, and they soared skyward, leaving Florida below them. He let his mind drift, only partially aware of the banking turns of the aircraft. Soon they'd be over the Gulf and headed toward Mexico.

Before he landed, he needed to come up with what he would say to *El Escorpion* about recent events.

He was still going over some possible excuses and

defenses he'd come up with earlier when he became conscious of the wide, circling turn the aircraft was making. Opening his eyes, he looked out the window. They were nearly at cruising altitude now, the tufts of clouds beneath them like pillows of cotton candy.

Except the water was on the wrong side of the aircraft. And they were flying away from it rather than toward it.

What the *hell*?

Snapping his head around, Carlos looked between the seats. Antonio was sprawled out against the window, legs stretched out across the seats, arms folded across his chest and the brim of a ball cap pulled low over his eyes as he slept. "*Antonio*."

At the abrupt tone, his head enforcer's head snapped up and he shoved the hat off. "What?" he asked, startled.

"We're flying in the wrong goddamn direction. Go to the cockpit and find out what the hell's going on."

Face blank with surprise, Antonio shot out of his seat and hurried up the aisle while Carlos glared at his back. This was all he fucking needed, another goddamn headache. If he showed up late to the meeting, it would look like a deliberate show of disrespect. And people who disrespected *El Escorpion* tended to disappear without a trace.

Forever. Unless body parts started turning up in various waterways.

Antonio shut the cockpit door behind him. Carlos kept sipping at his drink, willing the mellow burn of the alcohol to quell the nerves in the pit of his stomach.

A loud thud sounded from the cockpit.

Carlos froze, his drink inches from his lips, eyes darting to the closed door at the end of the aisle.

Another thud, this one even louder.

Without looking away from that door he set the drink down, dread curling inside him, his heart rate accelerating. His muscles drew taut and he set his hands on the edge of the seat, ready to shove to his feet.

The cockpit door flew open.

Carlos jerked in surprise when a dark-haired man strode out, aiming a Glock dead center at Carlos's chest. Recognition splintered through him.

Special Agent Reid Prentiss.

The FAST agent stalked toward Carlos with measured strides, his expression so deadly it sent a chill racing up Carlos's spine. "Where's my daughter, asshole?"

REID STRUGGLED TO keep his rage in check as he aimed the pistol at Ruiz's center mass. From the moment he'd seen the bastard step out of that rented car earlier, he'd wanted to smash the fucker's face in.

Ruiz shot to his feet, expression set.

"*Where is she?*" Reid bellowed, stopping a stride away, the barrel of his weapon level with Ruiz's chest.

"Where are you taking me?" Ruiz said, not even bothering to ask about Antonio. His chief enforcer was either dead or incapacitated, of no help whatsoever to Carlos.

Reid had never wanted to put a bullet in someone so badly. "D.C., asshole. Where a team of federal agents is waiting to lock you up in the darkest hole they can find." Savage satisfaction ripped through him at the flash of fear in Ruiz's eyes. Every Mexican cartel member's worst nightmare was being extradited to the U.S. to face trial and imprisonment where the officials, judges and guards couldn't be paid off. No way out.

But rather than spill his guts, the bastard put on an oily smile Reid itched to wipe off his face. "My team of lawyers will have me out within a week. You've got no evidence against me."

No evidence?

Reid lunged forward and drove his fist into the fucker's smug face. Bone crunched. Pain flashed through

Reid's hand as Ruiz's head snapped back and he yelled, both hands flying to his busted nose.

Blood trickling out from beneath his hands, he glared up at Reid with utter loathing through watering eyes. "You'll fucking pay for that, *cabrón*."

Reid grabbed the front of Ruiz's shirt and yanked, twisting the fabric so it dug into the bastard's throat. "Where *is* she?" he bellowed, on the verge of out of control, lungs heaving, hands shaking. He would kill Ruiz if Autumn was dead. Kill him right here and now even if it meant rotting in jail the rest of his life. If she was gone he was dead anyway. At least killing Ruiz would avenge his little girl and give him a tiny amount of peace.

"Go fuck yourself," Ruiz snarled, lips peeled back over bloodstained teeth.

Reid's finger twitched on the trigger guard as they stared each other down in the tense silence, both of them breathing hard.

He almost pulled it. He *wanted* to pull it. Wanted it so bad he shook. But until he knew what had happened to Autumn, he couldn't kill Ruiz.

With effort, he pushed his rage down deep and shoved Ruiz. Ruiz slammed back against the seat with a grunt and quickly scrambled to face Reid, giving him a lethal glare.

"Maybe you'd rather talk to my associate instead." Instead of shooting him, Reid pulled his cell phone from his pocket.

Keeping his eyes on Ruiz, he pressed send on a text he'd had ready long before Ruiz's bodyguard had entered the cockpit—where he now lay trussed up like a Christmas turkey and tied to the copilot's seat, missing a few teeth and one eye swelling shut.

"What? Who are you calling?" Ruiz sneered up at him, the lower half of his face and the top of his shirt covered in blood.

Reid didn't answer, just stood there facing him down

with the Glock aimed at his chest.

Moments later the cockpit door opened. Ruiz's eyes shot to it, his face tense.

Reid's pulse beat faster as the booted footsteps thudded lightly on the carpet behind him. He watched Ruiz's face carefully, searching for signs of recognition—and terror. Anticipating the exact moment when he realized how truly fucked he was.

Triumph roared through his veins when Ruiz sucked in a breath and paled, his eyes growing wide. The blood drained from the fucker's face as he stared at the big, scary son of a bitch coming up behind Reid.

Ruiz's throat bobbed, a confused frown tugging at his eyebrows. "But you…you're supposed to be…"

"Dead? Yeah." The dark-haired ghost set his hands on the backs of the seats, caging Ruiz in as he leaned closer. "Boo."

CARLOS WAS FROZEN solid, unable to take his eyes off the dark-haired, dark-eyed man towering over him. It couldn't be, but…

The ghost shot Prentiss a sideways glance. "He not talking?"

Prentiss's dark blue eyes bored a hole straight through Carlos. "Nope."

Before Carlos knew what was happening, the second man raised his hand. Light flashed on the silver switchblade as the blade sprang free, a heartbeat before that lethally sharp blade came at him.

Carlos sucked in a breath and cowered away, but at the last moment the blade changed course. His lungs compressed as instead of carving into his skin, the blade sliced into the back of the leather seat in front of him and withdrew.

He stared at the oval shape slashed into the leather, and the irrefutable proof of who he was dealing with made the blood congeal in his veins.

El Santo.

Helpless to stop himself, he lifted his eyes to meet the bone-chilling gaze of Miguel Bautista. The deadliest and scariest motherfucking enforcer in the entire cartel world. Everyone had thought he'd died in a shootout with the FBI a couple years ago.

"You need to tell him where his daughter is," Bautista said, his quiet tone and the utter lack of emotion in his eyes making Carlos's bowels cramp. The stories of what *El Santo* had done to his victims with his blades were legendary. It was said they broke long before Bautista killed them, unable to stand the pain and terror of being expertly filleted while still alive.

Carlos's gaze darted away from that terrifying stare to the deadly blade in the man's hand and back again. But terrified as he was, part of him wondered whether it would be better to die here and now than to rot in a maximum security American prison until he took his last breath.

Gathering the last of his courage, he raised his chin. "Fuck you all."

He tensed, bracing for the moment that blade began carving him up, prepared to fight for as long as his strength lasted.

Instead, he jerked in surprise when the blade retracted into its sheath. To Bautista's right, Prentiss holstered his weapon and reached up to undo one of the overhead bins. Carlos's eyes pingponged back and forth between the two men, confusion clouding his brain as Prentiss pulled something out.

Two parachutes.

"You've got three minutes to tell me everything I want to know," Prentiss said in a clipped voice as he and Bautista began putting on the harnesses. "Then we're turning this plane hard to the right and ditching it into the Atlantic after we bail out. Your choice, jail or death."

Carlos started to laugh at the absurdity of it, but the utter conviction on both their faces made it die in his suddenly bone-dry throat. He had no fucking idea how to fly this thing. And though he was pretty sure he could get out of whatever charges they had waiting to lay against him in the States due to lack of evidence, he didn't want to die. But he would if they jumped, because he would plunge into the water with the jet and be torn apart.

Bile rushed into his throat, hot and acidic.

Both men had the parachutes on. Prentiss set his hands on his hips and raised a taunting brow at Carlos. "Well? You're down to less than ninety seconds."

They were bluffing. No one was crazy enough to bail out of a jet without oxygen at this altitude.

As if hearing his thoughts, Bautista reached into another overhead compartment and withdrew two oxygen tanks with masks. Holding Carlos's gaze, laughter lurking in his dark eyes, he handed one to Prentiss. "Seventy seconds."

Prentiss already had the mask in place. Carlos stared at them, heart thundering beneath his ribs, mind whirling frantically. He was trapped, forced to choose between jail and a terrifying death.

When he didn't say anything, Prentiss spun around and stalked up the aisle, Bautista following him.

Carlos automatically half-rose out of his seat, unable to believe they would actually do it. But Bautista disappeared into the cockpit as Prentiss reached the door in the side of the aircraft.

The jet turned sharply to the right. Banking out to sea just as promised.

Then Prentiss grabbed the handle on the aircraft door.

Carlos's heart shot into his throat. "Okay! Okay, I'll tell you!"

Chapter Nineteen

───────◇◇◇◇◇───────

"**W**hoa there, Wonder Woman," her sister said, hurrying through the connecting door of their Alexandria hotel rooms as Tess came out of the bathroom struggling to get her damn bra strap over her bandaged shoulder.

Tess sighed and lowered her left arm in frustration, her plain white bra dangling from her left hand. "I hate this damn thing," she grumbled, glaring down at the sling that kept her right arm immobile and useless against her chest.

"Well that damn 'thing' is currently keeping you from being in even more pain," Shannon said, efficiently easing the strap into position over Tess's bad shoulder, choosing a spot where it wouldn't rub the surgical site. Two years younger than Tess, Shannon was a natural mother and had jumped a flight to be here for Tess when she'd arrived an hour ago.

She paused, meeting Tess's eyes. "Do you, um… You wanna do the honors, or shall I?" she asked, lifting the cups, eyeing Tess's bare breasts.

Tess grunted and sat up straighter, hiding a wince as

the motion pulled at her newly fixed collarbone. It hurt, but not so much as not having any more information about Autumn. And she was worried as hell about Reid since their last call this morning. "Go ahead. It's not like you haven't seen them about three minutes ago while you were in there helping me wash my hair."

"True." Shannon tucked a strand of golden-blond hair behind her ear and wiggled the cups into position, then reached down and quickly scooped each breast into place. "There. Voila," she said, reaching around Tess to hook the bands together between her shoulder blades. "What shirt do you want to wear?"

"Whatever hurts the least to get on."

Shannon dug through Tess's duffel on the floor. "Let's try this one." She pulled out an oversize plaid, button-down, flannel shirt.

"Is that Reid's?" It sure wasn't hers. She grabbed it, brought it to her nose to smell it and caught the scent of his soap on the fabric. A pang hit her. He must have put it in here when he'd thrown the bag together for her last night.

"And it does double duty, because not only do we not have to pull it over your head," Shannon said, carefully easing the right sleeve up Tess's curled arm, "but it also put a smile on your face."

"He's a good man." They'd talked about him a lot while Tess had been back in Texas. Shannon had listened patiently while Tess had poured her heart out, talking about her concerns, her fears. And that she had already pretty much been a goner as far as Reid Prentiss was concerned.

"So you've told me, alcohol and ex problems included."

"I know, but he's so much more than that, Shan." He was also brave and strong and caring. "He rescued me yesterday. And he was there waiting for me when I woke up in the recovery room. He even packed me a bag and called you to arrange your trip."

"Gotta love him for that," Shannon said.

All that in spite of the hell he was going through with Autumn. He amazed her. "God, I miss him." So damn much, especially with all that had happened yesterday. She'd relived those stomach-curdling moments before the crash so many times since, and the terrifying attack in the woods. If not for Reid and the men he'd recruited to come in after them, she and her crew might be dead right now.

Or, she might be in a cage like those other women, about to be shipped out to the highest bidder. Cold swept through her just thinking of it.

"Well, I'm sure as hell looking forward to meeting him when this is all over. I'm going to hug the hell out of him for saving my big sister."

"Get in line, Shan. He's mine, so I get to hug him first." Tess eyed her phone sitting there charging on the desk across the room. It had been hours since she'd gotten word from Reid about the operation happening right now, but he'd been so evasive and there'd been no updates since.

She pushed off the bed to walk around, the pain in her shoulder making it impossible to get comfortable. They'd given her meds to keep on top of it before leaving the hospital but she didn't want to take any with the current situation going down. Her boss had told her that the DEA and FBI had hatched some kind of sting to nab Ruiz and get a lock on Autumn's location. Reid was involved, but she wasn't sure in what capacity and it was driving her nuts to be cooped up here waiting for word.

Her cell rang, making her heart rate skyrocket. She grabbed it from the desk, hope inflating her ribcage when she saw Reid's number. "Reid?" Her entire body was on alert as her sister watched her anxiously.

"Yeah, sweetheart, it's me."

The endearment hit her straight in the chest. "Are you okay?"

"More than okay. I think we've found her, Tess." His voice cracked with emotion.

Tess closed her eyes and leaned against the wall, praying Autumn was all right. "Thank God." She opened her eyes, mind working fast. "Where is she?"

"An address in the Tidewater region. Analysts are working on it now, and the taskforce is putting together a team to go after her."

She was already grabbing her ID and jacket from the closet. "Where are you right now?"

"I'm in the air, about two hours out of Alexandria. Will you go with them? They're going to pull the trigger soon, and Autumn knows you. She's gone through hell already, and if she's there it—"

"Reid, of course I'll go. You don't even have to ask." After signaling to Shannon that she'd call, she was out the door and headed down the hallway with rapid strides, the pain in her shoulder all but forgotten. "Where are they meeting?"

"Quantico."

"Okay, I'm on my way."

His heavy sigh tugged at her. "Thank you."

"No thanks necessary." She paused as the elevator carried her down to the lobby. "Are you sure you're alright?"

"Won't be okay until I know for sure she's safe."

"Yeah, I can understand that. You're going to fill me in on what happened, right?"

"As soon as I see you." Voices sounded in the background. "I gotta go. But look, Tess…"

She smiled even though he couldn't see her. "It's okay, Reid. I'm going to get her and bring her back to you."

"God, I want to kiss you so bad right now."

She wanted that too. So much it shook her. "I'll take a

rain check. See you in a while."

"I can't wait to hold both my girls again."

A bittersweet sting spread beneath her ribs as she climbed into the cab and directed the driver to take her to Quantico. She hadn't expected Reid and his daughter, hadn't been even remotely prepared for them to crash into her life and burrow their way into her heart. But they had. She was emotionally committed to them both now, for better or worse.

And she was going to get that sweet baby back to her father today.

The head of the taskforce was waiting for her when she arrived on base a little over thirty minutes later, and took her directly to the briefing room. Two FBI SWAT teams had already been assembled. The head of the taskforce introduced her to the team leaders, and informed them that she would be going into the building directly after the breach. If Autumn was alive, they were to give Tess immediate access to her, and Tess would stay with her while the scene was secured.

Everything moved fast after that. Soon she was riding shotgun with a group of DEA agents behind the SWAT vehicles as they made their way across base to where four Blackhawks were waiting to fly them to the target location.

Tess's pulse beat faster at the sight of them, her palms turning sweaty as she climbed aboard. She mentally shook herself. *No.* This was her aircraft and she loved it.

But the memory of yesterday's events was all so fresh in her mind. The loss of control, those moments before the wheels touched the road and they'd been going too fast and there wasn't a damn thing she could do to slow them down. That sickening moment of impact, the instant her collarbone snapped.

She refused to give into the fear, took slow, steadying breaths as they lifted off and gained altitude. After a few minutes, she was able to relax, the hope that she might be able to get Autumn in a little while helping to dispel the lingering anxiety.

They landed several miles from the target location and drove the rest of the way in a convoy. When they arrived on scene, police and special FBI units had locked the surrounding area down, giving them a buffer in which to operate. Tess got out of the vehicle she was riding in and followed behind the SWAT teams with three other agents, her left hand on the pistol holstered at her hip.

Up ahead lay the target house: a stately private residence located along the Chesapeake waterfront. Worth at least a few million for the location and view alone, the imposing white colonial home on immaculate grounds stood on two acres of land that overlooked the bay. The agency had investigated the owners, but if they were connected to the *Veneno* cartel, that info was buried deep.

Time slowed as everyone got into position. Tess waited tensely just beyond the interior security perimeter with some FBI agents while the SWAT teams stacked up at the front and rear entrances to the house. The team leader in charge gave the command to breach, and they stormed the house.

Tess counted to ten, then twenty, and ran for the back door with the other agents.

Inside the back entry she stood in the mudroom, weapon in hand while the teams swept the house. It was so quiet. No shots, no shouts except for the brusque communication between team members.

Rapid treads above her head made her look up at the ceiling, and then the team leader in charge appeared around the corner from the kitchen. "Main floor's clear," he said to them. "Other team reports the upper floor's clear as well."

Unease and crushing disappointment hit Tess. Autumn

had to be here. She *had* to be. God, this nightmare had to end—happily.

"We're gonna search the basement and the outbuildings."

The two teams split up, one going to check the garage, pool house and garden shed, while the other searched the basement. Tess stayed with the latter, standing at the top of the steps as they opened a door in the hallway and rushed down another staircase into the darkness beyond.

Her heart beat faster, her ears straining to make out any sounds coming from below, and her mind spinning with all kinds of horrifying possibilities. They'd caged women. Chained them naked to the floor. Starved, beaten and raped them. What the hell had they done with Autumn? Had they killed her and buried her body somewhere on the property?

Tess swallowed and started down the stairs, praying with each step. *Please let her be here. Please let her be okay.*

"Dubrovski!" a male voice called up to her.

"Here!" She broke into a jog, heart clattering against her ribs as she rushed down the stairs. What had they found? Not Autumn's body. *Not her little body, please.*

She rounded the corner, able to see because one of the men had switched on a flashlight. "Did you find her?" she asked, desperate to know.

"Yeah." The team leader pulled off his balaclava, his eyes grave. "In there." He pointed to a utility room off the basement hallway. "Let her in, guys," he said to his men.

Tess immediately moved past him, the pain in her shoulder forgotten, a dull throb in her ears and her legs wooden as she walked to that open doorway. Someone was inside it. One of the SWAT agents.

His back was to her as he did something with his hands. And he was speaking softly, his tone soothing. Cajoling, as though talking to a frightened animal.

Or a terrified little girl.

Tess rushed inside and stopped dead when she took in the sight before her. The agent moved back enough for her to see Autumn as he gently sliced through the tape holding her hands behind her.

Elation slammed into Tess, so sharp and powerful the floor seemed to tilt beneath her for a moment. "*Autumn*."

The little girl's eyes swung toward her, and the moment they locked on Tess, her face crumpled and she burst into tears. "Tess," she choked out, reaching for her.

Oh my God, oh my God... Tess pushed past the male agent and grabbed her, wrapping her left arm around those frail little shoulders.

Autumn clung to Tess. Tess winced and hissed in a breath when Autumn's face pressed against her surgical site, but she didn't care about the pain. "Oh, sweetheart, it's so good to see you," she murmured against that soft brown hair.

Autumn continued to cling to Tess as she cried, her whole body shaking.

Tess held her tighter, gathered her up and sat there on the floor just holding her. "It's okay. It's okay now." She smoothed her left hand over Autumn's hair, down her shuddering back. Was she okay? Was she hurt anywhere that Tess couldn't see? "I'm going to take you home."

"W-where's my dad?" she quavered.

"He's coming, sweetie. He's on a plane right now, coming to get you." Tess cupped the girl's face in her hand and tipped it up. Autumn's eyes were puffy and swollen, but in the dim light it was hard to see if she had any cuts or marks on her. "Are you hurt anywhere?" It made Tess's guts clench to think of what they might have done to her.

Autumn shook her head, her frightened gaze darting past Tess to all the uniformed men standing in the basement.

"It's all right, they're with me," Tess soothed. "Honey, look at me."

Deep blue eyes exactly like Reid's focused on her.

"That's better." Tess put on a reassuring smile. "Are you hurt, Autumn?"

"N-no." Her lips quivered and more tears flooded her eyes. "I want to go home. I want my mom and dad."

"I know you do. And you'll see them real soon." Tess hugged her close again, clamped her teeth together as her injured shoulder protested with a searing pain. Autumn had been through something unbelievably traumatic, and Tess didn't want her to suffer even a moment's more distress. "I'm going to take you outside now, okay? There are lots of police officers and federal agents waiting for us outside, just to make sure you're safe. Some of them will want to talk to you, ask you questions about what happened, and the paramedics will want to check to make sure you're okay."

"I just wanna go home."

"I know, sweetie. But I'll stay with you the whole time, okay?"

Autumn focused on her again, searched her eyes a moment, then nodded.

Tess smiled at her again. "Ready?"

Autumn burrowed closer and wrapped her arms tight around Tess's neck, and this time she couldn't hold back a hiss of pain. Autumn's head came up, her gaze moving from Tess's face to her shoulder and back. "What happened?"

"Well, it's kind of a long story."

"Are you alright?"

Tess huffed out a laugh. It was funny, for Autumn to be asking her that right now after everything she'd been through. "Yes. Now let's get you out of here, huh?" When Autumn nodded, Tess gathered her tight and wrapped her left arm around the girl's hips. "You're gonna have to hold on tight because I've only got one arm to hold you with."

"Okay." For good measure Autumn wrapped her legs around Tess's waist.

The SWAT agent nearest her helped Tess to her feet, then followed her up the stairs. She squinted at the brightness when they emerged into the main floor hallway, and paused a second to let Autumn's eyes adjust. The little girl was peering over Tess's shoulder, her face apprehensive.

"Everyone out there is here to help you," Tess reminded her.

"And you'll stay with me."

Just let someone try to take you from me. "I'll stay with you."

The next hour passed in a blur as Tess helped Autumn through all the questions and physical examination. To Tess's relief she seemed to be unharmed, but the EMTs insisted Autumn be taken to the hospital so a doctor could do a more thorough exam. Thankfully the doctor was kind and quick, and Tess expelled a breath of thanks when he confirmed that she was fine other than a few bumps and bruises, and hadn't been sexually assaulted.

"Can we leave now?" Autumn asked, reaching for Tess's hand.

Tess squeezed gently. "You bet." She cleaned Autumn up with a quick sponge bath and changed her into a pair of pajamas one of the FBI agents had brought her.

Autumn held tight to her hand on their way to the main doors. Outside, an agency vehicle was waiting to take them to FAST headquarters. Tess was halfway to it when a familiar male voice called out to her left.

"Autumn!"

They both looked up in time to see Reid sprinting toward them, his face a mask of naked emotion as he ran from an SUV that had just pulled up.

"Daddy!" Autumn tore free of Tess's grip and raced toward her father as fast as her little legs could carry her.

Chapter Twenty

Reid's heart was about to explode as he raced toward his daughter. When Autumn was a step or two away, she launched herself at him. He caught her and crushed her to his chest, burying his face in her neck.

At the feel of those little arms clinging to his neck, he crumpled. His knees gave out and he dropped to the ground, barely even feeling the impact.

Autumn was here. She was safe.

He knelt there on the ground holding his daughter, and something inside him shattered. All the fear and anguish he'd bottled up came bursting forth in a rush of tears. Hard, wrenching sobs ripped out of his chest, raw and agonizing.

"Don't cry, Daddy," Autumn said, her voice stricken.

He couldn't stop, couldn't do anything but hold her and cry, his entire body shaking.

He was dimly aware of another vehicle pulling up close by and a door popping open a minute later.

"Autumn! Oh, my God, Autumn!"

Autumn and Reid both looked up as Sarah ran toward them, tears streaming down her face. Reid dragged in a shaky breath and lifted one arm out to her.

Sarah dropped to her knees beside them, reaching for their daughter as Reid wrapped his arm around her and dragged her close. Locking the three of them together again, united in this joyous moment when their daughter was returned to them.

"Oh, baby," Sarah whispered, still crying, squeezing Autumn and peppering her head and face with kisses. "Oh, baby, I missed you so much."

"I missed you too, Mom."

Reid didn't know how long they stayed like that. Minutes. Hours. But even after his tears dried and all three of them had calmed, he still couldn't let go. He couldn't bear that he was the reason Autumn had been taken. Couldn't stand that he'd posed this kind of risk to his family—a broken one, but still a family.

Finally, he was able to relax his hold on both of them and cup Autumn's precious little face in his hands. He'd ached to see it so badly, and the sight of her now with her puffy, bloodshot eyes would forever be burned into his heart and mind. "You okay, baby girl?"

She nodded. "I'm not hurt. The bad man who took me tied me up and gave me to another man, and he brought me to a big house. He put me in a closet downstairs and left me there. I don't know why."

Reid's entire body stiffened at his daughter's words. He knew exactly why. Javier, the bastard who had kidnapped her, was one of Ruiz's most ruthless *sicarios*. News of her abduction had rapidly spread through the *Veneno* grapevine, all the way up to *El Escorpion*.

Maybe because of her young age, maybe because he was rumored to have children, the head of the cartel had intervened on Autumn's behalf, and sent another enforcer to step in. That enforcer had taken Autumn to what had turned out to be a kind of safe house, where she'd been placed for the impending rescue before the details had been passed on to the DEA.

In the meantime, *El Escorpion* had reached out to the legendary *sicario* Miguel *"El Santo"* Bautista through some back channel to set up a hit on Ruiz. Because of his ties to DeLuca and Colebrook through the women in their lives, Bautista had contacted them about the situation, and offered to be part of the op.

That was still something else Reid was trying to process. Why had Bautista volunteered for the stunt on the private jet? Maybe it was some kind of cartel justice or payback. Reid didn't know what kind of compensation DeLuca had offered the man, but Reid would have given the man everything he owned in return for getting Autumn back safely.

And for the satisfaction of knowing that Ruiz, now in federal custody, was going to rot inside the deepest, darkest hole they could put him in. After they grilled him day and night until he spilled every last dirty secret about the cartel, its operations, and its shadowy head.

"The bad men who did this won't ever scare or hurt anyone again," he told Autumn, because it was important she know that. As for Javier, Reid suspected that piece of shit's dismembered body would turn up over the next few days in a swamp somewhere down south. He hoped that before Javier died the bastard suffered the kind of torture Bautista had once been famous for.

All in all, he was just pathetically grateful that *El Escorpion* had stepped in and prevented his daughter from suffering the same kind of fate that Victoria Gomez had endured. Or worse.

Releasing a shuddering breath, Reid kissed the top of his daughter's head, breathing in her soapy, clean scent. Someone had cleaned her up and given her new pajamas.

"Just glad you're okay, baby girl."

"I was really scared because I was alone in the dark. And they'd tied my hands and feet together behind my back so I couldn't move, and put tape over my mouth so no one could hear me screaming."

Oh, fuck, he was gonna have nightmares about that for months. Years. "You were so brave."

"Then some more men came in and found me. Agents, kind of like you when you're in your uniform. I was scared at first, because I thought they were more bad men, but then Tess was there."

Tess.

Reid's head came up, searching for her. God, he'd been so focused on Autumn, he'd forgotten she was there. He was such a shithead.

He spotted her halfway up the sidewalk leading away from the main entrance. He released Sarah and Autumn and shot to his feet. "Tess!"

She stopped, seemed to hesitate a moment before turning around. Why did she hesitate?

"Wait!" He broke into a jog, his chest filling with emotion as he took in the sight of her there, her face blotchy as though she'd been crying, her right arm secured to her body in a sling, and she was wearing his shirt.

She didn't move as he ran, looking uncertain. Uncertain about what?

Reid ran straight up to her and wrapped his arms around her, carefully drawing her into his body so he didn't hurt her arm. "Thank you," he whispered fiercely, his mouth against her ear.

TESS SLID HER left arm around his waist and squeezed, resting her cheek against his shoulder.

"Don't thank me," she said, thrilled to be in his arms but hating to intrude on such a private, family moment.

Her eyes were swollen and gritty from crying. She'd managed to hold it together during the emotional reunion until he'd buried his face in Autumn's hair and lost it, and the sounds of those sobs ripping from him had just destroyed her. "I'm just glad she's okay and back where she belongs."

"No, I mean it. Having you there made all the difference. She said once she saw you, she wasn't scared anymore."

"I'm glad."

Reid lifted his head and brushed a lock of hair away from her wet cheek, searching her eyes. "You were just going to walk away?" The hurt in his voice was reflected in his eyes.

"I thought you guys could use some privacy."

"Not from you. That's the last thing I want." He hugged her tight to him, kissed the top of her head.

Oh, damn. She'd thought she was all cried out, but maybe not.

"Tess?"

At the quiet, feminine voice behind Reid, Tess pushed away from him and looked past him as Autumn's mother approached, holding her daughter's hand. Sarah Prentiss had light brown hair and a slender build, and her daughter had inherited her delicate features. "Hi."

Sarah's brown gaze flicked between her and Reid before focusing on Tess. "I'm Sarah."

Tess cleared her throat. "Yes, hi." She stuck out her left hand in an offer to shake, feeling awkward.

Sarah smiled at her, and it transformed her from pretty to beautiful, even with her red, puffy eyes. Instead of shaking Tess's hand, she grasped it and pulled her into a hug, careful of her bandaged shoulder. "Thank you for what you did for Autumn. She told us all about it."

"It was nothing," Tess murmured, uncomfortable with all the thank yous.

Sarah pulled back to meet Tess's gaze, her expression somber. "It wasn't nothing to her."

Well. "I was glad to be there." She smiled at Autumn. "Wasn't I?"

The smile she got in return squeezed her heart so hard it hurt. "Yes. I kept praying that my dad would come, but when I saw you I knew he'd sent you instead."

God, this kid just slayed her with her words. "Yeah, he did."

Reid moved in close and closed his arm around Tess's shoulders. She stiffened, her gaze automatically darting to Sarah, but Reid's ex was smiling softly at them.

"You better be good to her, or else," she said to Reid, startling Tess before she turned to her daughter. "What do you say, time to get you to the hotel? We can order room service."

Autumn frowned. "We're not going home?"

Sarah and Reid exchanged a brief look. "Not tonight. But yes, we can have room service."

"Cheeseburgers and root beer floats?"

"Anything you want."

"Two root beer floats?"

"Have three. Or four. I don't care, whatever you want."

Autumn grinned then it faded and she looked at Reid, uncertainty in her eyes. "Are you coming with us?"

"Absolutely I am."

Autumn relaxed visibly at that and Tess inwardly let out a relieved breath. He and Sarah must have come to some kind of an agreement before meeting here at the hospital, because there was no sign of any animosity between them. And not letting Autumn go to either parent's house was probably for the best right now, at least until the agency could figure out how extensive the information breach for the team was.

"Can Tess come too?"

All three adults looked at Autumn. A slightly awkward pause followed, but Tess was the first to speak, rushing to smooth it over. "I'm sorry, honey, but I can't tonight. Your parents need some time alone with you, and I need to go take my medicine for my arm and get some sleep."

"Are you going back to Texas soon?' Autumn asked, worry clouding her eyes.

"Not for a few more days at least."

"I'll make sure you see her again before that," Reid said.

"If that's okay," Tess added quickly, looking at Sarah, who smiled and nodded her consent. Tess smiled back and shifted her attention back to Autumn. "That sound good?"

"Yes."

"Okay, baby girl, say goodnight to Tess," Reid said.

Autumn stepped forward and wound her arms around Tess's waist, her little cheek resting against Tess's stomach. "Thanks, Tess, for saving me. Hope your arm gets better."

Aw, hell, there went that lump in her throat again. "Thanks, sweetie. You have a good night with your parents, and have a good sleep." *Because you're safe now. And no one will ever hurt you again. Your daddy will make sure of it.*

Reid stayed where he was with his arm tight around Tess's shoulders as Sarah and Autumn walked back to the SUV. The driver's door opened and Kai stepped out. A huge grin lit his face as he bent down and opened his arms. Tess heard Autumn's delighted "Uncle Kai!" as she ran for him, and couldn't help but smile when those huge arms gathered her up in a bear hug that lifted her four feet off the ground.

"Just when I thought I was all cried out," Tess said on a shaky laugh, wiping at her wet cheeks.

Reid gently turned her around and took her face in his hands, doing the wiping for her. His eyes were intent on hers, burning with too many emotions for her to decipher. She gazed up at him, heart hammering, a tiny bit afraid of what he would say next.

But he didn't say anything at all, just bent his head and kissed her softly. Slowly. A tender claiming in front of his daughter, ex and teammate, and whoever cared to watch. "I have to go with them now, but I need to see you tonight. Call you later, once everything's settled down?"

She nodded, needing him desperately too. "Okay."

"Good. Then I'll see you soon." With one last kiss so full of promise it made her ache, he shot her a loaded smile and jogged away to rejoin his family.

Chapter Twenty-One

"**B**reaking news out of Virginia this evening."
Abby McKinley looked up from her plate as the breaking news banner appeared on her TV screen. "The amber alert issued for nine-year-old Autumn Prentiss is now over."

She stopped chewing her mouthful of lasagna. *Oh, God...* She'd been following the story since it broke days ago. The entire state was out looking for the little girl, but there'd been no sightings since she'd been abducted from the strip mall parking lot.

"The nine-year-old girl is now home safe with her family after a brazen daytime raid conducted by the FBI this afternoon at a private residence on Chesapeake Bay."

Fantastic. Abby raised her glass of wine to the screen in salute. "Here's to you, little one." And fuck whoever had taken her in the first place. Abby considered herself to be fairly liberal when it came to politics, except in cases of terrorism, and crimes involving kids or animals. Then she was as right wing as they came.

She finished off her dinner and sipped at her wine

while the newscast wound down. It had been a long week of business meetings for the pharmaceutical company she worked for as a rep. Normally she met up with some girlfriends on Friday night, but since most of them were now in relationships, it wasn't the same hanging out with them. She was an uncomfortable fifth wheel clunking along.

She eyed the pan of homemade lasagna sitting on the kitchen counter, tempted to eat another piece. Or three. Then she berated herself.

Turning to food for comfort had been her M.O. since she was a teenager. It never loved her back, and the weight she'd put on had plunged her self-esteem to an all-time low. Since breaking up with Garret last year she'd worked her ass off—literally—to dump most of the weight.

Thank God, she had the equivalent of a human garbage disposal living across the hall who seemed to adore her cooking. She could always count on Kai to eat up whatever she needed to get rid of, and he was a nice guy, so it was no hardship to visit with him.

Yeah, and his amazing body and smile have absolutely nothing to do with it, right?

"Shut up, conscience," she muttered under her breath, and carried her dishes to the kitchen.

After packing him up a few containers of leftovers to pop into his freezer, she headed across the hall to his place. He'd been gone longer than expected this time and had texted her that he might not get home tonight, so she'd drop the food off and feed Goliath for him.

His freezer was in sad shape, almost empty, so she put all but one helping of the lasagna in it and set the last one in the fridge along with some salad and garlic bread, and jotted down a quick note for him. She fed Goliath, bending down to meet his fishy stare, his little gills flapping in and out.

"Your dad's coming home tonight, buddy," she told

him. They had an understanding, her and Goliath. She fed him and cleaned his tank while Kai was away, and Goliath wasn't allowed to go belly up on her watch.

A key scraped in the lock.

She turned toward the door with a welcoming smile, expecting to see Kai, but it died on her lips when Shelley walked in.

The dark-haired woman froze and stared at Abby for a moment, the hostility clear in her eyes. "What are you doing here?"

"Just feeding Goliath."

"Why, where's Kai?"

Abby didn't see why it was any of Shelley's business if Kai hadn't told her. "He's away on business."

Shelley snorted. "Of course he is." Her gaze landed on the note Abby had stuck to the fridge. Those hard blue eyes flashed back to her. "You brought him food again?"

Abby shrugged. "Yeah."

Shelley crossed her arms, her mouth pursing. "What else do you do for him?"

Okay, she really didn't like that tone. "Sorry?"

"Are you fucking him?"

Abby's eyes widened. "What?"

"Because he's mine," the other woman snarled, stabbing a perfectly manicured pink fingernail into her chest for emphasis. "*Mine*, you understand?"

Abby generally had a long fuse, but she was sick and tired of this woman's bullshit, and they'd only met a handful of times. And if Shelley was any kind of freaking girlfriend, she should be the one coming to grab Kai's mail and feed Goliath for him instead of her.

She opened her mouth to tell Shelley to take her unsolicited opinion and shove it where the sun doesn't shine, but stopped when the door swung open again.

Kai's huge frame filled the doorway, his expression freezing when he saw Shelley standing there. His surprise and unhappy reaction told Abby he hadn't been expecting the woman, and for some reason that made her feel better.

Then his gaze slid to Abby and a tired smile broke over his face. "Hey."

"Hey," she said, wanting the hell out of here. Shelley's eyes were shooting daggers at her and Kai, her insecure, suspicious brain conjuring up God only knew what about them. She took a step toward the door, but stopped because Kai hadn't budged, his stare fixed on Shelley.

"What are you doing here?" he asked her.

"I came to surprise you," Shelley fired back, her expression all kinds of pissed off. "But instead I found out I'm interrupting." She threw a lethal glare at Abby.

Kai dropped his duffel on the hardwood floor and put his hands on his hips. He was a freaking big man, and his posture made him damn intimidating. "I told you, we're done. You were supposed to leave the key while I was gone. Or hell, throw it away, I don't care which."

Abby wanted to be anywhere but there. *Oh, shit, not in front of me, guys...*

Shelley's eyes widened in outrage, then hurt flooded her expression and the tears started. "Oh, but... Kai, I thought—"

"No," he snapped, his frustration evident in every line of his face and body. Everything Abby knew about Kai told her that he would never be doing this with an audience if he hadn't reached his limit. Or been shoved past it. "Done. Leave the damn key and go."

Abby didn't like Shelley much, but she couldn't help but wince inside at witnessing the other woman's humiliation. Ouch.

For a moment it looked like Shelley would burst into tears, but instead she drew herself up and nailed Abby with a nuclear glare. "You know what? You can fucking have him." And with that she dug in her purse for the key, flung it into the living room and stormed out.

Abby pressed her lips together as the door slammed hard enough to rattle the pictures hanging on the walls. Kai let out a frustrated groan and dragged a hand over his short, dark hair. Then he sighed and swung his head toward her. "Sorry about that."

"Hey, no worries. I'm sorry you walked into that." She studied him for a moment. "You look tired." And not just because of this recent drama. He'd been tired when he'd walked in.

"Yeah, I'm beat. Been a bitch of a week." Then he smiled. A soft, proud smile that transformed him from good-looking to *wow*, and made her insides heat up. "But it ended well."

It had? Even with the whole Shelley thing just now? "Yeah? Well I'm glad. And I'm not sure whether this will make your night or not, but I just put some lasagna and stuff in your fridge."

His eyes lit up. "You're seriously an angel. I'm starving."

"You're always starving." He reached down for his duffel and for the first time Abby noticed the bandage on his left forearm. "What happened?"

He followed her gaze, shrugged a shoulder. "Nothing. Just a scratch."

She didn't know what he did for a living, other than he worked for the government. And judging from the condition he was in and the way he moved, it was the furthest thing from a desk job. Whatever it was, it was dangerous, and she worried that he was hurting worse than he let on. She'd been around enough alpha males to know how they ticked. They weren't supposed to show pain or weakness of any sort, because that would be unmanly.

Right now, though, she should get out of his hair and let him unwind. "Goliath's been fed, and there's a notice there for a package delivery waiting for you at the post office."

"All right, thanks. Man, I owe you. Didn't think we'd be gone this long."

She wanted so badly to ask him what he did, but if he wanted her to know he would have told her by now, so she had to respect his privacy. "It's no problem." She paused a second, then picked up the key that Shelley had chucked onto the living room rug. "Do you, uh, think she has a spare somewhere?"

Kai crossed the room and took it from her. His skin was dark compared to hers, and he was so tall and broad, standing next to him like this made her feel tiny. Having fought body image problems most of her adult life, feeling petite and almost fragile around anyone was startling.

He stared at the key for a long moment. "Doesn't matter if she does. I won't be here long enough for her to use it anyway."

She frowned. "What do you mean?"

He lifted those deep brown eyes to hers. A mottled blend somewhere between dark chocolate and black coffee that was riveting against his bronze skin and dark lashes. "We had a major security breach at work. Two of us on the team had our personal information compromised. The agency feels it's in our best interest to leave our places this weekend."

"Oh…" The news was a shock, but more than that, the wave of sadness hit her hard. If he moved out of the building, she'd likely never see him again. And until that moment, she hadn't realized how attached she was to having him around. How much she looked forward to seeing him.

The same regret was written in his eyes as he stared down at her. "Yeah. It sucks."

It really did. She'd never be able to zip across the hall with a plate of something, or share a quick meal together again. He wouldn't be there to visit with or help her with little things around her apartment. More than that, she liked knowing he was just across the hall if she needed anything. He made her feel safe on an intrinsic level. "But everyone else in the building is considered safe? From the breach you mentioned?"

His gaze warmed. "Yeah. Especially once I'm out."

That…really didn't make her feel any better.

Kai searched her eyes for a moment, then sighed and motioned for her to sit down with him at the kitchen counter. Abby took a stool next to him and waited for him to continue.

"You know I work for the government."

She nodded.

"I'm with the DEA."

"Oh." Drugs. Dealers. Cartels. A warning shiver started at the bottom of her spine. "So this leak was to someone really dangerous."

He dipped his head. "Did you hear about the little girl who was kidnapped this past week?"

"The one who was just rescued tonight?"

A nod. "She's my teammate's daughter."

"Your…" She glanced down at his bandaged arm, then up into his face as understanding dawned. "*Oh*. So you're with some kind of a tactical team, then?"

His eyes crinkled at the corners in the hint of a smile. "Yeah."

"Were you the ones who rescued her?"

"Unfortunately, no. But I got to see her when she left the hospital tonight."

"Is she alright?"

"She's okay physically. Emotionally, I'm not sure." He shifted on the stool, the small piece of furniture creaking beneath his big frame. "I can tell you this now because the operation's over and the details are going to come out in the media over the next few days, but she was kidnapped by an enforcer of the *Veneno* cartel."

At the mention of that name, she cringed. Everyone knew about them. And how they murdered and tortured people at will to get what they wanted. Abby rubbed her palms up and down her thighs, pondering the knowledge that someone in the cartel might have Kai's personal info. "I'm really glad the FBI found her."

"Me too. She's such a sweetheart, you'd love her." His expression sobered. "But that's why I have to go. A *Veneno* lieutenant bought off a clerk in the agency, and she gave him my and my buddy's home addresses, information on next of kin, stuff like that."

Abby frowned, horrified. "So your family's at risk too?"

"Doubt it. They're all back on Maui, and the clerk's in jail, so there won't be any more leaks. And the sooner I pack up and get out of here, the sooner you'll be safe."

But I don't want you to go. She held the words back, because she was made of sterner stuff than that. "I'll miss you. It's not too often you get a neighbor you actually like."

He chuckled. "Truth."

Sadness filled her. "Who's gonna eat all the extra food I make?"

"Hey, if you still want to give it to me, we can meet up somewhere."

Finding Autumn Prentiss must have been a huge relief for him and the others, but there was a weariness in Kai's expression that tugged at her. "Well I'll be sorry to see you go. Have you got anyone to help you pack up?"

"A few of the guys are gonna come over tomorrow morning and help."

"I can help too, if you want. I can be here as soon as I get back from the gym."

His answering smile warmed her from the inside out. "You're a gem, Abby."

Oh God, she loved the way he said her name, his deep

voice like a caress.

The moment the thought hit her brain, blood rushed to her cheeks. Definitely time to go.

She cleared her throat and hopped off the stool. "Okay, I'll see you tomorrow. Hope you get a good night's sleep." Although how would he, when the most dangerous cartel in the western hemisphere had his freaking address? She wasn't going to sleep either.

He followed her to the door. When she started to twist the knob, he set a hand on the door to hold it closed. Abby froze, a rush of warmth licking along her skin. He was standing mere inches behind her, so close she could feel his body heat against her back.

"Can I get a hug goodbye?" he asked softly.

You could get anything you wanted from me. "Oh. Sure." Steeling herself, banishing her wayward thoughts, she turned around to face him, a pang hitting her at the loneliness she read in his eyes.

He reached for her, those huge arms coming around her back as he drew her to his chest. His crazy-hard, sculpted chest she'd imagined seeing naked—along with the rest of him—far more times than she cared to admit.

Slipping her arms around his ribs, Abby tried to get a grip on her body's reaction to the embrace, but it was no use. The feel of that big, hard frame pressed along her front sent tingles shooting to every nerve ending. Her nipples tightened and her stomach muscles pulled tight.

And he didn't just squeeze her and let go in the quick, neighborly hug she'd expected. No, he pressed his cheek to the top of her head and…cradled her.

It took a second for her to realize he was seeking comfort, rather than offering it. Her heart squeezed tight.

"Gonna miss you, short stuff," he said gruffly.

Her heart twisted. She leaned more fully into him, spreading her palms across the broad expanse of his back. His words sounded awfully final.

But she wasn't ready to say goodbye to him forever.

Chapter Twenty-Two

R eid's arm had fallen asleep at least thirty minutes ago, but he was afraid to move it in case it woke Autumn. So he lay there on the hotel bed with his daughter's back spooned up against his front, still drinking in the miracle of having her back safe.

"Man, she's a hot sleeper. The front of me's soaked through but I can't bring myself to let go," Sarah whispered from Autumn's other side. They'd forged a fragile truce between them, the reunion with their daughter helping to smooth their ragged edges.

"I know," he whispered back, smiling down at their daughter. She'd fallen asleep sandwiched between them after cheeseburgers and root beer floats from room service. They'd talked for hours about what had happened, and Reid had done his best to explain why the man had found her, and that none of them would be in danger anymore.

Or at least, not after he cleared out his apartment and found another place. The guys were splitting into two teams tomorrow morning to get it done, half helping

Maka, and the others helping him.

"Isn't she beautiful?" Sarah's voice was rough with emotion.

"The most beautiful thing in the world."

His ex-wife looked up at him over the top of Autumn's head and her smile faded. Regret shadowed her eyes. "I'm...sorry for what I said the other day. About it being your fault. I know you'd never do anything to put her at risk. And I'm sorry for lashing out like that. Truly."

Reid held her stare. "Thank you. And for the record, even though things aren't great between us, I'd never do anything to put you at risk, either."

She lowered her gaze. "I know that." She stroked gentle fingers over Autumn's dark hair. "She's really out cold."

"Not surprising." Every time he thought of her frightened and alone, tied up and locked in darkness, the helpless rage came back. He wasn't sure if it would ever go away.

"That reporter you found that night. Miss Gomez. Is she going to be all right?"

"I don't know." Though in all honestly, Reid wasn't sure how she could be, after all she'd endured at the hands of those animals.

"And what about Tess?"

Reid met her gaze. "What about her?"

"Is she going to be all right?"

"Yeah."

"You sound pretty certain of that."

He was certain. "She's strong."

"Maybe. But don't you think you should go check on her and make sure?"

Those were the last words Reid had ever expected to hear coming from Sarah's mouth. "What?"

Sarah rolled her eyes. "You think I couldn't see the connection between the two of you, even before you put your arm around her this afternoon? Please. And even if she is strong, she shouldn't have to be strong alone right now. Jeez, Reid. Sometimes I don't think you've learned anything about women and relationships at all."

He frowned. "I don't want to leave Autumn."

"Autumn is practically unconscious, and even if she wakes up, I can handle whatever she needs." Sarah raised her eyebrows. "You're telling me you don't want to see Tess?"

Of course he wanted to see Tess. He was dying to.

Her lips twitched. "That's what I thought. So go on. If something comes up that I can't handle, I'll text you."

He glanced down at Autumn, then back up at Sarah. "You sure?"

"Yes." She expelled a deep breath, seemed to summon her courage before meeting his eyes once more. "I saw an interview with Miss Gomez, a couple days after she was rescued. She was talking about what the men who saved her did, about how brave they were, and how she wouldn't be alive today without them. It made me stop and think. Gave me more insight and appreciation for what you guys do, and why you do it, despite the risks and the sacrifices."

Reid didn't know what to say. He hadn't expected any of this.

But she wasn't done. "And so on top of being sorry for how I reacted, I'll…try to be more understanding about stuff going forward. And I'll try not to be such a controlling bitch with the whole scheduling thing in future. Okay?"

He smiled, his heart swelling. "Okay." After carefully extricating his arm from beneath their daughter, he sat up and shook it to get the circulation going. Unable to help himself, he leaned over and kissed the top of her head, breathing in the scent of her shampoo. "I can be back here within thirty minutes if you guys need me."

Sarah waved his words away. "Go."

He did, driving straight to Tess's hotel. He'd thought about texting her first, but decided just to surprise her instead. He rode the elevator up to Tess's floor, the buzzing of nerves in the pit of his belly taking him off guard.

Because she mattered to him so much.

He'd never thought he would fall for someone again after such a bitter divorce, but Tess had somehow managed to blast her way through all the walls he'd put up around his heart. Tough as he was, it was terrifying to hand his heart over to someone. He just hoped Tess was as ready to receive it as he was to give it.

He knocked softly on the door, his heart thumping in his chest. It opened only seconds later, and Reid was surprised to see Tess standing there appearing fully awake, still dressed in his plaid, flannel shirt.

"Hey," she whispered, giving him a smile that warmed the center of his chest as she stepped back to let him in.

"I know it's late," he said as the door shut behind him, "but Autumn was gone to the world and I…" He tucked a lock of her hair behind her ear, let his fingers linger on the soft skin at the side of her neck. "I just needed to see you."

Tess reached up to curl her fingers around his hand, another soft smile curving her lips. "I'm glad you're here. How is she?"

"Better than I expected, but we'll see how things go over the next few days. We've got all kinds of appointments set up with doctors, psychiatrists and counselors."

"Was Sarah okay with you leaving?"

"She basically kicked me out to make me come here."

"She did?"

He nodded. "Because she knows me. And she can tell how I feel about you." He traced his thumb over the edge of her jaw, taking in the shadows beneath her pretty jade-green eyes, and the lines of fatigue around her mouth.

"You look exhausted."

She sighed and slumped against his hand. "I'm so tired, but I'm too uncomfortable to sleep."

He pulled her gently into his body, wrapped his arm around her waist and cradled the back of her head with the other, holding her cheek to his chest. "Did you take your meds?"

"Two pills about an hour ago. They haven't done anything so far."

He hated to see her in pain. Easing back a little, he cupped her cheek in his hand, bringing her gaze to his. "Can I do anything?"

One side of her mouth lifted in a crooked grin. "Wanna wash my hair?"

He grinned back and dropped a soft kiss on her mouth. "I'd love to."

She blinked up at him. "Really?"

He chuckled at her surprised expression. "Mmhmm." He'd love to do anything that would make her feel better. "Come on." Taking her left hand, he led her into the bathroom. The tub wasn't huge, but it was deep enough to hold both of them. "Do you like it warm, or hot?"

"Hot."

He started filling the tub, then turned to face her, tenderness flooding him when he noticed the way she shifted her stance and fidgeted with the hem of his shirt at her bare thighs. "Not nervous about being naked in front of me, are you?" he teased.

Her cheeks turned the prettiest shade of pink. "A little. This isn't exactly the scenario I imagined for when this happened next." She gestured to the sling.

"No? Then what did you imagine?"

"Something a hell of a lot hotter and more romantic than this."

"I'll show you romance," he promised.

Holding her gaze, he reached for the hem of his shirt

and stripped it over his head. Tess's eyes traced over his naked torso, leaving tendrils of heat in their wake that sent a rush of blood to his swelling cock. She wasn't in any kind of shape to do anything about it, but everything about her turned him on and he couldn't help his body's reaction to her.

He took off his boots and pants, sliding his underwear down his legs with them. Tess stared at him with open, unabashed desire, the pink in her cheeks intensifying and her lips parted. "Your turn, gorgeous."

Tess didn't move, just watched him with hungry green eyes as he undid each button of the shirt to reveal the white bra she wore beneath, and the strip of creamy skin all the way down to the dark blond curls between her thighs.

Shelving all the sexual impulses bombarding his brain for later, he took care extricating her injured arm from the sleeve, and dropped the shirt on the floor before gently removing her bra. She immediately moved to hold her right arm in place against her chest, and he wasn't sure whether it was from nerves or if it was more comfortable for her shoulder.

Settling his hands on her hips, Reid tugged her toward him and gently, softly kissed the curve where her neck met her right shoulder, just at the edge of the bandages. She caught her breath, goosebumps rising on her skin. He ran his hands over her hips and back while the sound of rushing water filled the air, kissing his way up to her jaw, her cheek, and finally her mouth.

Tess moaned softly and swayed toward him, her lips parting for the slow stroke of his tongue. He cradled her head in his hands, rubbed his fingertips against her scalp as he kissed her, caressing her tongue and the roof of her mouth.

When he pulled back a minute later, she was breathing faster and her eyes were a little glazed. But the nervousness was gone, and that's what he'd wanted.

Checking the temperature of the water, he shut it off and helped her into the tub, placing a rolled up towel beneath her head. He used the moveable showerhead to wet her hair, then spread the shampoo in his hands and knelt beside the tub to massage her scalp.

Tess groaned and closed her eyes, her gorgeous body relaxing in the water. "Oh my God, that feels incredible."

It made his dick even harder, seeing her all sleek and wet and hearing those pleasurable sounds in the back of her throat. But this was his chance to give her what she needed, and so he lathered and massaged her scalp while she lay there.

Once her hair was rinsed off he gently eased her into a sitting position and slipped into the tub behind her, drawing her into the curve of his body. She settled against him with a contented sigh that satisfied something primal inside him, her head on his shoulder.

Gently grasping her swollen right wrist, he pushed aside her left arm so she could rest it and kissed her temple.

"I never did thank you properly for what you did," Tess murmured, eyes closed while he ran the soap over her. "If you hadn't come in after us when you did, I'd probably be dead."

It chilled his blood to think of it, of losing this vibrant, amazing woman. "You don't ever need to thank me for coming after you, Tess. Anywhere, anytime, if you need me, I'm there."

She tipped her head back to meet his gaze. "That's nice to hear, thank you."

He wanted to tell her a whole lot more than that, but not while she was facing away from him in a tub. He spent some more time smoothing his hands over her wet skin, telling her without words how much he cared, how much she meant to him.

When she was half asleep, he rinsed her off and lifted her out of the tub. After setting her on her feet to dry her, he helped wrap her arm back up in the sling and scooped her up to carry her to bed.

"I haven't been carried like this since I was a kid," she said on a laugh, her left arm looped around his neck.

Her husband hadn't done this for her? Reid held the question back, not wanting to bring him up right now. He settled her on the bed, crawled in beside her and tugged the covers over her. "What way are you most comfortable?" he asked, stroking her hair back.

Her green eyes were full of mirth. "Honestly? They're all really damn painful."

"What about this?" he asked, gently turning her onto her side facing him and sliding a pillow between her bent knees. He shifted close and wrapped his arm around her waist, well clear of her injured arm and the sling.

"I like the view a lot," she murmured, lifting her left hand to stroke the side of his face.

Reid couldn't resist the temptation and moved in to cover her mouth with his. He kept it light even though he was so damn hungry for her, stroking her lips, caressing her tongue. When he pulled back she was breathing faster and her pupils were dilated.

"I wish I was feeling good enough to do something about this," she murmured, pressing her hips against his throbbing erection.

He grinned against her mouth and kissed her again. "What doesn't kill us makes us stronger."

She smiled back. "So true."

He came up on one elbow and stroked his fingers through her hair, his chest about to burst with everything he was feeling. "I know we haven't had a lot of time together, but I haven't felt like this in… Maybe ever. I think about you all the time, and I miss you like hell when we're apart."

He took a breath, let it out slowly, heart pounding. "I didn't see you coming, Tess. Didn't expect you at all, but I'm falling for you hard and I don't want to lose you. I realize we've all been through a lot here, and I know I come with a shitload of baggage and that we live in different cities, but I'm hoping that's not a deal breaker for you. I want to see where things go with us."

Joy flashed in her eyes, easing the constriction in his chest. "I don't want to lose you either. And believe me, you're the last thing I expected, too."

"And the baggage?" A young daughter, an ex-wife, and a drinking problem were a lot for a woman to take on.

"I can handle anything but you breaking my heart or drinking again."

He mentally winced at the reminder of what he'd done the night Autumn was taken. "I won't. Neither of those. I'm calling my sponsor tomorrow."

She smiled again. "That's good." She groaned softly and leaned her forehead against his chest. "I'm supposed to fly out the day after tomorrow with my sister, but I don't wanna go home."

Then don't.

Reid barely held the words back. Asking her to make that big a leap for him right now wasn't fair. She had at least six weeks of healing ahead of her, and other things to take care of back in Texas—like her job and family. He had to be patient, give her time to figure out what she wanted. "If we're both willing to try, we can make this work."

"I want this to work," she murmured sleepily. Then she yawned and he tucked her in closer to him, keeping another pillow between their chests to shield her arm.

He wanted to be there for her through her recovery, but he needed to be there for Autumn more. And Tess would understand that completely.

It was just another reason why she'd stolen his heart

so completely, so fast. And why he intended to claim hers for good in return.

EPILOGUE

"How's the view back there?" Tess asked via the headset from the cockpit as she flew them back to base.

"Great!" came the enthusiastic response from the back. "I can see the airfield out the side door window," Autumn said excitedly, then sobered. "It's so flat here."

"Welcome to Dallas Fort Worth, honey." Tess shared a smile with her copilot and eased the cyclic to the right to turn them, her feet adjusting the pedals to keep them steady.

Autumn had adjusted well into her normal routine after her ordeal. Autumn kept regular appointments with a counselor, but no longer had to see a psychiatrist, and Sarah had kept her word about loosening the reins with the schedule she and Reid shared. Even so, Tess had been stunned—and ecstatic—when Reid and Autumn had surprised her at the office this morning.

It had been eight weeks since the accident and her collarbone was fully healed. She still saw a physiotherapist twice a week but she had almost ninety-percent range of motion back in her shoulder already, and no more swelling in her hand.

The moment they'd cleared her to fly, she'd climbed back into the cockpit for various training missions out of her home base here in Fort Worth. The first few times had been hard, haunted by the memory of what had happened, but she'd refused to let it beat her. Imagining Ruiz despising life inside his max security prison cell was fabulous mental motivation.

"What can you see out the other side now?" Tess asked her.

A few seconds passed before Autumn answered. "My dad! I see him!"

Tess grinned as she lined them up on the runway and followed it in to the landing pad near the hangar. Reid stood there waiting for them, a pair of shades hiding his eyes as he watched them land.

Tess lowered them into a hover and gently touched the wheels down. "Touch down. Your first flight on a Blackhawk is in the books."

"It was so awesome! I can't wait to go up again."

"Think you might have created a monster there, Tess," her crew chief said, popping his head in from the back. "That's one excited little girl."

It warmed Tess inside and out to know that Autumn had enjoyed it so much. While she and the copilot went through shutdown procedures, she watched out her cockpit window as the crew chief led Autumn away from the helo, holding her hand. The moment they were clear of the rotors he released her, and Autumn went running to her father.

Tess's heart squeezed so hard it hurt when Reid grinned and bent to catch her as she jumped into his waiting arms.

"That's one adorable kid," the copilot said.

"Don't I know it," Tess murmured. "And I'm even

more partial to her dad."

The copilot chuckled and clapped a hand on her shoulder before undoing his harness and climbing out of the cockpit. Tess followed, hopping onto the hot tarmac beneath a clear blue July Texas sky. Reid stood there with Autumn, watching her.

Tess couldn't help but grin. "If I run and jump at you too, will you catch me?"

"Sweetheart, you know I will." Reid opened up his arms and raised his eyebrows, waiting expectantly.

She laughed and ran at him, jumping just as she reached him and sure enough, those big, strong arms not only caught her, but crushed her to his hard body and held her off the ground. Autumn was giggling like mad at the show. Grinning, Tess wound her arms around his sturdy neck and leaned her head back to look down at him. "Nice catch."

"Yeah, you're a helluva catch," he murmured, using one hand to pull her head down for a long, deep kiss that made every nerve ending in her body go haywire.

"Iiiick," Autumn said next to her. "Mush."

Tess laughed against Reid's mouth and kept her arms around him as he lowered her to the ground, not missing the solid length of his erection pressing against her lower belly.

She shared a naughty grin with him, a silent promise to take care of that later on tonight, when her parents, sister and the girls took Autumn for a sleepover so she and Reid could have a night by themselves at the hotel. She loved Autumn, but she couldn't wait to be alone with Reid. It had been over a month since they'd last seen each other and they were both impatient as hell to get naked again.

"So you loved it?" Reid asked Autumn, one arm locked around Tess's waist. She loved how openly affectionate he was, even around his daughter.

Her little face brightened. "Yes! I'm gonna fly a Blackhawk someday, too. Tess'll teach me. Right Tess?"

"Oh, wow, I really did create a monster," Tess whispered to him.

"Could be worse," he said. "You could've been a prima ballerina or something, and then I'd have to sit through recitals and whatever. At least flying a helo is badass."

Tess pressed a quick, hard kiss to his mouth. "Okay, who's starving for a chocolate milkshake?"

"Me! Me!" Autumn grabbed Tess's hand and started towing her to where Reid had parked his rental vehicle.

"And after that, it's sleepover time," Reid added, waggling his eyebrows at Tess.

"Yep. Right after you run the gauntlet of meeting my parents, sister, and nieces." They'd all flown in to stay the week at Tess's place, and she'd had no idea Reid was planning to surprise her by showing up. But this way, they had awesome babysitters for the next two days.

"I can handle it. As long as it doesn't cut into our night too much," he added in a sexy tone that made her toes curl in her boots.

After milkshakes at a favorite diner, then a BBQ dinner at Tess's place, they left an insanely excited Autumn to an evening of pedicures and movie sleepover with Tess's family, and headed for the rental vehicle.

Rather than open her door for her and put her inside, Reid caged her in against the door in the shadows cast by the detached garage. Tess hummed in her throat and threaded her hands through his hair to kiss him, but he merely brushed his lips over hers and eased back. Staring at her.

"What?" she asked.

"Autumn and I brought you a present. I told her I'd give it to you now."

She loved presents. "Where is it?"

"In my back pocket."

When he made no move to get it, she laughed. "You want me to get it?"

His lips curved into the sexiest smile, his deep blue eyes almost black in the shadows. "Yup."

With a light, teasing touch, Tess trailed her left hand down the hard ridge of his right pec, down his flat abs and dragged her palm over the bulge forming in the crotch of his jeans before sliding it over his hip to his ass. She squeezed for good measure, then stopped when the shape of something in his back pocket registered. Flat. Fairly small.

Holding his gaze, she slipped her fingers into the denim pocket and pulled out a small pink envelope. she turned the envelope over in her fingers. *For Tess, with love from me and my dad*, it read in Autumn's printing.

"Open it," he murmured, standing so close his breath brushed over her temple and his clean, spicy scent enveloped her.

A little dizzy, Tess did, and pulled out a key tied to a pink velvet ribbon with a tiny silver helicopter charm attached to the end. Awed, Tess looked up into Reid's eyes, afraid to believe what it meant.

He cupped her face in his hands, looking into her eyes as he spoke. "I'm in love with you, Tess Dubrovski, and I can't stand being away from you anymore. So Autumn and I went out and found a new two-bedroom apartment just being finished outside Alexandria. We want you to move in there with us when we get possession next month."

Her chin wobbled and her throat thickened. She'd already looked into getting a transfer to D.C. and they had an opening for her there if she wanted it. "You're in love with me?" She was still stuck on that part.

Reid nodded, a gentle smile tugging at his lips. "I love you so much it hurts."

"I love you too," she whispered, trying like hell to hold it together.

His teeth flashed as he grinned. "I'm damn glad to hear that, sweetheart. And what about—"

"Yes. Yes, of course I'll move in with you." She threw her arms around his neck and clung, laughing even as tears flooded her eyes. It seemed surreal, to have found a love like this after she'd become a widow and thought that part of her life was over forever. Reid had made her brave enough to love again.

He made a low, hungry sound in the back of his throat and then his mouth was on hers, his body pressing her into the side of the vehicle. Tess kissed him back with every ounce of love and passion in her, letting out a squeak when he hauled her off her feet and bodily put her into the SUV.

"Should we tell the others?" she asked breathlessly, shoving her hair out of her face as he climbed behind the wheel.

"Later." He started the engine and reversed, swinging them around so fast on the driveway that gravel spewed from beneath the tires. She laughed as he shifted into drive and shot them down the long, straight driveway.

"Looks like someone's in a hurry to get somewhere," she teased, climbing to her knees to lean over and nibble on the side of his neck. Her heart felt like it might burst from happiness. She felt free, the rest of her life with him a warm, beckoning glow on the horizon, full of possibility.

He groaned, reaching one hand up to clench in the back of her hair. "Wish we were in a Blackhawk instead. Would be way faster."

She laughed lightly, her hands busily undoing the button of his jeans. "Oh, but taking the long route is going to be so much more fun."

His chuckle ended in a tortured groan as she freed his

hot, hard length and curled her fist around him. "Whatever you do to me in this car, I'm gonna tease you twice as bad when we get inside that hotel room," he warned, not doing a thing to stop her.

"Who said anything about teasing?" she murmured, bending down to brush her lips over the swollen head. She knew exactly what he liked now, knew precisely how to take him to the edge…and over it. Just like she knew he would return the favor and then some once they reached the hotel, making her fly higher than she'd ever flown before.

He hissed in a breath, his hand clenching tighter in her hair. "Dammit, Tess, I'm—"

Whatever else he was going to say ended in a strangled growl as she parted her lips and started the real torment. Tess smiled inwardly and set to work driving her big, badass alpha male out of his skull. Because this was the first night of the rest of their lives together, and she was going to make sure neither one of them ever forgot it.

—The End—

Thank you for reading STRIKE FAST. I really hope you enjoyed it and that you'll consider leaving a review at one of your favorite online retailers. It's a great way to help other readers discover new books.

If you liked STRIKE FAST and would like to read more, turn the page for a list of my other books. And if you don't want to miss any future releases, please feel free to join my newsletter:

http://kayleacross.com/v2/newsletter/

Complete Booklist

ROMANTIC SUSPENSE

DEA FAST Series
Falling Fast
Fast Kill
Stand Fast
Strike Fast

Colebrook Siblings Trilogy
Brody's Vow
Wyatt's Stand
Easton's Claim

Hostage Rescue Team Series
Marked
Targeted
Hunted
Disavowed
Avenged
Exposed
Seized
Wanted
Betrayed
Reclaimed

Titanium Security Series
Ignited
Singed
Burned
Extinguished
Rekindled
Blindsided: A Titanium Christmas novella

Bagram Special Ops Series
Deadly Descent
Tactical Strike
Lethal Pursuit
Danger Close
Collateral Damage
Never Surrender (a MacKenzie Family novella)

Suspense Series
Out of Her League
Cover of Darkness
No Turning Back
Relentless
Absolution

PARANORMAL ROMANCE
Empowered Series
Darkest Caress

HISTORICAL ROMANCE
The Vacant Chair

EROTIC ROMANCE (writing as *Callie Croix*)
Deacon's Touch
Dillon's Claim
No Holds Barred
Touch Me
Let Me In
Covert Seduction

About the Author

NY Times and USA Today Bestselling author Kaylea Cross writes edge-of-your-seat military romantic suspense. Her work has won many awards and has been nominated for both the Daphne du Maurier and the National Readers' Choice Awards. A Registered Massage Therapist by trade, Kaylea is also an avid gardener, artist, Civil War buff, Special Ops aficionado, belly dance enthusiast and former nationally-carded softball pitcher. She lives in Vancouver, BC with her husband and family.

You can visit Kaylea at www.kayleacross.com. If you would like to be notified of future releases, please join her newsletter: http://kayleacross.com/v2/newsletter/

Made in the USA
Middletown, DE
10 October 2017